WEHRDRAGON: LIBERATION

Sarah Fisher

First published in Australia in 2021 by Sarah Fisher

Copyright © Sarah Fisher 2021

Website: www.sarahfisherauthor.com
Email: sarah@sarahfisherauthor.com

The moral right of the author has been asserted.

ISBN: 9780648182467 (paperback)

A catalogue record for this book is available from the National Library of Australia

Disclaimer

This is a work of fiction. Names, characters, places, incidents and events, other than those clearly in the public domain, are fictitious and any resemblance to actual persons, living or dead, is entirely coincidental.

To my Calliope crew – Kylie, Toni and Raelene

Acknowledgements

I am indebted to my family who continue to support my writing shenanigans – especially those of you who got up at 4:30 am … on Sundays … in winter … to help me set up my stall at the markets.

Thank you, Lucy for producing another amazing cover.

And to Patrice and Kirsty, I truly value your professionalism and gentle guidance.

Prologue

Newsfloor, Indigo Times Headquarters – Monday 22 November, 2021 – 12:17 pm

'Heads up!' Harry Jones cries as he ploughs his wheelchair through the bustle of the newsroom. His eyes are fixed on the footage of the tangled ruins on the overhead screens.

Journalists scatter, leaping out of the way of the veteran reporter as he zips across the floor.

'You people call yourself journalists?' Harry shouts. 'Have you not noticed the screens?'

Within a metre of the news wall, he yanks the wheel of his chair, spinning to a stop. The wiry female journalist at the desk closest to him snaps round to survey the screens, and gasps.

The government's prestigious science precinct is now just crumbled concrete, twisted metal and shattered glass. One screen shows a helicopter flying a low pass through the dust haze over the site. On another monitor, a first-aid truck with flashing lights manoeuvres its way painfully slowly across the debris-strewn landscape. Dust-caked people run, limp or stumble about. Some carry or drag injured colleagues.

A cameraman pushes his way through the crush of stunned journos to reach Harry's side. 'What the hell happened there?' Jasper asks, cocking his thumb at the screens.

'My money's on an earthquake or an asteroid strike,' Harry says, basking in the glow of the screens. He lives for this.

Jasper nods slowly. 'Either that or there's a demolition team out there that got the address catastrophically wrong.'

Harry shrugs. 'I'm happy to run with any of those stories.'

'Arrogant prick,' the young woman at the desk beside them mutters.

'What's that?' Harry says, a smile curling his lips.

The woman swipes her tablet off her desk and stuffs it into her knapsack. 'I love the way that you *assume* this scoop is yours.'

The PA system beeps twice, heralding an imminent announcement. Everyone freezes.

'Jones! Why are you still here?' the chief editor barks. *'Get on it!'*

Harry smirks at the woman whose name he doesn't remember. 'You really thought *you'd* get the scoop on this?'

She sneers at him. 'I reckon I'm due.'

'Then of the two of us,' Harry says, 'I'd say *you're* the arrogant one.'

The woman scoffs. 'How the hell do you figure that?'

Harry spins his wheelchair round to face her. 'I've been in this game longer than you've been alive – *and* I'm the best journo around. Actually, I can't decide if you're arrogant, stupid or deluded, thinking that you'd get this story over me.'

'You hate women,' she says.

'I don't care about gender, colour or religion,' Harry retorts. 'I just hate idiots.'

As the woman fumes to herself, Harry shouts at Jasper. 'Bring the car round! We're rolling!'

'I assume we're collecting Felix on the way?' Jasper says.

'Of course!' Harry yells. He pats his wheelchair, adding, 'Though this baby is top-of-the-range, it can't get me everywhere I need to be. We're definitely gonna need legs to get what we need for this story!'

Chapter 1

Felix

'Message on the bat-phone, Felix.'

I look up from my tablet to find Elvira staring intently at hers. Neither of us is actually working on our English assignments, but I hope we look like we are.

'Since we're in the library, Elvira,' I say, 'my *work* phone is on *Do Not Disturb*.'

Elvira looks up and squints at me through her pink glasses. 'Yes,' she says slowly, 'that's why *you* didn't hear it. But I know things.'

Elvira is the most infuriating person I know. Tight corkscrew ringlets sprout from her head, and though she's always cursing her unruly mop of wiry curls, if it weren't for the Sideshow Bob hairstyle, you wouldn't find her in a room full of hobbits. Her eyes, like her skin, are the colour of pecan nuts, but people rarely notice them since they are behind thick, round barriers of pink glass.

Elvira's wardrobe consists mostly of reinvented items from local op shops, so everyone thinks she'll be a designer one day but Elvira wants to be an actor. She's constantly trying out new personas, claiming that it is easier acting like someone else than pretending to be herself … whatever that means. Sometimes I have no idea who she really is, and we've been best mates for ten years, since I punched her and broke her nose when we were six. But I trust her; she's always had my back. And she's the only person I can say that about.

I shake my head and drag the phone out of my bag. She's always right about the phone – I don't know how she does it – and whenever Harry texts me with a job, it's best to respond pronto. He's not supposed to contact me when I'm at school, but Harry thinks I should prioritise my part-time job at the *Indigo Times* over my schoolwork.

'You better hope it's not a call-out,' Elvira says, returning her attention to her tablet. 'Your Unattainable Senior hasn't done her presentation yet.'

She means Liberty Fox. At least Elvira didn't refer to her as the Ice Queen, which is her other favourite name for Liberty, but I still glare at her before turning my attention to the conference room across from our workstation.

Liberty is working with five other seniors on a physics project. Only a few metres and a glass wall separate us. I ignore my phone for the moment. Harry can wait. Elvira is right about Liberty Fox being unattainable but I'm not willing to concede defeat yet, despite my recent encounter with her.

I interviewed her for the *Indigo Times* after she was accepted into an elite stunt training academy. Harry wasn't thrilled at the prospect of me interviewing my 'crush' as he calls her, but he eventually gave in and assigned me his cameraman.

Liberty had just finished a two-hour workout at the local karate dojo, but she looked so fresh she could have just arrived. Her black singlet and tights hugged her athletic frame and her blue eyes glowed in the freckled landscape of her face. And not a single strand of her red hair had dared stray from her ponytail.

She's like a cobra – mesmerising, radiating power. But I'd prepared for the interview. I would stay cool no matter what. I'd be the Ice King.

Epic fail.

My glacial armour didn't just melt under her gaze – it sizzled and hissed as it steamed away. For me, the interview was a blur. I had to watch the raw footage from the cameraman afterwards to find out what had actually happened. I'd stammered through all my questions and, as

Liberty had detailed the countless hours of weight-training, karate, rock-climbing, sky-diving and gymnastics that had paved her way to Lourdes Stunt Academy, my gaze had never strayed from her chest – where a shiny Liberty half dollar coin hung on a silver chain.

Across the hall, Liberty gets to her feet. I can't hear her but just watching her is awesome. My pulse rate quickens and I sigh.

Elvira groans. 'You're pathetic, you know that?'

'You're just jealous,' I say without taking my eyes off Liberty.

'Negative. She's not my type.'

'We're not in competition then,' I say. 'Lucky.'

'Yes. Lucky for you, Felix, because I'd win.'

'Uh-huh.'

'She might actually be more interested in someone like me,' Elvira continues, 'rather than someone like you.'

I ignore her. She's tried that angle before.

'Another message,' she adds.

Reluctantly I look at the phone. Two identical messages from Harry.

I frown. 'Crap.'

'Call-out?' Elvira says, one eyebrow arched.

'Yep.'

Elvira rubs her hands together. 'Where?'

'NSA,' I say, staring at the screen.

Her eyes widen. 'Ooooh! The National Science Agency! Please tell me it's something exciting! Has your stepmother been arrested? Did she blow something up?'

'Looks like something's blown up,' I say, tucking my phone in my pocket and reaching for my tablet. 'The whole precinct has been levelled.'

Elvira recoils. 'Really? I was just joking.'

I tap the phone in my pocket. 'Well, unless Harry's in on the same joke …'

'You're going there?'

I nod.

'If it's that serious,' Elvira says, 'you won't get past security.'

'Harry will get us in.'

Elvira adjusts her glasses. 'Keep me posted,' she says. 'I want to know everything.'

∞

The white van with the *Indigo Times* logo emblazoned on the side pulls up at the kerb. I hear the click of the automatic latch a second before the back side door slides open to reveal Harry Jones in his wheelchair in the dingy, cluttered interior. I swat an empty soft drink can and a crumpled burger wrapper from the bench seat behind the driver before I sit down.

Harry grins at me. 'How is my favourite apprentice today?' he asks as Jasper, the cameraman/driver, swings the van out from the kerb.

'I thought I was your only apprentice,' I say as I wrestle with my seatbelt buckle while avoiding knocking my knapsack off my lap.

The floor of the van is like the Great Pacific Garbage Patch and I'm afraid if my bag falls amongst the filth, I'll never find it again. And even if I did manage to rescue it, I'd never get the smell out of it. Harry bathes in patchouli aftershave but it does nothing to cover the van's signature aroma of greasy takeaway food. As always, Harry is immaculately dressed. He is all tailored suits and silk ties, and not a hair out of place. How he endures the filth inside the van is beyond me.

'Of course, you're my only apprentice,' Harry says, slapping his palm against his forehead. 'How could I forget?'

Harry Jones is the *Indigo Times'* chief weapon in the broadcaster's war on public ignorance. The Malaysian-born reporter is tolerated in media circles, feared in political circles, and ridiculed by pretty much everyone else; his obnoxious and offensive manner overshadowing his towering intellect.

He's been in a wheelchair since a diving accident when he was fifteen, but that doesn't stop him chasing down big stories. His wheelchair is a V6 four-wheel-drive, all-terrain vehicle that his rev-head younger sister built for him, which if NASA ever finds out about, will probably become standard issue for Mars missions.

Harry tosses me a plastic-wrapped package. 'Put those on,' he says. 'What is it?'

'EMT coveralls. Hopefully not too small for you.'

'EMT? I'm going undercover?' I say, ripping the plastic to get to the uniform.

Harry snorts. 'Let's not get carried away, Junior,' he says. 'We just need you to NOT stick out like a dog's balls when you're in the field today.'

'Do I get a first-aid kit?' I ask.

'Don't worry about that,' Harry says. 'It'll be such a shit-show out there no one will be looking that closely – lucky for you.'

'So, what's the shit-show about?' I ask as I place my knapsack on the seat beside me and unbuckle my seatbelt. 'And what exactly do you want me to do?'

'Well, something catastrophic has befallen the government's National Science Agency today,' he says officiously.

Jasper turns in his seat as he takes a corner. 'That's a bloody understatement!'

'All the buildings in the precinct have been reduced to rubble,' Harry says. 'It's like a war zone apparently. Army's on its way.'

'An explosion?' I ask.

Harry shakes his head. 'Implosion.'

'What caused it?'

Harry shrugs. 'That's what you're going to find out.'

'What will you be doing?' I ask.

'Interrogating whomever I can while adding to the general confusion. Jasper will wield his camera like Excalibur and get us some award-winning footage.'

'And my stepmother?'

Again, Harry shrugs. 'I can't imagine some bureaucrat who spends her days rubberstamping energy leases being of any interest to us.'

'I don't know that she would approve that many leases,' I say. 'I'm sure she'd rather deny stuff. She's an antagonistic, power-crazy bitch.'

'Well, in any case,' Harry says, 'you should probably prepare yourself for the fact that she is dead.'

I roll my eyes. 'Don't get my hopes up.'

∞

Liberty

As I make my way across the ruined landscape, a skulking figure appears from behind a giant slab of concrete about fifty metres away. I recognise him immediately, even though he's wearing an EMT uniform. It's the guy from school who interviewed me for the *Indigo Times*. When he spots me, he stops skulking and starts what is probably supposed to be a nonchalant swagger but ends up looking like a drunken pirate impression.

'Hello, Felix,' I say when he reaches my position.

'Li-Liberty,' he stammers. He clears his throat. 'What are you doing here?'

'Looking for my parents.'

Felix cocks his head to one side. 'What would your parents be doing here?'

Seriously? Does he not know that my parents are the lead scientists on his stepmother's project? Maybe the 'Cinderfella' rumours are true.

My folks say his stepmother, Karina Warhurst, talks incessantly about Felix's older brother, but rarely mentions Felix. Adam Warhurst joined the air force after school and although he's been there less than two years, according to Karina, he's close to becoming the Air Commodore. Felix is – allegedly – the result of an affair his father had with a local hairdresser, and when Felix's birth mother died, he had to go live with his father. Karina pretends he doesn't exist, while blatantly lavishing her time and energy on Adam. That's what has earned Felix the nickname, 'Cinderfella'.

'My parents work here,' I say.

'Really?' he says, eyes wide. 'I hope they're okay.'

'I got a text from my dad,' I say, 'so once I locate him, I'll find out how they are.' I point to the uniform. 'You're undercover for the *Indigo Times,* I assume?'

His forehead crinkles and he breaks eye contact. 'Yeah, something like that,' he mumbles.

He's so awkward. Felix is easy to look at – take off his shirt and stick a puppy in his hands, he could be Mr July in the fireman's calendar – but his conversation skills are abysmal. He should stick to sport; his reputation on the cricket pitch, tennis court and football field is unmatched. Cinderfella might never *be* the belle of the ball but *give* him a ball and this bumbling goat becomes a gazelle.

'Okay,' I say. 'I'd best leave you to your job. Good luck.'

He frowns and nods. 'You too.'

I leave him and go in search of the best way to access my parents' lab. Eventually, I find the evacuation point and, once underground, I dispense with stealth. There'll be no security. It's a full evac and everyone who could escape – has. With only the *whoop-whoop* of the evacuation siren for company, I race along the corridors in the ghoulish glow of the orange emergency lighting, the shards of the original lights crunching under my boots. Apart from shattered glass, there is relatively little debris down here. These subterranean labs are designed to withstand seismic shocks, so the air here isn't filled with concrete dust like the upper levels.

Perspex panels line the corridors, and a glance in each dimly lit lab reveals no movement. The federal government's top-secret space, engineering and biosecurity research happens here, but it is only secret from the outside world. Anyone with access to these levels can view the workings of any lab. Dad's text message said Lab 17. As I check off the numbers I pass, I wonder what my fellow physics students would think of this. Much more interesting than our presentation which is due tomorrow.

I slide around a corner and my skin puckers into goose bumps. I'm close. Three labs down, the perspex is bowed outwards. I slow to a jog and steady my breathing.

I reach the lab, and I see it. The portal.

The massive vertical steel ring – my mother's creation – draws my gaze. It's big enough to drive a truck through. Sketches and design specs for this monstrous cosmic gate have littered our house for years. I used to find mathematical equations scrawled across my bedroom mirror when I came home from school. Mum would have been in my room performing some mundane domestic chore, had an idea and then written on whatever was at hand to preserve her inspiration. Having a quantum physicist for a mother has had its moments.

None quite like this one though.

The lab could accommodate a football field if required but, at the moment, it resembles the set of a Hollywood sci-fi disaster. The pliable, shock-proof putty used for the walls and ceiling appears to have melted. Elongated teardrops of gelatinous goo hang from the ceiling, the bulbous ends suspended at different heights like creepy Christmas baubles. Goo from the walls has congealed on the floor, carpeting the mass of cables snaking their way from the power grid to the portal. The portal itself is showering white sparks, which turn orange in the intermittent flashing of the hazard lights.

I dismiss those details to focus on the only thing moving inside the lab. In the dark belly of the portal, a glowing nimbus surrounds a pulsating mass. It's like a knot of eels made of fluid metal. But it's unstable, glitching like a television picture during an electrical storm.

This is the source.

All the devastation at the NSA precinct can be traced to here. Lab 17.

And whatever happened here … I don't think it's finished yet.

I step forward and press my hands on the perspex. It's soft under my palms and I pull them away again, rubbing my fingers together, the sticky residue balling on my fingertips. As I wipe my hands on my trousers, I return my attention to the lab and notice a body lying on the floor amongst the cables.

'Dad,' I whisper.

There'll be no back up. There's no option but to go in.

I wrench the sliding door open – thank God all locks are released in an emergency evacuation – and step inside. It is zero Kelvin cold in here – okay maybe not quite that cold, but it's definitely chilly – and it smells like cinnamon. I cup my hands over my mouth, trying to warm the air on its way to my lungs, and pick my way carefully across the floor so I don't trip on any cables.

As I kneel beside my dad's body and take his icy hand in mine, the glowing mass in the portal blips and I look up. The superfluid snakes slip around each other and I squint to study the mass more carefully. It's more chilling up close. And not actually metallic. Nor are the writhing ribbons uniform in shape or size.

I notice something beyond the glowing mass now. Stars. Thousands of them. I don't recognise any of the constellations – Dad would know them. He's been gazing at the heavens since he was a boy. It was no surprise to anyone he became an astrophysicist.

Something pokes free of the jumble, catching my eye. A flailing arc of … skin? Though I can almost feel ice crystals in my lungs slicing the delicate tissue with every breath, I don't take my eyes from the seething mass. I squeeze my father's unresponsive hand as another protrusion breaks free. It looks like a tiny arm. A tiny human arm.

'Liberty.'

Dad's voice. I drop my gaze but his eyes are closed. Did he say my name or did I imagine it? It doesn't matter. The priority is to get him out of here, then look for Mum. I try to stand but my legs refuse to cooperate. Weakness consumes me. I collapse on top of Dad, my head resting on his chest. He's still alive. I count his heartbeats as I reach into the pocket of my trousers. My fingers close around my phone and I try to muster the strength to pull it out.

But I can't.

'What the hell is happening to me?' I whisper.

No one answers.

Chapter 2

Felix

I scan the ruined landscape. I need to find the cause of the devastation here and locate my stepmother. Even wearing the EMT uniform, I feel exposed. Not having a first-aid kit seriously compromises my disguise.

I skirt the perimeter of the rubble looking for clues while rescue teams with sniffer dogs clamber over the collapsed buildings. The incessant *whoop-whoop* of the evacuation alarms and the percussive thrum of helicopters is like the rhythm section for today's disaster soundtrack. Sporadic blasts of unintelligible human voices through megaphones punctuate the chorus of police, fire and ambulance sirens. Occasionally the ground rumbles, like the rousing canon-fire of a dramatic orchestral piece, and it feels like the end of days.

After quarter of an hour, I've found nothing useful and I wonder if I need to revise my strategy. I'm on the clock. Harry is waiting. I can't stuff around out here.

As I consider climbing the mountain of mangled steel and rubble in front of me, a gigantic concrete slab shifts. Instinctively, I jump back behind a block of broken mortar to avoid becoming another casualty, but peek around the side to keep an eye on the slab.

Then I see a large, scaly foot emerge from underneath it. My immediate thought is that it's a crocodile, but we don't get crocs in downtown

Indigo. Not the amphibious kind anyway. The temperate climate doesn't suit them.

Movement beyond the slab catches my attention. A security guard is approaching. She's spotted the shifting slab and is running towards it. Well, lumbering towards it. The woman has the physique of a whiskey barrel, and given that her cropped hair is more salt than pepper, has probably been aged for at least half a century.

I maintain my position but flick my gaze back to whatever is emerging from the ruins. A coppery snout … followed by a long, shingled neck. I squeeze my eyes closed, sure that I'm hallucinating. I count to three before opening my eyes again. The creature is still there. Now I can see its body, its wings and its tail.

A dragon.

It's a small dragon. It wouldn't be much longer than I am tall.

My concern that I'm hallucinating evaporates when I look at the security guard's face. Her wide-eyed stare indicates that she too is seeing something inexplicable.

The dragon shakes its head and flutters its wings, sending a swirl of dust into the air. The creature doesn't seem to have sustained any injuries, even though it has emerged from underneath tonnes of rubble.

The guard draws her weapon but, before she can take aim, the dragon's tail whips around and flicks the pistol from her hand. The Glock 9 mm lands only a couple of metres away from me. I freeze. Should I kick it back to her?

I glance at the dragon. It's on all fours, snout up, sniffing the air. It seems more intent on its surroundings than the security guard, now the threat has been neutralised.

The guard sidesteps towards her weapon, not taking her eyes off the scaly creature. She squats. I want to shrink back further behind my cover but don't dare move in case I distract her. I can see her ID badge. Jo Higgins. Her hand fumbles the pistol and she cries out a second before the dragon's tail slams across her face. Jo crashes to her knees, clutching her cheek.

I glance between Jo and the dragon, assessing options. My gaze lingers on the dragon as it rears up, standing on its two hind legs … and its scales start to melt away.

In my peripheral vision, I see Jo scramble for the gun again but I maintain focus on the dragon. Its wings fold in behind its back as the tail retracts and the neck shrinks. Its limbs lengthen and the snout flattens. Within moments the dragon is gone and in its place is a woman.

A naked woman.

My stepmother.

'K-Karina?' Jo stammers. 'What … are you?'

It's an excellent question and I hold my breath as I wait for my stepmother's answer. Karina doesn't respond straight away. She's still surveying her surroundings – tracking the path of an army helicopter as it does a low pass. I shield my eyes from the dirt the whirring blades whip across my face.

Dispensing with words, Karina takes half a dozen steps to stand before Jo. She smiles before snatching the pistol from Jo's grasp and shooting her between the eyes.

As the woman's body slumps to the ground, Karina says, 'Jo, I'm afraid that's a secret.'

My heart hammers inside my chest as my stepmother removes the woman's shirt. I'm thankful my stepmother's nudity issue will be resolved, but her interfering with a corpse is a whole other problem. The shirt is like a short dress on her and once it is buttoned, Karina retrieves Jo's pistol before lifting a concrete block – effortlessly – and dumping it on top of the security officer's head.

My stomach rolls violently as I imagine the mangled skull beneath the concrete. Moments ago, Jo was a person. A person who had a home to go to after her shift. She might have stopped for takeaway on the way home and eaten some of the fries on the drive. But that life is gone. Bile burns the back of my throat.

Karina rips the ID badge from the stolen shirt and tosses it on the ground. 'Ought to keep the brains trust busy for a while trying to figure out what happened here.'

I slink further down in my hiding spot, holding my breath, even though I know she could never hear me over the noise out here. Or could she?

I peep around the stonework to see her stalking away from the remains of the buildings. Without thinking, I spring from my spot to follow her. It's easy enough while we're in the disaster zone; there are plenty of hiding spots. I can pursue her from a distance with relative protection. When she continues past the boundary of the building precinct though, I hesitate. Crouching behind a mound of rubble, I watch as she jogs north across open ground.

I squint, tracking ahead to see where she's heading. About two hundred metres away, there's an open trapdoor. An evacuation point from underground. Karina disappears into the opening without hesitation and, though it's probably a bad idea to follow her underground, I have to find out what's going on here. I can't afford to lose her, so I race across the exposed ground to the evac point.

I slide on my knees to the opening and, with a glance into the gloom to make sure she's not checking for pursuit, I make my way downstairs. At each level I find a locked fire door. On the sixth level, the door has been pulled from its hinges.

'Must be it,' I mutter aloud.

I scoot along the corridor, the evacuation siren blaring and the strobing orange hazard lights engineering an epileptic's nightmare. I turn left at the next corner. This corridor is different. There's a solid wall on one side but the opposite wall is perspex. Karina is nowhere to be seen. Either she's made it to the end of this corridor or she's in one of these rooms.

I check each room – each lab – as I jog past. No sign of Karina. At the next T-intersection, I stop and peek left then right. I catch a fleeting glimpse of her as she disappears around the next corner to my left.

I hesitate. Karina just killed a security officer and she is armed.

A more chilling thought occurs to me. Liberty is on site.

I dash around the corner and skid to a stop at the next intersection. A glance around the corner reveals Karina standing only a few metres from me. With her back to me, she's focused on one of the labs; one where the perspex is bowed out like a bubble. She still has the security guard's pistol in one hand, but she lifts the emergency handset from the wall fixture with the other as she stares into the room. A strange light dances around her. In my mind, I see a copper-coloured dragon.

Finally, she taps several buttons on the handset before lifting it to her ear. She raises her voice to be heard over the evac siren.

'Lab 17,' she says. 'Two bodies. Dispose of them, then secure the perimeter.'

She listens for a moment, then, 'Yes. Caspian Fox is here but his wife isn't. I'll find her.'

Karina replaces the handset and sighs. 'Shit.'

She stalks away down the corridor – thankfully in the opposite direction to where I'm standing. If she'd caught me here … I'd probably suffer the same fate as the security guard. When Karina disappears from sight, I venture round the corner to inspect the lab. Could this be the story Harry is chasing?

I pull my phone from the pocket of the EMT coveralls as I approach the bowed perspex.

'What the hell?'

Either they're filming a *Dr Who* episode here or they're experimenting with alien tech. I'm assuming it's option B, and while everything I know about alien tech comes from movies, I'd put money on the fact that this *thing* is malfunctioning. Crazy as it sounds, it looks like a portal. The ring itself is spewing sparks, there's a glowing glob of plasma in the centre winking in and out of existence, and the walls and ceiling have … melted.

Something went wrong here. Very wrong. This must be what has brought down the entire precinct. This *is* Harry's scoop. I snap a couple of photos, aware that someone is on their way to dispose of the bodies and secure the room.

Bodies.

I scan the floor and my heart seizes inside my chest. Liberty is slumped over a man's body. Looks like she found her father. Stuffing my phone in my pocket, I race through the open doorway. The cold ambushes me but I ignore it. Carefully, I roll Liberty onto her back and lay my ear against her chest, but it's difficult to listen for her heartbeat when my heart is pounding so loudly in my ears. The delicate wisps of steam that leak from between her blue lips tell me she's alive though.

I scoop Liberty off the floor, cradling her limp form in my arms, and retrace my steps – taking care not to trip on any cables on my way out.

Once outside, I confront a conundrum. Someone is coming to dispose of these bodies. Or possibly *someones*. Since all the buildings aboveground have collapsed, access to the labs is limited. Will the clean-up crew come through the evac point I used? Or is there another way in? Karina didn't leave the way she entered, but she went looking for Liberty's mother.

I stare at Liberty's face. What would she do in this situation? Assess it logically, then act calmly. Okay. I've got two bodies, very little time and a fifty-fifty chance of picking the safe escape route. Holding Liberty against my chest, I slink around the corner and into another lab. I lay her on the floor behind a stainless-steel island workbench.

'Wait here,' I say. 'I'll get your father and be right back.'

I creep to the doorway, but a glance down the corridor reveals six figures in military fatigues marching towards me. I scurry back behind the workbench, breathing hard.

Liberty moans. I reach to put my hand over her mouth to quieten her but decide the troop won't hear her over the sirens so I pull my hand back. Once they pass, I slide my arms under her shoulders and knees and lift her up.

'We've gotta go,' I whisper to her.

When the crew finds one body, they'll know they have a problem. Karina told them there were two. I need to get Liberty out before they organise themselves to look for her.

With Liberty's limp body in my arms, I retreat as fast as I can. I race along the corridors and then take the stairs to the evac point two at a time. Once aboveground again, I suck in a deep breath. I've got a lot of ground to cover. My uniform says EMT so I need to do justice to my disguise. If I look like an unauthorised undercover reporter scurrying away with an unconscious and equally unauthorised civilian in his arms, there'll be trouble.

Within five minutes, we're bouncing over the uneven terrain in an ambulance. Having found one unattended and with the engine running was almost too good to be true, but now I wish there'd been an ambo inside this one when I stole it. They'd have known how to turn on the sirens. I glance in the rear-vision mirror for the fifteenth time. Liberty is on the stretcher, still unconscious.

A horn blasts beside me a second before impact and the jolt returns my attention to the front. Too late, I jam my foot on the brake.

A soldier waves at me from the passenger side of the Mercedes G-wagon that has emerged from the curtain of dust and smoke swirling over the precinct like a flamenco dancer's skirt. 'Watch where you're going!' he yells.

I salute as the army vehicle roars off across the road in front of me, leaving me with a crumpled front corner on the driver's side of the ambulance.

I scan the dashboard, muttering, 'I need lights and sirens. Then *they* can get out of *my* way.'

The chaos around me seems to amplify as I search the control panel for the signal switches. When I finally activate the lights and sirens, I hit the accelerator.

'Hold on, Liberty,' I call over my shoulder. 'We're on our way!'

I pull the wheel to the right and head for the procession of vehicles making their way to the main road. Orange, red and blue lights punch through the smoky haze, reminding me of a disco I attended at the PCYC when I was thirteen. The Police and Citizens Youth Club held a biannual dance to keep the city's youth off the streets. How anyone thought reducing gang crime could be achieved by locking young people in a room for two nights of the year with dodgy music, a smoke machine and strobe lighting is still beyond me.

I join the convoy of vehicles, pulling in behind another ambulance, and once we hit the public road, I floor it. I'm happy to let the ambulance ahead of me bulldoze its way through Indigo's afternoon traffic and drag me along in its wake.

We reach the hospital in under fifteen minutes and I swing into a bay beside the ambulance I tailed. The truck sways as I wrench on the handbrake. I shove my door open and jump out to see half a dozen people racing across the carpark towards the hospital's emergency entrance. It could be the next shift coming in but it's more likely the hospital has called in everyone they can to deal with the NSA emergency.

Two of them peel away from the pack and head for the ambulances that have just pulled in. A woman in drill trousers, a Nike t-shirt and a baseball cap meets me at the back of my truck. She helps me open the doors.

'You're a doctor?' I say.

She glances inside the ambulance before turning back to me.

She frowns. 'I *am* a doctor – Doctor Palmer,' she says, raking her gaze over me. 'But you're clearly *not* a paramedic.'

'Well, I … um … it's … a – it's a long story,' I say at last.

'Which I don't have time to hear,' Dr Palmer snaps. 'Just tell me about the girl.'

I feel like I'm in one of those emergency room television shows. 'Liberty Fox, seventeen-year-old female,' I say. 'I found her unconscious in an underground lab at NSA.'

'Lab? Potential contamination risk,' she mutters. 'Right. Clear the way.'

Dr Palmer pulls the stretcher from the ambulance and the supports snap into place. I trot beside her as she wheels the trolley through the hospital's front door.

The doctor calls out to a nurse behind the desk. 'I've got this one.' Then she points at me. 'Get the details from this guy.'

Dr Palmer scoots the trolley down the hall and disappears around a corner. The lobby is swarming with people. Nurses in different coloured scrubs are flitting about while a doctor with a blood-spattered gown threads his way through the sea of casualties. But for all the gore and groaning in the waiting room, there is no panic. Today is going to stretch the hospital's resources but the staff here are professionals. As I survey the injured, I'm thankful Liberty has jumped the queue.

The nurse snaps on a fresh pair of gloves before stalking towards me like a praying mantis.

Pen poised over her clipboard, she says, 'Patient's name?'

'Liberty Fox, seventeen-year-old female,' I say.

'You her boyfriend?'

'Yes,' I say reflexively, and instantly regret it. I'm supposed to be undercover. 'How did you know I'm not a paramedic?'

She doesn't look up from her paperwork. 'No ID, old uniform, no partner and … no gloves. And seventeen-year-old girls don't work at NSA.'

'Her parents do – she was looking for them. I found her unconscious in an underground lab.'

As I'm defending Liberty, a real ambo scuttles past me. I watch as she presents her gloved fist to the doctor at her side. The doctor mutters as he records the stats scrawled on the latex. Gloves aren't just for protection apparently; they are a vital data source in the patient transfer process.

'Your name?' the nurse asks.

'Steve Rogers.'

The lie is unexpected and I feel a surge of adrenaline. Maybe I'm finally getting the hang of this undercover thing.

'Her parents?' the nurse says without looking up.

'Missing.'

She glares at me. 'Their names?'

'Oh. Right. Mr and Mrs Fox,' I reply slowly. Belatedly I remember Karina calling Liberty's father Caspian, but it's too late to plug that in now.

The nurse's eyes narrow. 'Does Liberty have any medical conditions?'

'No. She's fit, active, … healthy.'

'Allergies?'

'None known,' I say, praying I'm right.

'Given you don't know your girlfriend's parents' full names, I guess there's no point asking you about the family medical history?'

'I haven't met her parents yet,' I say defensively, adding, 'we haven't been together long.'

'Uh-huh.' The nurse finishes scrawling. 'Wait here,' she says. 'I'm going to grab a Geiger counter to run over you.'

'A what?'

'You've been in a lab,' she says as she turns her back on me. 'I'm gonna make sure you won't glow in the dark. Don't go anywhere.'

She returns quickly and scans me with her handheld device. It sputters briefly around my knees but then remains silent for the rest of the screening. I refrain from sighing with relief. Just.

'You're clear,' she says at last.

I nod. 'Thanks. When do you think I'll be able to see her?'

'I'd suggest you take a seat and get comfortable,' she says as she fiddles with the power switch on the Geiger counter. 'Unless you want to keep pretending to be an ambo?'

I feel the heat in my cheeks. 'Probably not the best idea,' I mumble.

'Thought not,' the nurse says with a sniff.

'There's a spare ambulance out there,' I add. 'Someone might be able to use that.'

'Yep.'

I pull my personal phone from the pocket of my coveralls and slump into a seat as the nurse stalks away. I'm sure Harry will have bombarded my work phone with messages, so I ignore that one for the moment. Three missed calls and five messages on my phone. The calls are all from my father, along with a voice message and a text. I read his text first.

Hi Son. If you haven't seen the news, there has been a major incident at NSA. Your stepmother is fine. Only a couple of scrapes and bruises.

I roll my eyes. The voicemail probably says the same thing so I don't listen to it. I send a reply to his text. *Heard about it. A girl from school was injured there and I'm at the hospital with her now. I'll be home later. Talk to you then.*

Again, an image of the dragon flashes in my mind. That's a level of weird I can't deal with right now, so I move on to Elvira's three texts.

Her first message was two and a half hours ago. *Your US has left the building. Headed for NSA!*

US. Unattainable Senior.

'Her name is Liberty, Elvira,' I say aloud.

The second message. *What's doing? Are you okay?*

The third message sent only twenty minutes ago says, *If you get captured, I should be your ONE phone call.*

I send back to her. *I'm at the hospital. Liberty's hurt.*

Her response will be quick so I leave my phone on my lap as I drag my work phone from another pocket. A dozen missed calls and seventeen texts from Harry.

Where are you?

What are you doing?

Report.

Report.

Report.

Report.

Report.

Report.

Report.

Report.

Report.

Report.

Report.

Report.

Report.

Don't ignore me.

As I type my response, I wonder if Harry has some kind of psychological disorder. I send, *I'm at the hospital. Liberty Fox is hurt. I have info for you. Talk in person later.*

Both phones ping simultaneously when Elvira and Harry respond.

Harry's text says, *Stay there. I'll come when I finish my last cross.*

Elvira's message is, *I'll be there as soon as I can.*

I check the time. 15:04. If what the nurse said is true, I'm in for a long wait for news about Liberty. I hope Elvira and Harry stagger their visits, but I also hope I've got some time to get my story straight before they arrive. I need to decide what information to share with whom. One thing is sure. I won't be telling either of them about the dragon.

Chapter 3

Elvira

My father's face appears on my tablet. He's in his office, half a world away from me. The whiteboard behind him – framing him – is a canvas of indecipherable equations. Aeon Elegand owns every colour of whiteboard marker available and he isn't afraid to use them. His brain is wired for theoretical physics but he has the soul of poet.

'Daughter,' he says. 'How are you?'

I grimace. 'Horribly conflicted.'

His brow creases. My father is a handsome man, even when he frowns. On my screen, I trace the outline of his angular jaw with my finger, wishing that I could feel the stubble of his five o'clock shadow graze my fingertips. I haven't felt that in over ten years. Nor have I felt the warmth of his embrace or smelled the scent of his ylang-ylang shampoo. I want to ask him if he still uses that shampoo, but now is not the time. Now, we have important matters to discuss.

His eyes, like dark butterscotch orbs, study me. 'I too am conflicted, Daughter,' he says, 'but we must both put our feelings aside for now. We need to focus on the big picture.'

I sigh. 'I know.'

'I need to know I'm talking with Elvira,' he says into the long pause that follows.

'It is me,' I whisper.

Father knows – and understands – that my characters are shields. Elvira is dangerous, alien, someone who must be hidden from humans. She was born on Earth but doesn't belong here. She belongs to Rhybor – a world she's never known. Her cast of characters deflects attention, keeping her secret safe.

'Where are you, Daughter?' my father asks.

'In a park,' I say. 'School's done for today. I'm on my way to see Felix.'

'I see,' he says, nodding and leaning back in his chair. 'You'd better tell me what happened at NSA. Was it Karina's portal?'

'I think so,' I say. 'I can't imagine what other projects they could have there that would make such a mess.'

My father glances to his left. 'Yes. I'm watching some of the footage. It just about couldn't be anything else.'

'You're getting coverage of it there?'

'Some,' he says with a shrug. 'Not much.'

My father has been in Russia for nearly eleven years. Since his release from jail there three years ago, he's been working on a secret intergalactic portal project. Worldwide, there are three teams in a race to open a portal to Rhybor, a world on the opposite side of the Milky Way galaxy to Earth. A world rich in elenium, which humans covet. But what my father and his kind know is that elenium is not Rhybor's only distinguishing feature. Rhybor is the world of wehrdragons.

'Can you access the site?' he asks.

'Felix has been on site. He's currently at the hospital – the Fox girl was injured looking for her parents – so I'll go and see him once we are done here. I'm sure I can convince him to go back.'

My father nods. 'Good. I need first-hand intel on—'

'I think we should recruit him.' I blurt out the words before I change my mind.

'Daughter, we—'

'He's ready.'

My father leans forward, peering directly into his tablet's camera. 'Elvira, I agree with your assessment of Felix. I believe, in time, he will be an asset to our cause – but I do not think that time is now. I understand you're protective of him, but we are at a delicate juncture and we cannot afford to compromise this mission. Patience, Daughter.'

'Patience,' I say and sigh.

'You know we cannot let Karina be the first to return to Rhybor. She seeks to bring down the monarchy. *We* must be the first to return.'

I know. I've heard all this before. But my inner dragon can't connect to this narrative. Can't care about the 'cause'. Royal families, conspiracy theories, and the elenium trade – all be damned. All I care about is my father and my friend. Aeon and Felix.

'If he finds out what I know,' I say, 'we could lose him.'

My father smiles. 'I have faith in you, Elvira. You're a good friend to him.'

'But I'm a better spy for you.'

'You're not spying on him,' my father says. 'You're spying on his parents.'

'Yeah,' I say, 'and I'm sure he'll be really comfortable with that when he learns the truth about his family – and about me.'

My father shifts in his seat. 'Daughter, I need you to focus. We need information about the portal. Were the Foxes really close to a working portal and something unexpected went wrong? Or are they nowhere near a solution and have cocked things up completely?'

'Yeah, okay,' I say as I rifle through my character list for the one who can convince Felix to join me on a mission that I can't tell him anything about. 'I'll get the info you need.'

∞

Though the Emergency waiting room is packed, I spot Felix straight away. I really should put Harry in touch with some people I know at the theatre so his 'disguises' are more authentic. Felix is wearing ambo's coveralls but he's about as convincing as a turtle masquerading as a contortionist. If he's going to persist with the undercover journalist gig, he's going to have to do a lot better than that.

'Did you actually fool anyone with that getup?' I say as he looks up at me.

Felix stands and dusts himself off. 'I dunno. I didn't take a survey – I was kinda busy.'

'Busy rescuing a fair maiden?'

'Yes,' he says, folding his arms across his chest.

I manage to not laugh. 'Okay, Romeo, let's take it outside. It's too crowded to talk in here.'

I turn and retrace my steps, not bothering to check if he's following me. He will be. Once outside again, I follow a wide ramp – designed for wheelchairs – then turn left at the corner of the building towards the courtyard café. The café isn't as crowded as the ER; there are a few free tables. I wind my way towards one and dump my bag on one of the three black metal stools before plonking myself on another.

'I'll guard the table,' I say. 'You can order coffees. I'd love a small chai latte.'

'Yes, Your Highness,' Felix says before stalking away towards the counter.

I scan the café and my shoulders sag. One need look no further than a hospital café for proof that our 'health' institutions are actually focused on disease, rather than health. Upon entry, one is first assaulted with the smell of burnt coffee, grease and antiseptic. I've heard the coffee here is a bitter sludge, better suited to sealing roads than being consumed as a beverage. The food will, at best, stop hunger, but has the taste and nutritional value of a sponge. Even the ibises – or bin chickens as they are better known – don't eat it. And that's probably why the establishment is pest- and vermin-free too. The cockroaches and rats don't fancy the fare either. People would actually be better off eating the table napkins and drinking the hand sanitiser.

Today, the plastic walls are rolled up so we're not all festering inside a grime-encrusted pen. One would think fresh air and sunshine would improve the tone of the place. But no ... it's hollow in here, soulless. Everyone speaks in hushed, muted voices and no one smiles. The novelty surgical masks worn by some of the staff barely even get a second look, and I think I know why. Simply *wearing* pig snouts, shark jaws, crazy moustaches and zippered lips isn't enough. A performance is still required to bring them to life, and from what I've seen of this shift, the staff simply lack pizazz. I'd wager the most animated lifeforms in this café are microscopic. The only things partying in here are pathogens.

Felix will return soon so I don't have long to get into character. I plunge into my routine. I close my eyes and rummage around in my inner casting room where all my personas hang out. And I find Beth. Beth is calm, rational, and efficient, yet also kind and enthusiastic. Perfect for this role.

Felix returns with drinks and places a paper cup on the table in front of me, froth oozing down the side.

'Thank you, Felix,' I say. 'How much do I owe you?'

'Oh shit,' Felix mutters as he plants himself on a stool. 'Who am I dealing with now?'

I smile. 'Beth O'Brien – the forensic pathologist in *Bones of a Clown*. Remember?'

'No, I don't remember that one.' He sighs. 'Can you not leave your characters at the theatre, Elvira?'

'Life is a performance,' I say. 'How many times do I have to tell you that, Felix? And besides, one must work hard to become an actor. I need to practise every chance I get.'

Felix slurps his milkshake.

'So,' I say. 'Tell me everything … succinctly. Beth appreciates brevity.'

Felix's eyes narrow. 'Okay,' he says. 'I watched my stepmother escape from the rubble by lifting a slab of concrete that probably weighed several tonnes, like it was a piece of cardboard. She then murdered a security guard who witnessed her superhuman feat by shooting her right between the eyes. After that, I followed Karina underground where she inspected a lab that appeared to contain an unstable portal. She made a phone call ordering that the two bodies on the floor be disposed of, and that the lab be sealed. In the time between when she left and when the clean-up crew arrived, I recovered Liberty's body – she was still alive. The clean-up crew arrived before I had the chance to rescue her father though, so I got Liberty out and brought her here.'

My eyes widen, revealing Beth's surprise.

'That succinct enough?' Felix says before taking another long slurp of his milkshake.

I nod slowly. 'Yes.'

'So what does Beth think?'

Questions about the portal flood my brain, but I say, 'There is much to be considered here.' I frown. 'Firstly, it sounds like you could be in great danger, Felix. If your stepmother killed a security guard … and she finds out *you* know …'

I shudder. This is unexpected. I know the source of Karina's strength, but Felix doesn't, and Karina would definitely not want him to find out that she's a wehrdragon. My own dragon blood boils inside me. His heritage should never have been kept from him, though I kind of understand why it was.

Felix is different and not in a good way. He's a half-breed. His father is a wehr; it's his human mother's blood that is the problem. Crippled by the taint of human blood, Felix is doomed to be trapped in human form – never to experience the exhilaration of transforming into a dragon and sailing the skies.

'What are you going to do?' I ask, my heart chugging inside my chest. 'What will you say to her?'

Frowning, Felix places his drink on the table. 'I'm going to tell her that Harry knows about the portal and about the Foxes.'

'The Foxes?' I prompt when he stops.

He leans forward and runs his fingers down the sides of the metal milkshake container, leaving trails in the condensation clinging to the cup.

'Liberty's parents are scientists at NSA,' he says, 'and I think they were working on a portal. I found Liberty unconscious in the lab with a portal, and her father was in there as well. I overheard Karina on the phone telling someone to dispose of the bodies and seal the room while she tracked down Liberty's mother, who was missing – at that point.'

I feign a look of surprise. 'Well, that explains why Liberty went there.' I take a moment to fabricate Beth's response. 'You want to go back there, don't you?' I ask.

Felix nods. 'When Liberty wakes up, she'll want to know what happened to her parents. And I want to be able to tell her.'

'Hmmm.'

'You don't think I can do it?' he says, folding his arms across his chest.

I smother my own response, letting Beth handle this one. 'I don't think you should do it *alone*. I'll come with you.'

I sip my chai latte while I watch him consider my offer. I have to see the portal. Thankfully, Beth is more diplomatic than I am, so I am definitely in with a chance.

'It'll be dangerous,' Felix says, all male chauvinist bravado. 'I can't ask you to come with me, Elvira.'

'You didn't ask,' I say. '*Beth* offered. Completely different thing.'

'That doesn't change how dangerous it will be – for whoever is going.'

'Agreed, but you'll need backup, Felix. And Beth is perfect for this job. She's level-headed—'

Felix holds up his hands. 'Not a job interview.' He sighs. 'Fine. Beth can come.'

I grace him with Beth's winning smile. 'Great.' I erase the smile then, replacing it with a look laced with worry. 'But back to Karina … what's her connection to the portal? I thought you said she dealt with energy leases.'

Felix shrugs. 'Seems that's not all she does. She went straight to the portal – she must know a fair bit about it.'

I nod. 'So why tell her Harry knows about the portal? And *does* he, by the way?'

Felix shakes his head. 'He doesn't know yet,' he says, 'but he will by the time I get home tonight. He's going to drop by here later.'

'So why tell him?' I say, pressing him to reveal more.

'Insurance,' Felix says. 'A secret portal that levels the NSA – that's *massive* news. That means a lot of attention. With that much scrutiny, Karina can't cover it up.'

'Meaning you're trying to blackmail her into not killing you – or Harry – for what you know?'

'Something like that.'

'Risky play,' I say.

'Once the story is out … we should be okay.'

I shiver, equal parts excitement and terror. 'We should go now.'

'What? I thought you said Beth was level-headed. Don't you think this should be planned carefully?'

'The site is in chaos,' I say. 'This *is* the best time to go. Once they clear the site, it'll be much more difficult to sneak in and poke around. And you can talk to Harry while we're there.'

Felix's face betrays nothing as he considers my proposal.

Finally, he says, 'I want to be here if Liberty wakes up.'

I want to groan, then say '*if* she wakes up' but that's not Beth's style. Instead, I dip into her tank of diplomacy.

'I know you want be here for her,' I say, 'but do you want the trail to go cold? She'll want answers, and if you stay here – you'll have nothing for her.'

There's a flash – a spark – in his eyes. I've got him, but I don't have time to sit around waiting for him to admit it. Beth is calm but there is a limit to her patience.

'We could procure a couple of new paramedic uniforms here,' I say, 'and then steal a car from out front.'

His forehead barely creases at the suggestion of grand theft auto, which is disappointing. I thought that was a daring play.

'We should steal an ambulance,' Felix says. 'I know how to work the sirens.'

Chapter 4

Felix

Helicopters are crisscrossing the site as I trudge across the field, shielding my eyes from the sun as it slips behind the hills. Strips of cloud are tinged with the colours of a summer fruit salad – apricot, raspberry and mango – but I'm not here to admire the sunset. I've briefed Harry on what I've found out about the portal. Now I'm psyching myself up for stage two of my mission – speaking to my stepmother.

Hopefully, Elvira has been successful with her part of the mission – snooping underground for intel on Liberty's parents. I'd like to have gone snooping with her but talking to Harry was a priority and, to minimise our time onsite, the tasks for this mission needed to be split.

I hope she's okay. She was full of bravado, claiming that if she *were* to run into trouble her acting and improvisation skills would save her. I didn't think she needed to add that I would have been about as useful to her as a losing lottery ticket, but that's Elvira for you. I think I like Beth better.

I crest the hill bordering the field and make my way down the other side, winding my way between the trunks of the pine trees protruding from the mat of brown, dried needles carpeting the slope. From the pocket of the upgraded paramedics uniform that Elvira 'borrowed' from the hospital, I pull out my phone. 18:07. I scroll through the contacts until I find Karina's number.

When I find it, I press the telephone icon without hesitation and as the *brrrrp-brrrrp* starts in my ear, I consider how many times I have called her. I could probably count them using the legs of half a spider.

The call connects.

'Stepson,' Karina says. 'If you are calling to enquire after my well-being, I can assure you – as I believe your father already has – that I am fine. Now, if there is nothing else … I am rather busy here.'

I fail to suppress a shiver at my stepmother's tone. The lack of emotion is menacing. The vision of a gleaming dragon emerging from under a pile of rubble plays in my mind.

'Where are Liberty's parents?' I ask, pushing reptilian thoughts aside.

'Who?'

'Liberty Fox's parents,' I say. 'I pulled Liberty out of a lab earlier, but I didn't get a chance to get her father out.'

The silence that follows seeps out of my phone like an oil slick, threatening to smother me. My blood feels as though it has turned into a superfluid plasma, speeding adrenaline around my body and accelerating all my systems.

'Where are you now, Felix?' Karina asks.

'I'm on site,' I say, unwilling to give a specific location.

'You need to leave,' she says. 'This area is unsafe and unauthorised civilians compromise the rescue operation.'

'I am not an unauthorised civilian,' I reply. 'I'm here in my official role as cadet journalist for the *Indigo Times*. So, can I get an answer from you on the situation with the Foxes?'

'No.'

'What about the portal?' I ask. 'Do you have anything to say about that?'

She sighs. 'I have nothing to say to you about anything, Felix. What happens here is none of your concern.'

'Except that it *is* my concern,' I argue. 'It's my job to report on what happened here. I saw the portal and I reckon there's a good chance that something went wrong with it and caused this disaster.'

I stop myself from adding *and I have a strong suspicion that you'll try to cover it up.*

Karina snorts. '*Your* job is actually to report to a *real* journalist, Felix, so can I assume that you've shared your wild theory with Harry already?'

'Yes.'

'Well, that was imprudent,' Karina says, 'but Harry will, I'm sure, realise that he has a responsibility – as a *real* journalist – to corroborate *facts* before reporting on them.'

'Are you saying the portal doesn't exist?'

'What I am saying, Felix, is that I am not commenting on any projects here. The priority here is the rescue. Now please leave the site before Security finds you and detains you.'

'Detains me for what?'

'Trespass.'

'But I'm here in an official capacity.'

'Well, I'm happy for them to sort it out because I am certainly not going to waste any more time discussing it with you.'

'If rescue is really the priority,' I say, 'then surely Security would have better things to do than worry about me. It's not like I'm putting anyone in danger. It's not like I've shot someone or anything.'

The silence this time is surprisingly brief and when Karina responds, it is with a voice so calm she could lead a guided meditation.

'Felix, I don't know what your game is, but I don't have time for it.' She pauses before adding, 'And I assure you that nothing you dream up could possibly threaten me.'

The line goes dead before I can respond. I pull the phone from my ear and stare at the home screen. She's definitely gone.

'Bitch,' I mutter.

Provoking her might not have been a good idea but it felt great. I'm riding a wave of empowerment when a sudden thought makes me shudder. Phones have GPS. Security probably *is* on its way. I need to keep moving.

∞

Elvira

I kneel beside the concrete slab, careful not to touch the body of the security guard protruding from underneath it, and open the first-aid kit from the ambulance. As I snap on a pair of disposable gloves, I wonder why no one has found her remains. This place has been crawling with rescuers in the hours since Felix saw Karina shoot this woman and, as there is now less than half an hour of daylight remaining, EMTs are swarming to find what survivors they can before natural light deserts them. Not that this one is a survivor. Still, the body should have been attended to by now.

Luckily, there *is* no one else in this vicinity now. I don't need witnesses for this. I inhale deeply and exhale slowly before lifting and pushing the slab aside, disturbing the flies that are already feasting on the soupy mess. The insects *zzzzzrip* past my face like shrapnel from a grenade. This woman probably came to work today thinking it was just a day like any other. She couldn't have imagined she'd be shot dead by someone she was meant to protect.

'One job,' I murmur. 'Just get the thing and go.'

The gloves are a barrier to germs, but they can't shield me from the horrifying sensation of pulpy flesh and broken bone.

One thing.

The bullet.

Karina should never have left it behind. That's careless. Or arrogant. Or both.

I clench my jaw muscles in the hope that I won't scream or vomit as I gingerly sift through matted hair, shattered bone and lumps of brain tissue for the incriminating evidence. More distressing than the fact that I'm desecrating this woman's remains, is the knowledge that I'm potentially saving Karina's arse. I'd rather see Karina Warhurst burn, but none of us wehrs can risk having too much scrutiny. If humanity were to identify any of us, we'd all be hunted down.

I eventually find the mangled metal slug. I pinch it between my fingers and peel off the glove, bagging the bullet inside it. After tying it off, I put on another pair of gloves and retrieve the spent shell from the dirt nearby. Again, the evidence is sealed inside latex. I then tuck the gloves inside a pocket on my EMT uniform. I shudder.

'The show must go on,' I say aloud, willing my body into action.

I'm not religious but this security guard's fate needs to be acknowledged in some way. Closing my eyes, an act of avoidance rather than reverence, I offer a generic prayer that will hopefully find its way to the guard's god – if she has one.

'May your spirit be guided to peace,' I whisper.

∞

I've found the emergency exit Felix used to access the underground labs, but there is now a security patrol car parked next to it, which is vexing. A lone guard is in the driver's seat, engrossed in his phone. There is a lot of open ground to cover to reach it though. If he spots me racing across the field, he'll have plenty of time to deploy countermeasures.

I frown. 'I'll have to wait until dark,' I murmur.

As the minutes drag by, I consider how uncooperative the sun is. It's like someone has nailed it to the sky, a hostage in the heavens. A baleful bauble casting long shadows over the disaster zone with its ferocious gaze.

I wish someone would shut off the evacuation sirens. Those who could evacuate the site must have done so by now. Anyone who hasn't is either dead or trapped. Either way, the sirens are redundant.

A chopper makes a low pass over the field and I shield my face from the dust and dried pine needles that assault me. My heartrate almost matches the *whump-whump-whump* of the spinning rotors.

To kill time until the sun fades, I review the contents of the first-aid kit. Ear plugs? No, I need to be vigilant and that means all senses operating at full capacity. Face mask? Yes. Avoiding a mouthful of pine needles is a priority, and obscuring facial features is a bonus. I peel the packet open and secure the duckbill mask over my nose and mouth. Next, an Epipen. Unlikely to be useful, but not to be discounted. A couple of green whistles – could come in handy. Unfortunately, no tranquilliser gun loaded with darts. I shut the kit and seal the clasps.

While I wait for the final curtain of dusk to draw the day to a close, I study the patrol vehicle. It's probably a couple of tonnes but I will be able to move it. The guard will be a problem. I need to neutralise him. If I roll the boxy four-wheel drive just right, I might crush the frame enough so the doors are jammed shut.

I picture the look of consternation on the guard's face when the vehicle moves without his intervention. I smile. It's probably mean to take pleasure in such things, but I have to get my kicks where I can. Having so few opportunities to take my dragon form has been to the detriment of my sense of humour.

My blood heats up at the thought of Shifting and I squeeze my eyes closed, fighting to resist. That's all I need right now. After giving Felix a hard time about his woeful attempt at going undercover as a paramedic, I can't afford to be caught cavorting about in the sky – all wings, tail and bronze scales.

When the light finally bleeds from the sky, I race across the open ground towards the vehicle, first-aid kit in hand, and take cover at the rear. I'm panting, my breath warm against my face under the duckbill mask.

'Time to move,' I whisper.

I crawl to the passenger side of the vehicle and stand up, bracing myself with my gloved hands gripping the cool metal of the wheel rim. Adrenaline ignites my muscles and I heave … and the four-wheel drive rolls onto its roof. The guard screams but there's a chance he could crawl out the passenger side door, so I roll the car twice more for good measure.

The guard continues yelling as I wrench open the evacuation hatch, snatch up the first-aid kit and venture down the stairs into the gloom. I pull the metal door closed hoping the guard's phone has dropped out of reach and he can't call for backup.

I scurry down the steps in the stairwell's amber glow. At least there is no siren in here; the only sound is my tramping feet. Six flights down, with no sound of pursuit from above, I find a dislodged fire door.

This sublevel has the ambience of a morgue. I scan the upper wall for CCTV cameras but don't see any, so I set off again, following the directions Felix gave me to the lab where he found Liberty and her father.

'Bless you, Felix,' I say aloud when I find the lab. 'Would you look at that …'

The portal – or what's left of it – is visible through the bowed window. No one is around. Probably has something to do with the black and yellow radiation warning tape plastered across the door. A bit of radiation won't affect wehrs, so I push the door open and step into the room. I place the first-aid kit on the floor. My skin prickles into goose bumps at the change in temperature but I ignore that, keeping my focus on the flickering light in the centre of the portal.

I stop a couple of metres from the raised circular platform, at what I hope is a safe distance, to study the glowing nimbus. The jittery ball of light floats about a metre overhead. It stretches spasmodically into something flat, like a porthole on a ship, giving a tantalising glimpse of something beyond. But before I can decipher the scene, the disc snaps back into a roiling ball of slippery tentacles.

I slide my phone from my pocket ready to video footage for my father. I slide the focus to zoom in on the malfunctioning portal and press record. As the camera counts the seconds, I squint at the portal and when it flattens again I see … stars. I gasp. The Foxes were close to a working portal!

The stars disappear and the spherical mass, flickering like a hologram, returns. I briefly wonder whose stars I can see, when something un-tentacle-like catches my eye, something that looks like an ear. I step forward, peering into the mass. And then something peers back at me! An eye. Large, blue, bloodshot and framed with long, inky lashes. I flinch, blink, and when I look again, the eye is gone.

A shiver races down my spine. Someone is trapped in the malfunctioning portal and the eye suggests that someone is female. Rose Fox? I chew my bottom lip. It must be her. How many people would have been in here testing the thing? It is possible they had an assistant, and Rose went for help after the portal imploded, but—

I stop recording, stash my phone in my pocket and turn towards the door. After a final glance over my shoulder at the portal, I collect the first-aid kit and step back into the corridor, sliding the door shut behind me.

If my hunch is correct, I know where Liberty's mother is, but now I need to find her father. This would be easier if I could Shift. As a dragon, I could easily sense any lifeforms still down here. I'm going to have to do this the hard way though – walk the corridors and hope I don't get caught.

I retrace my steps and continue down the emergency stairs until I find an unlocked door. I slink into sublevel nine before finding what I'm looking for.

People.

I stand beside a large window with my back pressed against a solid wall, hoping to time a sneaky peek through the window so I don't get caught by whoever is inside. Through the wall, I can hear the beeping of electronic equipment and the hum of air conditioning. After counting to three, I turn my head slowly, keeping my body in the shadow of the wall.

It looks like an Ebola isolation unit. Beyond the back of a white Hazmat suit, I can make out a man lying on a gurney encased in a transparent plastic bubble. He has fair, wavy hair and his torso is dotted with round sticky pads connected to wires. A bag of blood and two bags of clear fluid hang from a drip stand on the far side of the bed, next to the heart monitor which is flashing frenetic green squiggles across the screen.

A beige leather recliner, which seems out of place in the otherwise sterile environment, lurks in the corner. The door in the wall adjacent to the recliner opens and I catch a glimpse of a shower recess before Karina appears in the doorway. I gasp but remain still. A sudden movement now might draw Karina's attention.

Felix's stepmother is dressed in grey jogging pants and a black t-shirt. Her shoulder length blonde hair is wet but combed, and her face and arms show no evidence of any injuries from her time under the rubble. Taking her dragon form when the building collapsed would have saved her delicate human skin. Scales make great armour.

'I'm ready for another withdrawal, Dr Costigan,' Karina says to her Hazmat-clad companion as she eases herself into the recliner and flicks up the footrest. 'I think we're on the left arm again this time?'

The doctor's reply is muffled by his face shield, but I can hear him.

'Are you sure?' Dr Costigan asks. 'This is your third in an hour. I'm concerned that—'

Karina waves one hand. 'I'm fine,' she says. 'I assure you my blood replenishes more quickly than the average person. We'll do the twelve withdrawals. Transfusions are Dr Fox's only chance.'

I turn my head slowly so I'm out of sight of anyone inside the room. I unlock my knees and slide my back down the wall until I'm crouching on the concrete floor. I rock forward onto my hands and knees and crawl along under the window towards the door. Once there, I drop flat onto the floor with my nose close to the base of the door. The concrete is pleasantly cool against my cheek, but it doesn't bring me any comfort. Though these doors have better seals than most, my wehr sense can still make out the distinctive smell.

Cloves.

Dragon blood is highly potent and does replenish quickly, but Shifting will make her recovery even faster. And Karina has Shifted. In the shower cubicle right here.

Dr Costigan is going to die.

Karina's plan is clear to me. To salvage her project she needs Caspian Fox, and a full transfusion of dragon blood is his only chance of surviving the radiation poisoning from the portal implosion. It's not guaranteed though. Whether or not Caspian survives, Dr Costigan's suspicions about Karina's miraculous ability to generate so much blood – and such potent blood – means that he will be a threat. Like the security guard who witnessed Karina's superhuman strength, Dr Costigan's fate is sealed. His lifespan can now be measured in hours.

There's nothing more I can do here.

Felix is the next priority. Hopefully, he has managed to stay out of trouble.

I crawl back to the first-aid kit and scoop it up before heading back to the surface. I had hoped the kit might come in handy if I'd managed to find either of Liberty's parents, and though it is not now going to be of use, I can't leave it as evidence of my presence here.

A potential battle with Security at the emergency exit point awaits, but I can't focus on it. Karina's plan to save Caspian Fox has merit. A similar transfusion is probably Liberty's only chance of survival too. But I can't see how that could happen.

Liberty isn't useful to Karina, so Karina won't risk exposing her secret to save her employees' daughter. And I don't know that I'm up for it either. Liberty is a fellow student and an innocent victim of an unfortunate accident. And I have the power to save her. But I can't afford my secret to get out either, for the sake of all wehrs. Unlike Karina, I'm not prepared to kill to cover my tracks.

Would Felix's blood be strong enough? He's only half dragon, after all. I sigh, shaking my head. Telling him his true heritage would clear my conscience – I hate keeping this secret from my best friend – but it would complicate so many other things. Besides, even if a transfusion would save Liberty, who could *perform* the procedure?

Suddenly, dealing with Security doesn't seem so difficult.

Chapter 5

Felix

After the chaos at the NSA, being back at the hospital should be a reprieve. It's not though. I've been waiting in this treatment room for over two hours now with no news about Liberty. I'm not sure why I'm in a treatment room rather than the waiting room, but I guess I should be grateful I'm not surrounded by sick and injured people.

Someone has hidden the remote control for the therapeutic recliner I'm sitting in – otherwise I'd have some entertainment. The pamphlets in the wire rack on the wall appear to have little value beyond campfire kindling, so I scan the plastic dishes on the benchtop for anything interesting. However, large paddle-pop sticks, alcohol swabs and gauze strips don't do it for me – I was hoping for syringes or scalpels. Not that I've got anywhere to stash stuff now. The EMT coveralls had lots of pockets, but my jeans and t-shirt don't offer many options.

While I wait for news about Liberty, I rehearse what I will say to her – assuming she's conscious. Elvira's mission at NSA was successful in terms of locating Liberty's parents, but the news isn't good. Caspian Fox is alive but in an isolation ward with severe radiation poisoning. He must be really important to the portal project if Karina's willing to expend the effort to treat him. And as for Liberty's mother ... I don't quite know how to explain that one. She's somehow trapped inside the portal? I've got no idea how that works.

A voice interrupts my thoughts.

'Steve Rogers?'

I look up thinking someone has got the wrong room before I remember the alias I had given the nurse when I signed Liberty in.

I swing my legs off the footrest. 'Uh, yep. That's me. Steve Roger. Steve *Rogers.*'

'I'm Doctor Rashad,' the woman says. 'You can stay seated. Just relax.'

Thin dark brows arch over eyes that gleam like polished chestnuts. Her skin tone and thick hair suggest Indian heritage. She is wearing a white coat and has a stethoscope draped around her neck, but she doesn't look old enough to be a doctor and I wonder if she's an undercover journalist like me. My eyes are drawn to her lips, painted with bright-red lipstick. She docks the tablet she's carrying in the desk station before seating herself on the wheelie stool beside the bench.

Turning to me, she says, 'You brought Liberty Fox in, yes?'

I nod. 'Yes. How is she?'

'She's very sick,' Dr Rashad says, her voice husky. 'Liberty has been exposed to some kind of radiation.'

'Oh. Is she going to …?' I can't finish the question.

The doctor sighs. 'Her prognosis isn't good,' Dr Rashad says at last, 'but we are doing everything we can for her. My problem at the moment though, is you.'

'Me?'

She nods. 'Has anyone checked you over?'

I shake my head slowly. 'No.'

Dr Rashad's lips press together into a thin red line until it looks like she's been slashed across the face with a scalpel.

She snaps on a pair of gloves. 'The fact that you're walking around suggests that you're probably okay, and that's my real problem. If you were where Liberty was – you should be in the same state as her.'

'I'm bigger than her – stronger,' I say, flexing one of my biceps for emphasis. When she frowns, I add, 'Not that Liberty isn't strong … for a girl. I mean … not that girls aren't strong. Liberty's fit. She does lots of—'

'Can you tell me how long she was in the lab?' Dr Rashad says.

I shrug. 'I don't know. I just found her. I wasn't with her when she went in, but …'

Dr Rashad rolls on her stool to sit right beside me. 'But?'

'I saw her before she went in,' I say, struggling to remember the timing of events, 'and then I went … looking for my stepmother while she went to find her parents. It couldn't have been more than about fifteen or twenty minutes.'

'Any how long were you in there?'

'A couple of minutes. I took some photos of the portal before I …'

'The portal?'

Shit. 'Um … pretend you didn't hear that.'

'How about I just examine you.'

'Yeah. Okay.'

Placing the earpieces of the stethoscope into her ears, Dr Rashad says, 'I'll listen to your heart first. Lift your shirt, please.'

She leans towards me and I catch the sweet scent of antiseptic, but as she listens to my heartbeat, she frowns.

'Something wrong?' I ask.

'Your heartrate is unusually slow,' the doctor says.

'I'm pretty fit,' I say. 'I play a lot of sport.'

'And syncopated,' Dr Rashad adds.

'Syncopated?'

'Irregular,' she clarifies. 'Has no one picked that up before?'

'I haven't seen many doctors,' I say with a shrug. 'I don't get sick much, and I've never broken any bones.'

'I thought you said you played lots of sport?'

I nod.

'And you've never broken any bones?'

'I *thought* I had a couple of times,' I say. 'I play hard – if you know what I mean – especially footy, but I just seem to recover from injuries really quick.'

Dr Rashad rolls her stool back to the desk and taps on her keyboard. Before she rolls back to me, she catches the metal pole of the stand with the heart monitor and pushes it in my direction.

'Blood pressure,' she says.

I pull up my t-shirt sleeve as she adjusts the armrest of my chair. 'Rest your arm there.'

Dr Rashad clips a plastic peg on my third finger before securing the inflatable blood-pressure cuff in place around my right bicep.

'Just relax.'

Relax? After everything that has happened today, that is not an option. I don't tell her that though.

'Blood pressure is ridiculously high,' she murmurs, frowning.

'What is it?'

'Two-fifty over one-fifty.'

'Uh-huh.'

That doesn't sound like the numbers I've heard in movies. One-twenty over eighty is more like normal, I think.

'Does radiation do that?' I ask.

'Not in my experience.'

I'm tempted to ask how much experience she's had with radiation, but she doesn't give me the chance.

'Open your mouth,' she says, brandishing a large paddle-pop stick and a torch.

I comply.

She presses on my tongue with the wooden stick. 'Say "ah".'

'Aaaaaaah.'

'Fine.'

From a container on the bench, she extracts a piece of black plastic which she screws onto the torch.

'I'm going to look in your ears now,' she says.

Seemingly satisfied with what she does – or doesn't – find in my ears, she tosses the used earpiece in a yellow plastic tub. She checks the glands in my neck, tests my reflexes and then makes me track a pencil tip with my eyes.

Once she's recorded her notes on the system, Dr Rashad says, 'I'd like to run a few blood tests.'

'Ooooookay.'

'Don't like the sight of blood?' she asks.

'It's not that. I've just never had a blood test.'

Dr Rashad frowns and shakes her head. 'It'll sting a bit, but you're such a strong, tough fellow that I'm sure you'll heal instantly.'

I feel the heat rising in my cheeks.

'Which arm?' she asks.

'Left,' I reply.

She straps the elastic tourniquet in place with hands that are warm and smooth before she swabs the crease at my elbow with an alcohol wipe. After disposing of the wipe, she picks up a needle. I watch the slender silver tip disappear into my flesh. She's right. It does sting, but I don't react as crimson fluid oozes into the vial.

'I'll get a rush on these,' Dr Rashad says as she labels the vials. 'I should have results within the hour. I'll come and find you in the waiting room once I've got them.'

I nod as the doctor gestures for me to leave.

'Okay.'

I return to the waiting room and find a seat in a corner with a view of the television screen mounted on the wall adjacent to the nurses' station. I pull out my phone to text Elvira. It's 21:30. She'll still be awake.

No change in Liberty's condition. She's got radiation poisoning like her dad.

Elvira's response comes less than a minute later.

Righto. How long you gonna stay there?

I send back. *Till I hear something – or they kick me out?*

Okay. Don't fall asleep. You might wake up in the morgue.

I roll my eyes. *Thanks for the advice. Very helpful.*

They might harvest your organs!

As long as I stay awake long enough to get my blood test results, I should be okay.

Why are you getting blood tests?

Standard procedure since I was in a contaminated lab.

This time there is a longer delay before Elvira's response comes.

Come to my place before you go home.

Why?

Please. Just do it.

It's an odd request, but Elvira being odd isn't anything new.

Righto.

I put my phone away, wondering what Elvira's grandmother will think when I turn up there late at night – or early in the morning. Winona has been Elvira's legal guardian since Elvira was five, after her mother drowned in a ferry accident and her father died in a Russian prison. Not that I should give a crap about their family situation since mine's totally screwed up, but Winona is special.

I used to joke that Winona was a vampire because she's pale and naps so often during the day, and because she's just a crazy old bat. But maybe I should stop the vampire jokes after what I saw my step-mother do today. *If* I really saw it. Who ever heard of people changing into dragons? That kind of stuff – werewolves, vampires, zombies – only happens in the movies.

It's not real life. It's *not* real life. *It's not real life.*

∞

Elvira

I cradle my phone in my trembling hands. The sanctuary of my bedroom theatre usually comforts me, but not tonight. From amongst the nest of cushions on my four-poster bed, I gaze out through the fine ivory netting cascading down over the frame as another tear rolls over my cheek. The stage lights are low, warm – perfect for an emotional monologue but I can't find a character willing to deliver it.

Blood tests.

'Shit,' I mutter.

This is a problem. A problem that wouldn't *be* a problem if Felix's parents had told him the truth about his heritage. I don't know exactly what kind of anomalies his tests will throw up but any doctor is going to be curious when they review the results.

'Shit.'

I dial my father's number. I fit my wireless earphones while I wait for him to answer.

'Daughter?'

I clear my throat. 'Hello, Father. I think we have a problem.'

'What kind of problem?'

I tell him about Felix's blood test.

'Which hospital?' my father asks.

'Calvary Public,' I say. 'Promise me you won't hurt him.'

'Daughter,' he says, 'do not worry about Felix.'

'That's not a promise. It's not his fault – he doesn't know.'

'I know it's not his fault, but we can't afford for anyone to get too curious. Any doctor who starts sniffing around Felix will ultimately end up on Karina and Joel's doorstep, and while I'm certainly no fan of theirs … to protect us all, I need to make sure they're not exposed.'

I close my eyes and warm tears slide over my cheeks. Not Felix. That's not fair.

'I understand,' I say.

'Good,' my father says. 'Take heart, Daughter. I'll deal with it and be in touch later.'

The connection goes dead and I let out a shuddering breath. I know protecting our wehr heritage is the highest priority but I can't let anything happen to Felix. I order an Uber.

In the four minutes I've got until my ride arrives, I change my clothes. Black jeans, grey t-shirt and Vans – not my preferred streetwear but desperate times call from drastic measures. I pull a dark newsboy cap over my curls and swipe my shoulder bag from the foot of my bed.

A silver SUV pulls up at the kerb as I close the front door behind me.

'Evening,' the driver says, eyeing me in her rear-vision mirror as I climb into the back seat.

'Evening,' I reply.

A prickly grey head mounted on a beanbag of a body is all I can make out from my seat.

'A trip to the hospital at this hour can't be good news,' the driver says.

Clearly not, so why say anything?

I decide to give her what she wants. 'My brother's been in a car accident,' I say. 'I just hope I make it in time …'

'That's terrible,' the woman says. 'Let's not dilly-dally then.'

She pulls out from the kerb and I'm thankful that the twenty-minute ride passes in silence – because out of the silence, an idea is born.

I clamber out of the car in the drop-off zone at the hospital. If the driver farewelled me, I didn't hear it. I'm still teasing out the details of a plan. I glance at the sky and a sliver of moon smiles down at me, as if in approval.

The glass doors slide apart soundlessly and cool air engulfs me as I enter the Emergency waiting room. Felix is sitting in the corner, intent on his phone. He doesn't notice me until I'm standing right in front of him.

'Elvira?' he says, looking up at me. 'What are you doing here?'

'You need to come with me,' I say.

'I haven't got my results yet,' he says. 'I—'

'Please trust me.' I perch on the moulded plastic seat beside him. 'We need to go.'

Felix frowns. 'I was hoping for an update on Liberty.'

I take a deep breath. 'I need to talk to you about that … but not here.'

Felix folds his arms across his chest. He doesn't realise it, but it's his barricade manoeuvre. I've seen it more times than I can count.

'Please, Felix.' I hesitate before adding, 'You're in danger.'

He waves dismissively. 'If you're talking about my stepmother, don't worry about that. I can handle Karina.'

I know he can't actually handle her but now isn't the time to discuss that. I have no patience left so I grab his wrist.

'If you don't come with me quietly, I will make a scene.'

Felix's eyes widen. He pushes to his feet.

'Fine,' he says, his voice loaded with annoyance. 'We'll go outside and you've got five minutes to tell me … whatever. And after that, if I'm not convinced, I'll be right back here.'

'Great,' I say. 'Let's go.'

I release my grip on his wrist and make for the door, assuming he'll follow me.

We find a bench seat in a courtyard at the rear of the building and sit with our backs to the hospital. If there are CCTV cameras mounted on the building's exterior, I don't want to be facing them.

'You're on the clock,' Felix says. 'Out with it.'

I have had this conversation with him hundreds of times in my head but now that it's imminent in reality, I hesitate. This secret has been mine for as long as I can remember. It's been both a boon and a bane. Being custodian of this knowledge has been the one thing that has tethered me to my father – a connection I have treasured. But withholding it from my best friend has eroded part of my soul.

'There is more to your father's heritage than you know,' I whisper, 'and if anyone were to find out about it, you and your family would be in great danger.'

Felix studies me, his green eyes boring into mine.

'You've lost me,' he says. 'What could you possibly know about my family that I don't know?'

Dispensing with subtlety I say, 'Your father and stepmother are wehrdragons.'

He frowns, accentuating the crease between his eyebrows. 'Where-what?'

'Shapeshifters,' I say. 'They are humans who can transform into dragons.'

Felix glares at me for almost half a minute before he rolls his eyes and smacks his forehead with his open palm. 'Okay. Righto,' he says. 'You almost had me there. Which character am I talking to and what the hell does she want? I gotta tell you – I'm not in the mood for this now.'

'No character. It is *me*. Elvira.'

Felix jumps to his feet. 'Yeah right. Look, I can't deal with this right—'

'You have to trust me, Felix!' I jump to my feet too.

'Really?' he fires back. 'Why? This is the craziest shit I've ever heard! Wehrdragons? What the hell?'

'They're real,' I say, reining in my temper. 'I know. I am one.'

He cocks his head to one side. 'You expect me to believe that you can change into a dragon?'

I nod.

'Yeah?' he says. 'Then prove it.'

Helplessness swamps me. 'I can't,' I say. 'Not here.'

'Then where?'

'Somewhere remote. Somewhere no one will see.'

'Sorry, Elvira,' he says, shaking his head slowly. 'You can't lure me away. Liberty is really sick and I'm gonna be here when she wakes up.'

Felix turns and heads back towards the hospital.

'How do you think Karina was able to survive the building collapse?' I call after him. 'Lift that concrete slab? Where do you think she got that kind of strength from?'

Felix spins back to face me, but when he folds his arms across his chest this time, it's not a gesture of defiance. It looks like he's trying to hold himself together.

'I don't know,' he says.

'I've never lied to you, Felix.'

'Never lied? Well, how come you never mentioned this before?'

'Believe it or not, it's kind of difficult to weave into a conversation,' I say.

'People don't turn into dragons, Elvira!'

Is he trying to convince me, or himself?

'Oh, wait,' I say. 'You *saw* her, didn't you? You saw Karina's dragon!'

Felix glares at me, says nothing for several seconds. 'Sorry, Elvira. I can't …'

'If you go back in there,' I say, 'they won't let you out. Once they see your blood test results, you'll be a lab rat. Please, trust me.'

'Go home, Elvira.'

As he turns his back on me again, I think about Caspian Fox and Karina's transfusion strategy.

I play my last card. 'I think I know how to save Liberty.'

'Go home, sleep it off, Elvira,' Felix calls over his shoulder as he resumes his walk back to the hospital waiting room.

Chapter 6

Elvira

Felix is such an arse! He *knows* what Karina is but he's in denial.

I don't have time for denial. I also can't believe he just dismissed me like that. But now is not the time for self-indulgent outrage. The stupid arse is in trouble – which means trouble for the rest of us – so somebody has to do something.

I feel my blood heating up, my skin tingling. My dragon is sending me a message. I can't fob off this responsibility to one of my characters. This job falls to me. *I* have to get Felix out.

I plonk myself down on a seat to think. I can't march in there without a plan. My watch shows 10:10 pm, which doesn't help me much. The time isn't useful unless I can pair it with something else – like what time the next shift change is. On any other night, there might be less activity inside the hospital but tonight is exceptional. The casualties from NSA have added an element of chaos to their usual procedures. Perhaps that's something I can work with? There are already more people around than usual, so maybe they won't notice one more.

I just need to divert their attention.

Setting off car alarms in the carpark might do it. Or I could Shift. I smile, imagining the reaction of the security guards who might be monitoring the CCTV when they see a large, winged reptile perched on top of an ambulance. I push that idea aside. As much as I'd like to do it, it's way too risky.

Setting off a fire alarm should do the trick. It always works in the movies.

With a plan coalescing in my head, I get to my feet, adjust my cap and make for the hospital's main entrance. Once inside, I scan the waiting area. Still a surprising number of people there. None of them seem to be in need of medical assistance so I assume they are waiting for news of relatives.

Felix is nowhere to be seen. Either he's visiting Liberty or a doctor has nabbed him. I imagine visiting hours are over so I'm left with option two. Not ideal. I approach the nurses' station.

'Hello,' I say. 'Excuse me.'

The lone nurse behind the counter looks up from her monitor. Feathery wisps of bronze hair have escaped her scrub cap, framing her freckled face, and her surgical mask is tucked under her three chins. The woman's glassy eyes are like topaz portals to the realm of boredom.

'Yes?' she says, punctuating her question with a sigh.

'I wonder if you could tell me how Liberty Fox is doing?' I say.

'You a relative?'

I nod. 'Cousin. Just flew in from interstate. So terrible what's happened. Just had to come here and see for myself.'

'You should have called,' she says, tapping on her keyboard. 'Visiting hours are done for today.' Scanning the screen, she adds, 'Liberty Fox is stable. You can see her from 10 am tomorrow.'

I put my hand over my heart. 'Thank goodness for that!' I say. 'Have her parents been brought in yet? Last I heard, they were unaccounted for.'

'Names?' the nurse says without taking her gaze from the screen.

'Uncle Cas … I mean, Caspian and Rose Fox.'

The keyboard clicks as she types. 'No. They're not here.'

'Oh. Well, thank you for your help.'

The nurse nods as I turn from the desk. Since visiting hours are over, I can't start roaming the corridors looking for Felix, but there must be toilets here somewhere. As I scope my surroundings, I notice a water cooler on the far side of the waiting area. The perfect procrastination point. Rather than taking the direct route between the rows of chairs, I skirt the seating so I can sneak a peek through the doorway to the wards. But as I pass the entryway, I'm nearly barrelled over by a laundry trolley.

'Sorry, Miss!' the young orderly says, catching my eye. 'Wasn't expecting anyone to be there.'

He pushes the trolley against the wall and hurries over to me, putting one hand on my shoulder. 'Are you okay?'

I did get a fright but he didn't actually hit me.

I smile. 'I'm fine. I guess I should watch where I'm going.'

'Are you *sure* you're okay?'

His voice is husky and I feel my heart flutter. What the hell? I suck in a deep breath. I need to focus.

'I'm fine,' I assure him.

'Well, if you're not,' he says, smiling, 'I might know some people who could help. I have a few contacts here, you know.'

Is he hitting on me? I study the orderly's face. He's probably early twenties. His face is pale, angular and lean, and hazel eyes sparkle with mischief under his thick, dark eyebrows. A spiky ebony ponytail sprouts from the back of his head.

'Really, I'm okay. I just need a drink of water,' I wave in the direction of the water cooler, 'and then, I'm off home.'

He turns his back to the nurses' station and leans in close to me. 'Aeon told me to look out for you.'

I recoil. 'What did you say?'

He grins at me. 'You heard me perfectly well, Elvira.'

My eyes flick to his name badge. 'Blake Rasmussen,' I murmur.

'You can call me, Gemini,' he says.

I look him in the eye. 'Is that your real name?'

He smiles. 'Sometimes.'

My father sent this guy to look out for me? Why? And also, why didn't he tell me?

'Anyway,' Gemini says, 'as lovely as it would be to stand around and chat, I have a corpse to dispose of and some beefcake friend of yours to rescue … wanna help?'

I stare at him. 'Did you just say a corpse?'

'Under the sheets,' he says, pointing to the trolley, 'is a doctor with a broken neck.'

'An accident?'

'No. Dr Rashad had information about the beefcake's blood that Aeon did not want her to have. I have taken care of it.'

'Are you talking about Felix?' I say as my brain scrambles to align with Gemini's train of thought.

'Yes. I have destroyed his blood samples and deleted the test results from the system. Next job is to get him out – along with a Miss Liberty Fox. You up for it?'

'Yes. Wait – how do you know about Liberty?'

Gemini winks at me. 'Let's discuss that later. Ready?'

'Yes. Ready.'

'Good.' Gemini gestures towards the water cooler. 'Take a drink, then meet me at the loading dock around back.'

'Okay.'

My brain is spinning inside my head so fast I can barely walk straight. My father sent an assassin? Gemini certainly doesn't fit the stereotype of a hired killer, but I guess that's the point. At least I've got help to spring Felix from the hospital's clutches, but I wonder how much I should trust Gemini.

When I've drunk my cup of water, I don't feel at all refreshed. In fact, the liquid is gurgling in my stomach, threatening to make a reappearance. I clench my jaws together and walk as calmly as I can from the hospital foyer. Keeping my head bowed, I make my way to the loading dock.

I find Gemini at the dock, filling out paperwork.

'Just out of curiosity,' Gemini says as he tosses the clipboard and pen on the beige laminate desktop, 'what was your plan to get Felix out?'

'Who said I was going to do that?'

He ignores my question. 'My guess is that you were going to trigger the fire alarm.'

I sigh.

'Knew it,' Gemini says, grinning at me. 'We can do better though. I have some toys—'

I hold up one hand, interrupting what promises to be a condescending little sermon. 'Let's just do this. Okay?'

Gemini nods once. 'Okay. I'll get Felix; you get Liberty.'

'Fine.'

As I turn to leave, he grabs my wrist.

'Here,' he says, pressing three metallic disks into my hand. 'Use these if you need to persuade or dissuade anyone who gets in your way.'

'What are they?'

'Teargas.'

'But won't I need a mask?'

Gemini raises his eyebrows. 'Really?'

He knows more than I thought. 'But you're not ...' I say.

'No,' he admits, 'I'm not one of you, but you can consider me an ally – a trusted human operative.'

'Uh-huh.'

'So, let me tell you the plan,' Gemini says. 'I'm going to black out the building and disable most of the backup generators. They'll have some emergency lighting and life support systems will continue to operate. Under cover of confusion, we can collect our treasures and be gone. We'll meet here and take the laundry truck.'

'So, I shouldn't need these?' I ask, displaying the metallic disks on my palm.

'No. I just want you to have something to take your mind off the fire alarm. Promise me you won't, under any circumstances, trip the fire alarm.'

'You seem to be really fixated on that. What have you got against fire alarms?'

'If anyone were to find out that I was associated with a job that involved the triggering of such an alarm,' he says, wagging his index finger at me, 'I'd be laughed out of the guild.'

'There's a guild?'

'Time to get to work,' Gemini says, pulling a smartphone from the pocket of his uniform. 'Ready?'

I shrug. 'Ready as I'll ever be.'

Gemini swipes and taps on his device and within seconds we're in darkness.

An alarm sounds.

'Is that the fire alarm?' I ask.

There's a snort from the darkness. 'It is NOT the fire alarm.'

'How many types of alarms are there?'

'A few,' Gemini says. 'The important thing is, this alarm will not bring the fire brigade, who will block our exit.'

'Ah.'

'Do you have a torch?' he asks.

I fumble in my bag. 'I have my phone.'

I feel cold metal on my forearm. 'Take mine,' Gemini says. 'It's got more range than a phone torch.'

He's certainly got all the gear.

'Throw your hat and handbag in the van,' he says. 'You don't want to attract undue attention.'

I do as he says before turning back to salute him. I don't know why I bothered. It's not like he can see me in the dark.

'Follow me,' he says.

I turn on the torch and find his sneakers. My attention is solely on Gemini's joggers as we make our way through the service corridors to the wards. We don't pass anyone on the way but when we reach the last door, Gemini pauses.

'Can you remember the internal route back to the dock?' he asks.

'Yes,' I say. 'I'm good with directions.'

'Good. Now Liberty is in ICU. Fourth floor. Take the stairs.'

'Roger that.'

'Good luck. I'll have the engine running.'

Gemini shoves the door open and breezes through the opening, dragging me along in his wake. Suddenly it feels like a race and though I'm not usually competitive, I'm keen to beat him.

People are screaming and shouting, almost drowning out the alarm. I keep the torch beam in front of me, trying to dodge the organic obstacles in my path. My eyes dart from side to side, looking for an entrance to the stairwell.

Something snakes around my waist. An arm. It pulls me back.

'Here!'

Gemini's breath is hot on my ear and my heart pounds as the wall beside me gives way. I stumble, crashing onto the concrete floor.

Bang!

In the aftermath of the slamming door, relative quiet cloaks me. I flick my torch left and right, up and down. I'm alone in the stairwell.

'Thanks, Gemini,' I murmur, wondering how he got behind me.

I race up the stairs two at a time until I reach the fourth floor. There is minimal lighting here, but enough for me to see that the ICU is a flurry of activity as nurses check patients and equipment. I kill the torch and crouch against the wall while my eyes adjust and I steady my breathing. The staff is calm and professional. It doesn't look like they're evacuating, which is unfortunate. I was hoping to drift with the current and slip off to the edges with my catch but that doesn't look like an option.

Gemini's teargas disks feel heavy in my pocket all of a sudden. Like they are trying to get my attention.

Not yet.

I crawl along the floor, keeping to the wall, until I am inside the ICU. In the dim light of the nurses' station, I snatch a gown, cap and facemask, and dress quickly, praying no one catches me.

'Update on the generators?' a male voice calls.

'No word yet,' another man responds.

'That's the priority,' the first voice says. 'Stay with it.'

Adjusting my mask, I stride out into the ICU scanning each bed I pass. The last time I saw this many bandages was in the Egyptian exhibit at the museum. Felix didn't mention that Liberty had burns so I move on.

Finally – as the lights come on – I find her. Inside a plastic isolation bubble.

I swear under my breath as I survey the tubes snaking from Liberty's arms and face. She looks like she's being smothered by a translucent octopus.

I lift the plastic barrier. 'I really hope you're worth this,' I whisper.

With my free hand, I toss one of the teargas disks behind me and the screaming begins.

I disconnect all the tubes tethering Liberty to the machines before scooping her off the bed and folding her over my shoulder. It's not the best way to carry a patient but I need one hand free just in case I need to access more teargas. I make it out of the ICU without resistance but I run into a nurse in the corridor.

'Hey!' the man shouts. 'What are you doing?'

He lunges at me and if it weren't for my floaty gown, I'd have dodged him. He wrenches on the fistful of fabric he's got and almost pulls me off my feet. I kick out at him, catching his knee. With a yelp, he crumples to the floor.

I toss another disk over my shoulder as I jog to the fire escape. Another alarm sounds as I hurry down the stairs.

'If that's the fire alarm,' I mutter, 'I'll never hear the end of it.'

There are more people in the stairwell this time and my heart races in panic. Even though the lights are dim in here, I still feel very exposed. I'm the only person carrying a patient like a sack of potatoes. And I've got only one disk left – and I still have to navigate the ground floor to get back to the laundry van.

I decide to bluff my way down. 'Stay left!' I shout, channelling the authority of a warden. 'Move swiftly but in an orderly fashion. Stay left!'

Someone moans. It could be Liberty but I'm not sure.

By the time I reach the ground floor, I am panting and sweating but I scoot along the corridor to the exit to the dock. I push my shoulder against the door but it doesn't budge.

'You've got to be shitting me,' I say, taking a step back.

A glance through the window shows nothing on the other side. I give it a moderate kick. The door rattles but doesn't open. I sit Liberty on the floor, propping her up against the wall before taking a few steps back for my run up. I launch a flying kick at the door, splintering the lock.

Gemini's face appears in the breach. 'About time,' he says, 'I was just about to come looking for you.'

'Did you lock that door?'

'Yep. Needed to keep the riff-raff out.'

I grunt in reply as I sling Liberty's arm around my neck and hoist her up from the floor.

'Was that you who set off the fire alarm?' Gemini asks.

I drop my last teargas disk on the floor at his feet.

'Oh!' he exclaims in between coughs. 'That's rude!'

'It's just what you deserve,' I retort as he scampers off towards the loading dock. 'You better have that motor running.'

It occurs to me that he might actually leave without me so I trot after him. When I reach the van, the side door is open and Gemini is in the driver's seat. Three laundry trolleys fill the back of the van.

'Lay her in the first trolley and throw a sheet over her,' he calls.

'Is Felix in here?' I ask, as I manoeuvre Liberty's body into position.

'Yes. Hurry up, would ya! I can hear sirens.'

I imagine that the doctor's corpse is in one of the tubs too – possibly under the sheets in the tub I've just dumped Liberty into – but I don't dwell on it. I can hear the sirens from the fire trucks too.

'Stay in the back!' Gemini yells as he guns the engine.

Tyres screech as the van rockets backwards. I fall back towards the open door.

'Shit!' I shriek, clutching at the bar behind the front passenger seat. 'Are you crazy?'

I catch the bar with my left hand, but my legs are dangling outside the van. 'Stop!' I cry. 'Let me get in.'

The van spins sharply as he yanks the steering wheel hard to the right. 'Hold on!'

'Thanks for the advice!' I yell. 'I hadn't thought of that!'

To my shock, he laughs. 'Don't be a sook, Elvira. You're a bloody dragon. You'll be fine.'

The van speeds along the roadway adjacent to the hospital carpark as the fire trucks approach. I need to get my arse inside the vehicle so I can deal with Gemini. He needs a lesson in humility.

Aeon told me to look out for you.

My father sent this angel of death to watch over me? I'm probably going to need all the help I can get. But only if I get myself back in the van without transforming. There are too many witnesses around.

Chapter 7

Felix

'I think he's waking up. Are you ready?'

It's a male voice. My eyelids refuse to open but my mind grinds into action. I remember being at the hospital. Dr Rashad had my blood test results. Though I wasn't displaying any symptoms of radiation poisoning, my irregular bloods suggested that I had absorbed a significant amount of radiation, so the doctor had put me on a saline drip and a prophylactic antibiotic in readiness for a transfusion. Neither of those things should make me feel this groggy. Did something go wrong? Am I allergic to something?

'Well, I'll be damned,' the male voice says. 'Would you look at that!'

Must be a nurse. Whatever he's looking at, it sounds like something he hasn't seen before. If my eyes would just open …

Felix.

That's Elvira's voice. What's she doing here? Memories of her story about shapeshifting dragons bubble out of the depths of my brain.

Felix. Wake up.

Here's another problem. I'm not actually *hearing* her – her voice is inside my head. I shudder. I really should wake up, if only to call security to have Elvira ejected from the hospital. Deciding it's worth a more concentrated effort, I force my eyelids open.

And instantly regret it. I squeeze my eyes closed again.

Felix, Elvira's voice echoes in the confines of my skull, *I know you're awake. Open your eyes.*

I peek out one eye. It's still there.

Ah, Felix, there you are. Welcome back.

I stare into the amber, gemlike eyes of the dragon. Delicate scales the colour of cinnamon gleam with a pearlescent sheen in the room's warm light while wisps of white smoke curl from her short snout, lacing the air with the scent of … cloves. She takes a step back, stands upright, exposing her pale underbelly. I thought Karina's dragon was small, but Elvira's dragon is even smaller. If I stood in front of her, she'd be staring at my solar plexus. The murderously sharp talons are not unexpected but the feathery tip of her whip-like tail blunts the otherwise fearsome image.

Do I have your attention? Elvira asks.

I nod as she unfurls her leathery wings, fluttering them gently like a lion might air its mane.

Good.

The dragon collects the robe from the back of a nearby recliner and drapes it around her shoulders as her tail vanishes, scales melt back into human skin and her snout retracts. Elvira secures the black robe around her waist with a sash.

'That was intense,' I say.

'Indeed,' Elvira replies. 'So, will you hear me out now?'

I sigh. 'I guess so, but first thing – where the hell are we? And,' I point to the nerdy freak hovering behind her, 'who's that guy?'

Elvira flicks a glance at the dark-haired man. 'You can call him Gemini. He's an … ally.'

'A friend,' Gemini says.

'A friend of my father's,' Elvira says.

Gemini clutches his chest. 'That's hurtful, Elvira.'

Elvira shrugs. 'We're in a safe house, about an hour out of Indigo,' she says to me, 'and our immediate priority is healing her.'

I turn my head, following her gaze.

'Liberty!'

My head whips back to the front as I leap out of my recliner. 'What the hell? Why is she not in the hospital?'

Not waiting for an answer, I step past the mobile stands and trolleys to be at Liberty's side. She looks so fragile. She's still wearing her hospital gown but, in place of a bed, she's been propped up in a plush leather recliner. Tubes snake from both her arms and she's on a respirator. Her skin looks impossibly pale and brittle, like a plastic shopping bag that's been left in the sun too long.

'I think *we* have got a better chance of healing her,' Elvira says.

'How did we get here?' I point to all the medical equipment. 'And who set all this up?'

'That would be me,' Gemini says.

I look at him. 'Pardon?'

'Me,' Gemini says. 'All me. I broke you out of the hospital—'

'With my help,' Elvira puts in.

'—with Elvira's dubious assistance,' Gemini concedes, 'brought you all here, set up the equipment and now I'm ready to do the transfusion. Unless, of course, you'd just like to stand around being all outraged as your precious little friend dies?'

My heart thumps inside my chest. 'Are you a doctor?'

'When I need to be,' Gemini says.

I fold my arms across my chest. 'What are you? Really?'

'Genius. Assassin. Spy. Dental hygienist.'

Elvira groans. 'You're an arrogant prick.'

'When the situation calls for it,' he says, with a smile.

'So why a transfusion?' I ask.

'Gamma radiation affects platelets and white blood cells,' Gemini explains. 'Infection is the biggest risk since the body doesn't have the means to protect itself. The best treatment is a complete transfusion. With new blood, her body stands a chance of fighting back.'

'Where's all this blood going to come from?'

Elvira walks over to me and rests her hand on my shoulder. 'You.'

'Can I assume you've checked that my blood is compatible?'

'Yes,' Elvira says.

I glance at her before returning my attention to Gemini. 'And the hospital didn't perform this procedure because …?'

Gemini studies the tablet on the trolley. 'According to hospital records, she's had several transfusions already.'

'But you can do it better?'

'Elvira,' Gemini says, 'all yours.'

'Perhaps I could explain … everything … once the procedure is underway?' she says. 'Clock is ticking.'

I glance at the oversized wall clock, which shows 12:20. The blazing lights in the room would indicate that sunrise is yet to come today.

I study Liberty's pallid face. 'Okay. What do I need to do?'

'Take a seat,' Gemini says, gesturing towards the recliner beside Liberty's. 'I'll take good care of you.'

'Just what I need to hear from an assassin,' I mutter as I ease myself into my seat. 'Hang on! Have you killed anyone … lately?'

'You'll just feel a small prick,' Gemini says as he inserts a needle into the crease at my left elbow.

'Felix,' Elvira says, as red fluid speeds through the tube connected to the needle in my arm, 'do you remember what I told you at the hospital?'

'How about we pretend I don't remember anything.'

'Fine,' Elvira says, nodding. 'Let's start with this. Your father, your stepmother and my parents are all wehrdragons – from Rhybor.'

Momentarily distracted by the lifeforce draining from my arm, I wonder how much blood they'll need for a transfusion. Will I be able to regenerate enough blood to fund my own survival?

'Rhybor?' I echo. 'The place Earth used to buy its elenium from before the portal collapsed – or was destroyed?'

'Yes,' Elvira says. 'Tell me what you remember from history class about Rhybor.'

'Well, I don't remember anything about dragons—'

'Let's start with what you *do* know, rather than what you *don't* know.'

'Okay,' I say. 'Rhybor is a planet on the far side of our galaxy. After the portal collapse, people assumed it was an accident, but when the Rhyborians didn't reopen the portal the conspiracy theories started. "They cut us off because a US diplomat insulted their king", "they felt threatened by our military advancements", or "the Rhyborians have been annihilated in an alien invasion". Reasons don't really matter though, do they? The fact is the Rhyborians never reopened the portal – and we didn't have the technology to do it from here. No more elenium.'

'Excellent summary,' Elvira says, massaging her temples with her fingertips. 'So the "history" that people don't know – and what your parents *should* have told *you*, but didn't – is that the Rhyborians had captured a small human spy force on their world, and sent an investigative/diplomatic team here in response. That team was still on Earth when the portal collapsed and was stranded here. My parents, your father and your stepmother were part of that team.'

As I digest this information, Gemini bags the first batch of blood and moves over to Liberty. With his back to me, he hangs the bag on a hook on the mobile stand and then bends over his patient. I shudder at the thought of an assassin's hands on her skin.

I catch Elvira's eye. 'Did you say this guy is a friend of your father's?'

She nods.

'I thought you were an orphan; that's why you live with your grandmother.'

'My mother's dead. My father lives in Russia. Stay with me – I'm getting to that.'

'Let me guess,' I say, 'the stranded wehrdragons went underground and tried to build their own portal?'

Gemini appears at my side with a fresh blood bag, which he attaches to my right arm this time.

'Initially they worked together,' Elvira says, nodding, 'but according to my father, there was soon an ideological divergence.'

'A what?'

'I need to back up here a bit,' Elvira says. 'Rhybor was a major intergalactic trading port for elenium. Huge. Aliens came from everywhere to trade. So, the fact that there were dragons on Rhybor was never a secret.'

'Because dragons are kind of hard to hide?' I say.

'Yes. And what do you think the first aliens to arrive on Rhybor looking for elenium thought of dragons?'

'A threat to be exterminated?'

'Correct,' Elvira says. 'The king way back then was keen to open Rhybor for trade but wanted to protect his citizens. So, while it was too late to keep the dragons a secret, there was something the aliens didn't know – and that's that the dragons could take human form.'

'Wehrdragons. Shapeshifters.'

'Yes,' Elvira says, nodding. 'The king decreed that the Shifting be kept secret. Wehrs could be in dragon form, but under no circumstances could anyone outside of Rhybor know that the indigenous population were shapeshifters. For many years, wehrs wandered about in human form and didn't attract any undue attention from visitors. All was well.'

Elvira pauses.

'Until?' I prompt.

Elvira sighs. 'Some wehrs weren't happy to have their "freedom" curbed. They thought wehrs should be proud of – and open about – their heritage. Society fractured. There was a line – Loyalists on one side, those who supported the king; Crusaders on the other side, those who wanted to overthrow the king for a more "progressive" society.'

'Karina's a Crusader?' I guess.

'Yep. And my father's a Loyalist. He's currently working in a lab in Russia. I haven't seen him since I was six.'

'Ten years and he hasn't got a portal yet?'

Elvira shrugs. 'He hasn't been working on it the whole time. He was in jail for quite a while.'

I study Elvira's face. This is really her – without any masks. She suddenly looks … vulnerable. But in light of the fact that she's harbouring a deadly reptile inside her, that vulnerability doesn't fit. Her family life is as messed up as mine and I should probably feel sorry for her. I don't though. Anger boils inside me. In my parents' absence, Elvira is the obvious target.

I glare at her. 'I can't believe I trusted you.'

'Trust?' She scoffs. 'Really? Is that what I saw when I told you the truth in the hospital carpark? Just a whole lotta trust? Honestly, when in the last ten years would have been a good time for me to tell you, Felix?'

I don't have an answer for that, so I say, 'Can I turn into a dragon?'

Elvira shakes her head, her lips pressed together in a thin line. 'No. You've only got half the genes. But your blood is more potent than regular human blood, so it's Liberty's best chance.'

'Surely your blood would be better?'

'I'm on the reserve bench.'

'If you kill me, you mean?'

'Get over yourself, kid,' Gemini says. He turns to Elvira. 'Can you please bring Felix some water. The quicker he rehydrates, the better.'

'How long will this whole … process take?' I ask.

'Strangely,' Gemini says, 'there isn't a lot of research to inform us. However, I've done some calculations based on Karina's schedule and adjusted for the fact that you have only half the genetic material of a full wehr.'

Somewhere outside, something bellows.

'What the hell was that?' I say.

'A cow,' Gemini replies calmly.

'Where *are* we?'

'Safe house,' Gemini says. 'Nestled in the rolling hills an hour west of Indigo. This property's a few thousand hectares and it has livestock on it. Birds, too. Wait till you hear the peacock.'

I scan the room. If it wasn't set up as a makeshift hospital ward, it would be a spacious and airy lounge room. The wide wooden floorboards look to be in perfect condition. Pristine white blinds cover the two adjacent walls behind me, shielding us from the darkness beyond the windows. The bricked fireplace is currently empty but its blackened belly holds the promise of a winter warrior – a fiery soldier to combat the frigid conditions that Indigo is famous for.

A long, stainless-steel island bench marks the boundary between the lounge and kitchen, where Elvira is currently perusing the pantry shelves. She loads several items in the crook of her arm before returning to the casualty area. With her free hand, she wheels a small table across to my recliner.

'Bottle of water at room temperature,' she says, placing it on the tray. 'A packet of Pizza Shapes and a chocolate bar. That should keep you quiet for a few minutes.'

My stomach growls, and I realise I haven't eaten in over twelve hours. I take a swig from the water bottle before opening the Pizza Shapes. After scoffing a handful, I lie back in my chair and close my eyes.

This is ridiculous. Who ever heard of shapeshifting dragons abandoned on Earth infiltrating top-secret human laboratories to work covertly to re-establish a gateway to their planet on the other side of the galaxy? I want to laugh at Elvira's story. But I saw a portal at NSA. I saw Karina's dragon. Elvira's too.

The next few hours pass with Gemini periodically stealing my blood and Elvira delivering me snacks. The sugar keeps my fatigue at bay and I watch Gemini administer Liberty's transfusions with metronomic precision.

As daylight peeks in around the blinds, Liberty stirs. I swing my legs over the edge of my recliner and push to my feet. Dizziness swamps me. I close my eyes to steady myself and once my brain stops somersaulting inside my skull, I open them again.

Liberty's eyelids flutter.

'Liberty,' I say, crouching beside her. 'Can you hear me?'

Her head flops to one side and I study her angelic face. 'Open your eyes if you can hear me, Liberty.'

Her eyelids flutter again and I catch a glimpse of blue. She squints, tries to raise her hand but it falls back to her side.

I shift to the left slightly, shielding her from the ceiling lights.

'Where am I?' Liberty whispers.

'Safe house,' I reply. 'You're going to be okay.'

Chapter 8

Liberty

'Felix?' I say. 'What is … Why are …?'

Finishing a question is more difficult than it should be. My brain feels like playdough that's been left out in the sun for a week.

'You're in a safe house,' Felix says. 'You're going to be fine.'

I blink several times to clear my blurred vision. And when I succeed, I regret it.

Felix is standing over me, leering at me.

'You're in a safe house,' Felix says again. 'You're going to be fine.'

His hair is scruffy, his t-shirt is crumpled, and he has bandages around both his elbows.

This is about as far from 'fine' as I can imagine.

'Where am I?'

'In a safe house,' Felix says.

'Okay. Right.' I sigh. 'Is there someone else here I can talk to?'

A girl with pink glasses and dark ringlets appears at Felix's side. She's from school too. Together, she and Felix are the school's 'odd' couple. I think her name is Elira?

'Hi Liberty,' she says. 'You're about an hour west of Indigo. You've just had a series of transfusions to give your body a chance to beat the radiation sickness you're suffering as a result of entering Lab 17 at NSA after the portal imploded.'

'NSA,' I murmur, memories of my father's body flooding back into my mind. 'Where are my parents?'

Elira nudges Felix who doesn't seem to register the cue. He just keeps grinning at me, so Elira continues. 'Your father is being treated on site and your mother … as far as we know, is still unaccounted for.'

I scan my surroundings. I'm in some kind of living room that appears to double as a pop-up veterinary surgery. It's clean, spacious, and the view of the imminent sunrise over the countryside through the glass sliding doors occupying two of the walls is serene. Two black and white Friesian cows are nibbling grass in the house yard against the backdrop of cherry blossoms, and there's a peacock sitting in one of the eucalypts, his tail a blanket of jewels cascading down from a low-hanging branch.

'Why am I not in a hospital?' I ask.

'You were in a hospital,' Elira says, 'but they were totally overwhelmed by the number of casualties coming in from NSA.'

'I can imagine that,' I say, 'but what makes you people think – given that I needed blood transfusions – that you could provide superior treatment?' I shudder. 'Where did the blood come from?'

Felix raises his hand.

Geez, are we at school?

My heart thumps inside my chest, like it's trying to break out, pumping Felix's blood through my veins. Though I should probably be thankful I'm alive, I can't help but feel violated. This is totally wrong. I need to get out of here – except that I don't know exactly where 'here' is. I'm going to have to play along and take the first opportunity to escape.

I manufacture a smile. 'Well, in that case, I guess I should say "thank you".'

Felix bows, hitting his head on the heartrate monitor as he does so. 'You're – ouch! – welcome,' Felix says, rubbing his forehead.

Good grief! I really need to get away from these freaks.

Aloud, I say, 'So, what's next?' As I swing my legs over the side of the recliner, I notice another young man in the room. 'Who are you?' I say.

'Gemini Holmes,' he says, extending his hand. 'Genius. Assassin. Spy. Doctor in residence.'

Felix frowns. 'I thought you said you were a dental hygienist.'

'I *can* be,' Gemini says. 'But one must adapt to new circumstances.'

'Dare I ask if you have any formal qualifications?' I say.

Gemini smiles. 'I have an IQ of 185 and a photographic memory.'

'So, you *don't* have any qualifications then.'

'On the contrary,' he says. 'I have an extensive CV.'

Gemini's words echo inside my head. *Genius. Assassin. Spy. Doctor in residence.*

'You have a heap of false documentation for your different covers then?' I say.

His smile broadens. 'You're not just a pretty face, are you.'

Felix clears his throat. 'There is more to Liberty than just looks, you know,' he says.

I refrain from rolling my eyes, barely. As if I need *his* help.

Gemini is clearly the brains here, so he's the one I need to deal with to get myself out of this mess. He's obviously dangerous – but in a focused and intentional way; as opposed to the other two, whose stupidity poses a threat to society.

'If you're an assassin and a spy,' I say, 'firstly, why are you babysitting this pair? And secondly, why are you "helping" me?'

'Excellent questions!' Gemini exclaims. 'Let me answer them by saying this … my employer has a keen interest in your parents' portal so I am here to ensure that the project gets back on track. Each of you – for reasons that I am not authorised to share – is connected to the fate of this project, and it falls to me to ensure that you do what is expected of you.'

'And if we don't do what is expected of us?' I ask.

'I have a plan for that contingency too,' he replies.

I suspect this means his employer has authorised him to terminate us so I will have to play this carefully.

'Great,' I reply. 'So, what's your master plan?'

'Well,' Gemini says, 'Elvira's going to school.'

Elvira recoils. 'What? Why?'

'Because it's a school day, and you're not sick – so you're going,' Gemini says.

Right. Mental note. Her name is *Elvira*, not Elira.

Elvira squints at him through her pink glasses. 'You don't seriously think you can tell me what to do, do you?'

'Elvira,' he says, 'shower. Go.'

Elvira storms off down the hallway as Felix says, 'And what about me?'

Gemini checks his watch. 'You need to "clean out" the van, so you can drive Elvira to school and then report in with Harry Jones. Get on it. Clock is ticking.'

Felix's face loses several shades of colour and he swallows hard. 'Clean out … the … van?'

'This is required of you, Felix,' Gemini says brusquely. 'You'll find all the tools you need in the shed.'

'Do you really expect me to—'

'Yes!' Gemini says. 'I really do expect you to!'

Felix looks down at his outfit. 'Well, once I've finished "cleaning out" the van – I can hardly go into the newsroom looking like this.'

'Agreed,' Gemini says, 'which is why I'm awaiting a delivery that will fix that problem. So … van … now! Chop! Chop!'

Felix clenches his fists as his face reddens. Gemini ignores him. Turning to me, he says, 'Liberty, you will shower, then rest up until we get an update on your parents.'

I snort as Felix slams the front door behind him. 'That's not—'

'What's that around your neck?' Gemini asks.

Surprised by the question, I say, 'It's an American half dollar.'

'Uh-huh?'

'A *Liberty* half dollar.'

'Riiiiight.'

'My *name* is Liberty.'

'Okay … And?'

Is he serious?

'Do you wear it for identification purposes?' Gemini asks.

'Sorry?'

'The *Liberty* coin,' he says. 'Is it in case you forget your name?'

'No,' I say. 'It's a good luck charm.'

Gemini rubs his chin. 'Wouldn't have picked you for the superstitious kind.'

You know nothing about me. I found my coin on a bouldering excursion to Bear Mountain with my father when I was seven. Having only done indoor climbing before that, I was keen to do some 'real' rock-climbing. For me, it was the perfect day. Although Dad chewed off every fingernail he owned, I found clambering up rocks, finding increasingly difficult hand- and foot-holds as I traversed the slope, nothing short of magical. And on one spectacularly difficult hand-hold – for a seven-year-old at least – I found my Liberty coin.

I remember clutching the craggy rock and my fingertips registering something smooth, hot and loose. Carefully, I pinched the object between my fingers so I could inspect it. When I saw it was a Liberty half dollar, my heart had pumped faster inside my chest. It was a rare find – a sign. Definitely a sign. How had this foreign coin made it to this obscure ledge in the first place? How long had it been waiting for someone to find it? For *me* to find it.

It was actually Dad who suggested it was my good luck charm. He'd probably used every law of physics to calculate how many ways I could have died that day, and the fact that I'd survived could only have been explained by something that defied natural law, something supernatural. He had the coin polished and set in a pendant for me, and so far it had proved its worth as a lucky charm.

And now, it seems it had saved me from radiation poisoning.

'Look,' I say. 'As much as I'd love to sit around here "resting", I really need to go home. So … what's the best way out of here?'

'Doors work for me,' he says with a shrug.

'You know what I mean. What's the best way back to town?'

'Oh. Do you have a car?'

I shake my head.

'A helicopter?'

'Seriously?'

'Well,' he says, 'unless you want to ride one of the cows, you might have to walk.'

'You have a van!'

'I *do* have a van,' Gemini says, 'but it is *my* van, and I have plans for it at present.'

'I'll pay you for a lift back to town.'

'How much?'

Now we're getting somewhere. We haggle for a minute before settling on a price.

'Well, Gemini, if you ever tire of dentistry,' I say, 'you have a flair for extortion.'

He grins. 'Thank you.'

I shake my head as a phone beeps.

'That sounds like mine,' I say, 'but I didn't …'

'Felix brought it,' Gemini says. 'You wait right there – I'll get it for you.'

I'm hooked up to the heartrate monitor and an IV drip so racing him to the kitchen bench isn't an option. He returns and hands me my phone. I open the message and read it three times before looking up.

'Gemini,' I say, 'I'll double my price for a ride to town if we can go now.'

He rubs his hands together. 'Really? Why?'

'My father is okay – and at work,' I say, waving my phone.

'Well, that does change things,' Gemini says. 'New plan! You can go and shower, and once Felix has finished with the van and dropped Elvira at school, he can escort you to NSA.'

Once Gemini has disconnected the IV and removed the canula from my hand, he points to the hallway adjacent to the one Elvira took. 'There's another bathroom down there. You'll find spare clothes on the shelf.'

In the bathroom, I quickly strip off my hospital gown and install myself under a steady stream of warm water. I scrub my skin and wash my hair, not bothering with conditioner. The white towel is princess-grade, and though I dry myself quickly, I still revel in its softness. I find disposable underwear, track pants and a t-shirt on the shelf. The haute couture is far from boutique but at least it's clean and comfortable – better than a hospital gown any day.

I return to the kitchen to find Gemini with Elvira, who looks me up and down. 'Well, I'm glad we're not going to the same party,' she says.

'That's a problem with safe houses,' Gemini notes. 'The wardrobe is pretty grim.'

'Help yourself to something to eat, Liberty,' Elvira says, gesturing towards the pantry.

My stomach rumbles as I peruse the shelves. 'Everything is canned or in a packet,' I say.

'Another problem with safe houses,' Gemini says. 'Never much in the way of fresh produce.'

The doorbell rings as I slip a protein bar into each of the pockets of my trackpants.

'That'll be Felix's suit,' Gemini says, leaping to his feet and heading for the front door.

I open a protein bar and take a bite.

Elvira puts her phone down on the kitchen bench. 'I hear that Felix is going to escort you to NSA, Liberty.'

I sigh on the inside. 'That is Gemini's plan, yes.'

'Felix means well,' she says. 'Please be nice to him – or at least … don't be awful to him.'

'I'm never awful to anyone,' I say.

Elvira's eyebrows arch over the rims of her glasses. 'Did you know he's the one who pulled you out of the lab? And took you to the hospital?'

How did he know where I was? Was he stalking me?

'A smile would go a long way,' Elvira adds.

A smile? Felix might have pulled me out of the lab, but he left my father there to die. Then, after taking me to hospital, they subsequently abducted me and gave me blood transfusions without my consent. The blood was from an unregulated source, potentially contaminated – who knows what diseases Felix might be harbouring – and the transfusions were performed in a non-sterile environment. And she wants me to smile?

'And you're what?' I say calmly. 'His nanny? His manager?'

'I'm a creditor,' Elvira says. 'He owes me a nose job.'

'Pardon?'

'He broke my nose when we were six and promised me corrective surgery one day. I intend to make sure he honours that promise.'

These people are seriously weird. Elvira acts like she's Felix's mother. Creepy. And I used to think Felix was just awkward but there might be more to it than that – something more sinister. This whole thing has a definite stalker vibe about it.

I turn to Gemini, who has returned with a suit bag. 'And what's your plan?' I say. 'What are you going to be doing?'

Gemini taps the side of his nose. 'That's for me to know and for you to not find out.'

Chapter 9

Liberty

As Felix swings Gemini's van into one of the few vacant spots in the NSA carpark, I say, 'It really is a mess, isn't it?'

'Yes,' Felix agrees.

I check the clock on the dash. 09:27. It's been less than twenty-four hours since the portal imploded.

Cranes dominate the rubble-strewn landscape. Some are unloading relocatable buildings from trucks. The truck convoy stretches past the bend in the roadway as the haulers wait – engines running – for their turn to unload. Other cranes are lifting twisted steel girders and giant concrete slabs, then dumping them in massive rubbish skips.

We exit the van and make our way to the makeshift check-in point.

Felix and I look completely out of place, being the only ones who aren't wearing hi-vis vests. Felix's shoes are polished, his dark trousers and blue business shirt are perfectly pressed and his mauve and yellow tie makes him look every bit the cadet reporter he's supposed to be. I just hope he doesn't ruin the image by opening his mouth.

The checkpoint is a portable picnic table and a folding chair under a portable gazebo. The lone security guard has a tablet, a small printer and an Esky.

'Help you?' the security guard asks, his tone implying that 'helping' is not really on his agenda.

'I'm here to see Caspian Fox,' I say. 'I'm Liberty Fox, his daughter.'

The portly middle-aged man pokes at his tablet with pudgy fingers. Finally, he says, 'Okay, your pass will print out there.'

He glances at the small printer on the table before transferring his gaze to Felix. 'And you?'

'Here to see Karina Warhurst,' Felix says. 'I'm her stepson, Felix Dangerfield.'

'Didn't realise it was family day at the office,' the guard mutters. 'Given the circumstances, you'd think they'd have cancelled it.'

'Thanks,' Felix says as he collects his pass. 'You have a nice day.'

The man rolls his eyes. 'Follow the path to the next checkpoint. They'll direct you from there.'

'Well,' I say, 'at least they haven't lost the "government department touch". We've got to have our paperwork in order and then jump through lots of hoops.'

'Yeah,' Felix says.

After four more checkpoints, we get a personal escort to Karina Warhurst's temporary office. She's sitting behind a grey melamine desk, scowling at her laptop screen. In the corner, six slabs of bottled water are stacked up, supporting a pizza box that could serve as another table. Aside from that, the office is bare.

'Your visitors, Karina,' the security officer announces.

Karina looks up and gestures for us to take the two empty seats across from her. 'Thanks, Briony.'

'Y'welcome,' Briony says with a wave as she departs.

Karina leans back in her chair, interlacing her fingers over her abdomen. 'So, Felix … busy night?'

'Yes,' he says.

Her face morphs into a sour frown. 'Too busy to come home?'

'I told Dad I wouldn't be home.'

Karina sneers. 'He said you sent him a *text*. Do you really think that is satisfactory?'

'Yes.'

She snorts derisively. 'And *why* are you dressed like *that*?'

Felix straightens his back. 'I'm here in my official capacity as a cadet reporter for the *Indigo Times*.'

'Really?' she says, her voice loaded with sarcasm. 'What a joke! You'd be better off at school, but anyway …'

My stomach clenches into a hard knot as Karina turns her attention to me. My mother would never speak to me that way – and would never belittle me in front of other people. Maybe the rumours of Felix's 'evil' stepmother aren't as far from the mark as I'd thought. Perhaps he's weird with good reason. Maybe a smile – as Elvira suggested – isn't too much to ask for after all.

Karina leans forward and rests her elbows on the table. 'Liberty, I'm glad to be able to give you good news about your father – he'll be along presently to join us – but we are still working to locate your mother, I'm afraid.'

I keep my hands folded in my lap. What are the odds my mother is still alive?

'Was it the portal that caused this destruction?' I ask.

Karina's eyes flick to Felix and then back to me. 'If you hadn't brought your newshound with you, Liberty, I might have been able to speak a bit more candidly, but …' She shrugs apologetically.

'Felix,' I say, turning to him, 'wait outside for me, would you?'

His face and neck flush with red, igniting a fiery flash in his eyes. 'Fine.'

I cringe inwardly. I sound like Karina. I could at least have said 'please'.

When he's gone, I say, 'So, *was* it the portal that caused the destruction here?'

'Yes,' Karina says. 'Something went wrong. At this point, we don't know what.'

'Was my mother working on the portal at the time?'

'Yes.'

I take a deep breath. 'Is it possible my mother *entered* the portal?'

'Yes,' Karina says.

'When can I—'

'Liberty!' My father's voice interrupts my question.

I leap from my chair and spin round, into his embrace.

'Dad!' I say, hugging him tightly.

I squeeze my eyes closed, fighting tears. I have every right to cry – from relief that my father is fine to fear that my mother isn't – but I won't let Karina see that. I won't show weakness in front of her.

Reluctantly, I release my father from my embrace. I grasp his hands. 'Are you okay? Really?'

'Right as rain, Liberty,' he says. 'I'm so sorry to have worried you.'

I shake my head. 'You don't need to apologise, Dad. We're both fine – now we just need to find Mum.'

'Caspian,' Karina says, 'have you made any progress locating your wife?'

My father nods his head slowly. 'I think she's entangled in the portal.'

'Entangled?' Karina drums her fingers on the table. 'What does that mean?'

'In simple terms,' he says, 'it means that she entered the portal, but it hasn't spat her out anywhere. She's still … in it … somewhere.'

Karina's eyes narrow. Then she sighs. 'Do you need an assistant?'

My father screws up his face. 'An assistant? For what?'

'To fill Rose's place – until you can extract her. Someone to *help you* extract her.'

'I don't know who could do that,' he says, his frown deepening. 'Filling such a specialised role will be extraordinarily difficult.'

Karina shifts her gaze to her laptop. 'I have no doubt, but I will forward you three applications I have received this morning for the position.'

'You've advertised it already?' my father asks, incredulous.

Karina shakes her head. 'Didn't need to. These are unsolicited.'

I'm not sure I believe that, but that's irrelevant.

My father harrumphs. 'I don't need CVs,' he says. 'Just tell me their names. Anyone of note in the field I will know by reputation.'

'Fair enough,' Karina says. 'Your three contestants are … Emmanuel Forrester, Jyarenesha Singh and Gemini Holmes.'

Gemini Holmes. My blood runs cold. *Felix's blood actually,* I remind myself. After so many transfusions, I doubt any of the blood in my system is actually my own. That thought prompts a question. Since I assume my father underwent a similar treatment to mine, whose blood did he get?

'I've heard of the first two,' my father says, 'but the last one – I've got a complete blank.'

'Dad,' I say, 'you should get back to work. Locating Mum is the priority now.'

'Yes, yes,' he agrees. 'Splendid, yes.' To Karina, he says, 'I will contact the applicants.' To me, he says, 'Walk with me?'

I smile. 'Of course.'

I turn to Karina. 'Thank you so much for your time and for looking after Dad. I will get out of your hair now.'

Karina stands and, to my surprise, extends her hand to me. 'Anything I can do to help,' she says, shaking my hand firmly, 'please let me know.'

'I will.'

Once we are outside, Felix is lurking only metres away. Inwardly, I curse myself. I'd forgotten he was waiting. Talking to my father privately is a priority but I'd like to do it without offending Felix this time. I really don't fancy being like Karina.

'Felix,' I say, beckoning him over. 'I'd like you to meet my dad.'

Unsmiling, he approaches us.

'Felix Dangerfield,' he says, extending his hand to my father. 'Nice to meet you, sir.'

'You're a friend of Liberty's, are you?' my father asks, accepting the handshake warmly.

'We go to the same school,' Felix replies. 'Just a coincidence that our parents work together.'

My father's eyebrows arch in surprise. 'Your parents work here?'

'Karina is my stepmother,' Felix explains.

'Oh! You're *that*—,' my father begins, catching himself too late.

Felix frowns. I cringe. So much for not offending him.

'Your stepmother is a generous woman, Felix,' he says. 'She gave her own blood to save my life.'

Well, so much for asking that question in private. Now that I've got my answer though, I need time to process how I feel about it. I have

Felix's blood; Dad has Karina's. I should be grateful Dad and I are both alive. But the whole blood-sharing thing is totally creeping me out.

I kind of feel sorry for Felix though. Seems his home life is probably as messed up as the rumours at school suggest. It wouldn't kill me to be pleasant to him, but I'll need to be careful not to fuel his neediness. I'm not in the market for friends.

Craving a distraction, I say, 'Felix, how about we go to school? We can catch the afternoon sessions.'

'Happy to drop you there,' Felix says coolly. 'I have other orders … um … plans.'

Chapter 10

Felix

I press the button for the third floor as the lift doors close. The carriage shudders before lifting off, and the creaking and grinding noises outside my metal box are disturbing. I'm thankful it's only three floors. Today is not the day to get stuck in an elevator.

When the doors open, I make a hasty exit and scan my security pass at the door. The glass doors with *Indigo Times* plastered on them slide apart and I stride into the news hub. It's the middle of the day and it's quiet. Most of the journos must be in the field. Not Harry though. He's in his corner kingdom to the left of the entrance, presiding over the newsroom from his wheelchair. He waves me over.

'Felix,' Harry bellows. 'Attend!'

Only when I reach his spot do I notice Jasper perched on a footstool, slumped over his camera.

'Is he okay?' I ask, pointing to the cameraman.

'Yeah,' Harry says, 'he's just having a nap.'

I shake my head in disbelief. 'How the hell can he sleep in here with you yelling like that?'

'Yelling?' Harry says, cocking his head to one side. 'I'm not yelling.'

'I'm not sure you actually know what yelling is then,' I say.

'Do you have news?' Harry asks as Jasper stirs.

'Not as much as I'd hoped,' I reply. 'Caspian Fox is alive; Rose is entangled in the portal. Karina is possibly going to employ another scientist to help Caspian.'

Harry's hands hover over his tablet. 'Help Caspian to do … what?'

'Retrieve Rose, then fix the portal I guess.'

'You guess?'

'It was difficult to hear. I was eavesdropping from outside.'

Jasper places his camera on a nearby desk and stretches his arms over his head. 'Don't suppose you managed to get an *unblurred* photo of the portal this time?'

'No.'

Jasper sighs. 'This story would be so much better with clear pictures.'

Anger bubbles in my gut. 'I got one of Dr Fox hugging his daughter,' I say, dragging my phone from my pocket. 'Captured, the "human element" of the story, as you like to say.'

'Well, that's better than nothing, I suppose,' Jasper says with a shrug.

Condescending wanker. I want to throw my phone at his head.

'Jasper,' Harry says. 'Go get us a couple of cappuccinos – minus the chocolate.'

Jasper squints at Harry. 'Do I hear a "please"?'

Harry glares at him. Unsurprisingly, Jasper backs down immediately. He knows he's wasting his time in this battle.

'Cappuccinos coming up,' he says, shuffling off.

Too late to make a difference to the order, I say, 'I like the chocolate on top.'

Harry ignores my comment. 'I thought you'd be here earlier. You met with Karina nearly three hours ago. Where have you been?'

'Fighting with my father.'

'Fighting?' Harry says. 'Fists or knives?'

I roll my eyes. 'Okay, not *fighting*. Arguing.'

'About what?'

'Why? You gonna publish a story on it?'

Harry shrugs. 'Unlikely, but it depends. If it's interesting …'

'It was nothing to stop the presses for,' I tell him.

'Humour me. What did you argue about?'

'My stepmother,' I say. 'Apparently I don't show her enough respect.'

Harry scoffs. 'You're right. Not newsworthy.'

What we argued *about* wasn't newsworthy, but the real *reason* we argued would be. No way I'm sharing that with Harry though. My father accused me of only coming home to pick a fight. And he probably wasn't wrong about that. After what Elvira told me about my heritage – and showed me of hers – I could barely look at my father, let alone have a reasonable conversation with him. I was angry with Elvira for withholding what she knew about me, but when I saw my father, I found a whole new level of fury. The fact that *he* never told me … is unforgivable.

Facing my father, pretending that I didn't know the truth, was astonishingly difficult. I really wanted to tell him what I knew but that would have compromised Elvira, and she doesn't deserve that – even if she did only tell me to save her own skin.

Jasper returns with two cans of beer. Harry winks at me as Jasper hands one to me.

'Still want chocolate on top?' Harry asks.

'How is this a cappuccino?'

Harry grins as he cracks the seal. 'It's got froth on top, it counts.'

'Uh-huh.'

'It's more hops than caffeine,' he admits, 'but you need to keep your fluids up.'

'You do know that alcohol dehydrates you, don't you?'

'Oh, for Christ's sake, just drink it, Felix!' Harry says. 'One beer won't kill your sporting career.'

I look at Jasper. 'You're not joining us?'

Jasper shakes his head. 'Might have to drive.'

The last twenty-four hours have been totally insane and arguing with my father, has left me pretty wired. Maybe a drink will take the edge off.

I open the top and raise the can. 'Cheers.'

Harry winks. 'That's my boy.'

That's my boy?

Really? I don't belong anywhere, or to anyone. I'm an outcast. I'm not human, but I'm not a dragon either. Wehrdragon. Whatever.

Harry takes a swig of his beer then belches loudly. 'Got that photo?'

'What?'

'The photo of Caspian with his daughter. You said you had one?'

'Oh, right. I'll drop it to you.' Beer can in one hand, I negotiate my phone with the other. 'Done.'

Harry wipes his mouth with a handkerchief. 'Great,' he says, scanning the photos I took outside Karina's temporary office. 'I'll do a follow-up article on the portal. The original piece got mega-hits.'

'I'll bet.'

'Would have got more hits if there'd been a sharp photo,' Jasper adds.

'Jasper,' Harry says, 'go and do an audit of the cappuccino supplies, would you?'

'You're trying to get rid of me,' he says.

Harry nods emphatically. 'Yes.'

While Harry and Jasper trade barbs, I text Elvira. Maybe she *had* protected me by not telling me the truth earlier. At least she *did* tell me though. I was a prick about it. I need to make it up to her a bit.

Meet at Hoogey's after school?

Her reply comes as Jasper concedes defeat and retreats to wherever the pseudo cappuccino supplies are held.

Yep. See you there.

There are no emojis. She must be really mad at me. I frown. I'm not the only one in the indignation zone, apparently. I still think I've got more right to the space than she does though and, no doubt, we'll argue about it when I see her.

'Problem?' Harry says.

'Nothing I can't handle,' I say.

Harry's face cracks into a hyena-like smile. 'It's a girl, isn't it? I can tell by the look on your face.'

I groan. 'Well, I won't be taking any advice from you on that, so save your breath to cool your porridge.'

Harry laughs uproariously, prompting vocal protests from the few other journos in the office.

'Save your breath to cool your porridge,' he echoes, still chuckling. 'I've not heard that one before. Consider that stolen.'

'Hmmm.'

'What's your next move?' Harry asks once he's recovered his composure.

'I'm meeting Elvira after school,' I say. 'Until then, I've got some time to kill.'

Harry checks his watch. 'I can keep you busy.'

'Great,' I say, happy to have something to keep me occupied. 'What have got for me?'

'Social media detail,' he says. 'You can respond to all the comments from my ... admirers.'

When he says 'admirers', he means 'haters', but that's okay. They're more fun to respond to. And with the mood I'm in today, I'm totally up for it.

Chapter 11

Elvira

It's always worth waiting for half an hour for the second bus. I take a seat in the back section – I prefer the elevated seats – and drag out my phone in order to text Felix to let him know I'm on my way. Message sent, I turn my attention to my fellow passengers. Imagining people's backstories is one of my favourite pastimes. Life is a stage and, for the characters currently sharing my stage, it's fascinating to think who they might be, where they've come from, and what they've done.

The young man sitting directly behind the driver catches my attention. I truly believe that people who choose that seat all share a certain psychology but, in all my bus-travelling days, I have discovered it's far from a stereotype. His back suggests tantalising details. Dark, wavy hair is pulled back in a ponytail, which caresses the collar of his pink business shirt, and his skin is the colour of macadamia nut shells, so he's possibly of Asian heritage. Wireless earbuds are wedged in his ears.

From these scant details, I deduce that he is the only son of wealthy parents who run a successful import business. This young man isn't interested in the family business though; he's focused on a career in real estate. Today, he has done battle with grubby tenants who did a runner from their rental, leaving a festering mess behind. One day though, he won't deal with filthy ferals. He'll deal solely in luxury properties, selling to the rich and famous, and living the high life on a stream – no, a river – of fat commissions.

When the bus pulls in to the next stop, a young Sudanese woman gets on. Faded stretch jeans hug her long, slender legs and I love her vintage leopard-print top. Her long braids, dotted with colourful beads, cascade from a high ponytail and end halfway down her back. She strides up the aisle, like she's on a catwalk – until she stumbles at the step up to the back section of the bus.

Embarrassed for her, I look away. I'm still looking out the window when she plants herself next to me. Why is it, when there are vacant seats available, that people choose to sit right next to someone else? I sigh. Though I am fascinated by people, I don't necessarily want to talk to them. Their realities are often disappointing. I prefer my imagined backstories.

She studies the screen of her phone as she inserts her earbuds. At least she won't talk to me. It's only another half a dozen stops to the café where I'm meeting Felix so I give up on the people inside the bus and commit myself to the view outside.

Two stops later, I'm interrupted by a scream.

'Smoke! Fire!'

The bus driver slams on the brakes and I'm flung forward, crashing painfully into the seat in front of me. I groan as I scramble to my feet. Smoke wafts around me and I cover my mouth and nose with my hand. I clutch my bag against my chest as a hand encircles my wrist and yanks it hard.

'Whoa!' I yell as I'm dragged into the aisle.

I crash onto my backside.

'Come on! Get up!' the Sudanese girl urges. 'We need to get out!'

'Yeah,' I say. 'Okay.'

'Back window!' she cries. 'Back window!'

I'm no sooner on my feet than someone crashes into my back, winding me. I struggle to suck in my next breath, now I'm wedged between my Sudanese saviour and another passenger.

'Back window!' she yells at the people streaming towards the front. 'The fire's in the middle of the bus! Go back!'

Breathing is my sole focus as she braces herself against the tide of panicked passengers, using me as a shield. Long moments pass as my struggle to breathe becomes more frantic, then suddenly the pressure on my chest eases as the passengers at the rear of the bus finally turn back. I suck in a lungful of smoke and instantly regret it. Coughing uncontrollably, I follow the frenetic stream towards the emergency exit.

When I reach the back row of seats, an athletic-looking thirty-something hooks the crook of his elbow under my armpit and almost launches me through the opening where the rear window used to be.

I scream as I plummet to the bitumen below.

'AAAAAAAAAAAHHHHHH!'

Traffic behind the bus is stopped; several cars are concertinaed together. The adjacent lane is crawling on account of the rubberneckers, as are the two lanes going in the opposite direction. My Sudanese travel buddy appears at my side.

'Off the road,' she says, pointing towards the footpath.

It's only once we're on the footpath that I see it.

'Look out!' I cry.

I'm shoved out of the way of the approaching traffic control truck and into a garden bed. However, before I have time to recover and get to my feet again, a man in a council uniform leaps from the passenger side of the truck and crouches in front of me.

'You okay?' he asks.

I inhale slowly. 'Yeah, I think so.'

'Good.' He extends his hand. 'Let me help you up.'

I accept his help, but the moment I'm out of the garden, I'm barrelled into the truck.

I manage to say, 'What—' before a cloth is stuffed into my mouth and there is a sharp sting in my thigh. As my consciousness seeps away, my bones turn to rubber, rendering my muscles useless and the last words I hear are …

'Target acquired. Let's go.'

∞

Consciousness slithers back like a geriatric eel through peanut butter. My body aches. I'm lying on my side on a hard, frigid floor. My hands are tied behind my back and my ankles are bound. Something tight around my throat makes it difficult to swallow. When I force my eyes open, the first thing I see is a pair of black Doc Martens.

'Finally,' a male voice says, then there's a pause before, 'Boss, she's awake.'

The boots pick their way through the debris on the concrete floor before disappearing through a doorway. In the musty silence, I crane my neck to scope what I can of my prison. It looks like an abandoned storeroom. Yet, judging by the mess, I'm guessing it wasn't simply abandoned, but has been subjected to an amateur demolition job or it's been a project for local vandals.

When the next pair of shoes arrives, I turn my head to identify the owner.

'Elvira,' Karina purrs. 'We meet at last.'

This isn't the way I pictured my first encounter with Felix's stepmother. I've curated a significant digital dossier on Karina Warhurst for my father over the years and, even without the murder of the security guard that Felix witnessed, it could still be the basis for a Hollywood thriller.

As a spy for my father, I am predisposed to focus on Karina's traitorous machinations in the great game – the wehrdragon conflict between Loyalists and Crusaders. Having studied her for so long though, I would jump at the chance to play the lead role in any biopic of her life. It certainly wouldn't be a heartwarming tale, but it would be intriguing.

Feminists would laud her as a shining example of what modern women should aspire to. This ambitious woman is a portrait of career success against a backdrop of the responsibilities of being a wife and mother. An inspiration. A glittering bauble on the Christmas tree of equal opportunity.

But one doesn't get to be the director of a government department overseeing secret intergalactic projects by being a nice person. She's tough, fearless, focused on outcomes – and does not suffer fools. Employees who can meet her dizzyingly high standards admire her tenaciousness, but those who fall below the benchmark and are 'cut' from her ranks see her as a ruthless troll. And as for being a mother, she's a ripping non-example.

'Karina,' I croak, 'I'd like to say it's nice to meet you but …'

She squats down in front of me. 'Well, I think it's just a shame it took so long.'

'It wouldn't have taken so long if you'd shown more interest in Felix's friends,' I say.

'Hmmm,' Karina says, settling herself to sit cross-legged on the floor. 'That's true, but until yesterday, neither he nor his friends were of any interest to me.'

I wriggle to try to get into a more comfortable position, something that will ease the pressure of the heavy chain around my throat.

'Why the change of heart?' I ask. 'Afraid he'll expose you?'

Karina chuckles. 'Regardless of what he *thinks* he knows, I can deflect whatever mud he tries to fling my way. Felix is irritating, but not a threat.'

'You're not worried about his relationship with Harry Jones?'

'Thankfully, Harry Jones is a smart man,' Karina says. 'He *appears* to want to disseminate truth to the masses, but he is actually more focused on protecting his own arse. He knows better than to go after me.'

'Because you'll discredit him?'

'Yes.'

'And what about me?' I say. 'Why am I here – getting this special treatment?'

Karina leans forward. 'Because after our little "meltdown" yesterday, this site was swarming with witless imbeciles – like Felix, Liberty Fox … you. Not that I would have wished any of you any harm, but I was relieved when security finally confirmed you had all vacated the site.'

Though I am sure her wish that we not suffer any harm stems from potential insurance claims rather than concern for our welfare, I don't quiz her on that.

'And yet, here we are,' I say. 'What gives?'

'To be honest,' Karina says, 'it wasn't until Felix and Liberty visited me this morning that I gave any of you any more thought. Liberty's amazing recovery after you'd witnessed Caspian's treatment—'

'How did you know that?'

'Some security cameras were still operating, Elvira. I reviewed everything I could. It was the only way I could track you and confirm when you'd left the site.'

My heart sinks. I didn't think I'd left anything incriminating behind. Father will be furious.

'It's a simple chain to follow then,' Karina continues. 'You tell Felix about the treatment and how Liberty can be healed. Where does the blood come from though? Felix's might do it, but how would he know to use it? Who could tell him about what his blood might hold? It wasn't me or his father, so who else?' Karina leans over and taps me on the forehead. 'It could only be you.'

This is a problem. I've misjudged Karina. I didn't doubt she'd figure out the link but I thought she'd play it cool. Monitor, rather than act.

Karina traces my jawline with her index finger. 'So, the question is, who do you belong to, little dragon?'

I glare at her, the only answer I'm prepared to give at the moment.

'Looking at your hair and your complexion, I am guessing that your mother is Rhianna Lindstrom. She was the only one on the original mission to Earth with skin colouring strong enough to account for you. And now the fun part – guessing the father … because, as I recall, Rhianna wasn't interested in men.'

My body twitches involuntarily as blood ignites in my veins.

'Are you going to Shift?' Karina says, goading me. 'I reckon I'll pick your father if I see your dragon.'

'Aeon Elegand,' I say through clenched teeth. 'Aeon Elegand is my father.'

Karina rocks back on her haunches and smiles. 'Aeon, huh? Wily old bugger. He's more ruthless than I gave him credit for – willing to kick his baby out of the nest because he'd rather have a spy than a daughter. Even I don't put the crusade ahead of my family.'

I picture myself in dragon form, sinking my teeth into Karina's throat … watching her life force drain out onto the dirty concrete … exulting in her final, rasping breath.

Her words echo my thoughts. 'You want to kill me.'

I don't confirm or deny. Instead, I say, 'Are you going to kill *me*?'

'Not yet,' Karina says. 'This moment marks the beginning of a new phase in this game of ours and, to be honest, I'm quite excited at the prospect of hosting you.'

'Hosting me?' I say. 'Gotta say, your idea of hospitality needs some work.'

'With the site in the state it is,' Karina says, 'we all have to make sacrifices. You should see *my* temporary office. It's appalling.'

'I bet no one ties you up and leaves you on a concrete floor, though.'

'True,' she admits, 'but I just haven't had time to organise appropriate accommodation for you, Elvira. Once I do though, I'll have you moved right away.'

'Can't wait.'

'Until then, I'll leave you here. The security cameras are working just fine, so I'll know if you need any … attention. As an extra precaution though, I'll leave Heston here to keep you company.'

'Who's Heston?' I ask.

'He escorted you here.'

'Abducted me, you mean.'

Karina shrugs. 'It's all a matter of perspective, I suppose.'

Something occurs to me. 'What about the girl on the bus? Is she one of yours?'

'Emmaline?' Karina says, pushing to her feet. 'She doesn't belong to me, but she's a very reliable freelance operative.'

I replay the bus ride in my mind. The dark-skinned girl tripping in the aisle before taking her seat beside me, then being surprisingly committed to helping me off the bus and then onto the footpath where the council truck was waiting.

'She was responsible for the fire on the bus?'

'There was no fire, just a smoke bomb,' Karina says, brushing the dust from her jeans. 'Anyway, would love to stay and chat but lots to do.'

She turns and heads for the doorway. She's no sooner out of sight, than the Doc Martens return. I close my eyes, ignoring Heston, and wonder how long it'll be before Felix misses me.

Chapter 12

Liberty

The cafeteria is quiet. It always is at this time of year. Seniors are on exam block so we only show up for our exams and then disappear again. It's so peaceful, anyone wanting to do some last-minute cramming would be better off in here than in the library.

I spot Felix at a corner booth. He's not studying. Correction, he's not studying for exams. He does seem preoccupied with his milkshake container though, contemplating it like a clairvoyant might examine the remnants of someone's teacup to divine the future.

I hesitate. He hasn't noticed me so I could easily turn around and leave. *Coward,* my brain snarls. *He saved your life. Don't be like his step-mother.* I buy a bottle of mineral water and a bag of chips before making my way to his table.

'Mind if I join you?'

He looks up, startled, then clears his throat nervously. 'Sure.'

I slide into the seat opposite him and twist the lid off my drink. 'Elira not here today?'

Felix frowns, still staring at his milkshake. *'Elvira* … is missing.'

'Oh, yeah. *Elvira.* Missing? Since when?'

'She was going to meet me after school yesterday. She never showed. I went to her house but …'

When he looks up, I study his face. His eyes are bloodshot, his skin pasty, but it's the deep creases on his forehead that document his concern most clearly.

'Did you go to the police?'

Felix nods as he pushes his milkshake container aside. 'I took her grandmother to the station last night to file a missing person's report.'

'She's into drama though, right?' I say. 'Might this be a … stunt?'

The way Felix narrows his eyes makes me want to rewind what I've just said.

'No,' he says flatly. 'Not a stunt.'

I have my doubts, but I don't press. I regret my decision to join him but, given the circumstances, I don't feel that I should abandon him now. I need to play this straight and cool.

'You've checked with the local hospitals?' I ask.

Felix nods. 'Yep.'

I sip my water as I marshal my thoughts. Again, I study his frown lines and find something more than worry etched there. There is fear.

'You have a theory,' I say.

'Yes.'

His lips press together into a thin line, a barricade. He doesn't want to tell me his theory. Probably not a surprise given that he barely knows me and I just accused his best friend of disappearing as a stunt. And if I'm honest, I don't really want to know. I've got enough to worry about with my mum.

'Seems we have something in common,' I say at last.

Felix leans back in his seat and folds his arms across his chest. 'What's that?'

'We're both missing someone.'

Felix holds my eye for a long moment before turning his gaze to the window. 'Any progress there?' he asks.

'Dad thinks she's trapped inside the portal.'

Felix's attention flicks back to me. 'How does that work?'

'Well …' I say slowly.

He frowns and raises both hands. 'No – wait – sorry. Forget I said that. That was really … bad. Look, I'm sorry. I don't want to know how it works. Well … what I *mean* is … I don't *need* to know how it … Look, I'm sorry you haven't found your mum.'

'Um. Thanks,' I say. 'I'm … sorry about Elvira.'

'Uh-huh.' Felix appears to think for a moment, then sighs. 'I think my stepmother has something to do with it.'

Somehow, I manage to maintain a straight face. 'What makes you think that?'

'I know something.'

'What do you know?'

Felix shakes his head. 'I told Elvira what I know and now she's missing. I don't think it's a good idea to tell anyone else.'

My spidey senses are tingling – warning me that with every question I ask I am approaching the event horizon of the Warhurst/Dangerfield stepmother/stepson black hole. I don't want to get sucked into that nightmare but I can't help thinking that bigger things now are in play – and that what I want, doesn't really matter. Karina, the portal, my parents, Felix – they are all intertwined. There is no turning back.

'How much do you know about Gemini Holmes?' I ask.

Felix winces. 'Not much – he's a "genius", apparently; an assassin; a spy … and whatever else he feels like by the sounds of it.'

I ignore the sarcasm, saying, 'He said his "employer" was interested in getting the portal project back on track. Do you know who he was talking about?'

Felix picks up his milkshake container again, slurping the remaining contents through the metal straw. 'Why is that important?'

I pinch the coin on my pendant between my fingers. 'Because he's found himself a *new* employer,' I say. 'Gemini is now working for your stepmother – on the portal project.'

'Seriously?' Felix says, his forehead creasing in confusion. 'Since when?'

'Since yesterday. His CV must have been really convincing for my dad to hire him, given Gemini was the only applicant Dad had never heard of.'

'But Gemini couldn't actually *do* the job … could he?'

I shrug. 'Quantum physics is a long way from blood transfusions, but who knows what this guy is capable of? At this point though, I think Gemini is less of a concern than who else he is working for.'

'How do you mean?' Felix says.

'Well,' I say, trying to knit my ideas together as I think them, 'someone clearly wants to get the jump on restarting the elenium trade. Anyone who'd hire an assassin to infiltrate a secret project involving an intergalactic portal is pretty hardcore. I don't reckon you'd want to mess with someone like that.'

'I *don't* want to mess with someone like that,' Felix says. 'I just want to find Elvira.'

To be honest, I don't want to mess with someone like that either. I just want to make sure my father is safe and that we find my mother. Felix doesn't need to hear that though – he's clearly got his own issues to deal with.

'Well, I think Gemini's the key to finding Elvira,' I say. 'He said we all have a role to play on this project. Surely he'd be keeping tabs on where we all are and what we're doing?'

'Sounds logical, I guess.'

'I'll talk to my father,' I say, 'and see if I can get a message to Gemini.'

Felix's eyes narrow in suspicion. 'What kind of message?'

'I don't know yet,' I admit. 'I'll have to be careful. My father is terrible at subterfuge – and we can't afford for Karina to intercept any correspondence.'

Chapter 13

Liberty

I drive past the front of the school on my way to the student carpark and spot Felix loitering just inside the gates. Talking to him again isn't on my bucket list. However, the sooner I get it over with, the sooner I can focus on my own problems – like the fact that my mother has been stuck in a portal for almost four days now.

I pull into my usual carspace, my head feeling like it's packed with cottonwool. I've had very little sleep.

My phone rings in my pocket and I flinch. *Damn.* I need to control my reactions. I retrieve my phone. Private number. Hoping and simultaneously dreading that it's Gemini, I swipe the answer button.

'Hello?'

'Liberty,' the voice says, 'it's Gemini. I need you to follow my instructions. Are you ready?'

'Yes.'

'Get Felix, drive to the safe house – you remember where it is, don't you?'

'I remember,' I say.

'Good. Do it now, please.'

'Sounds like you're in a hurry,' I say. 'How about *I* just come now? It'll be quicker.'

'Felix shouldn't be difficult to find, Liberty. He's tall and athletic – and his face will go traffic-light red as you approach him,' Gemini says. 'Anyway, he's less than fifty metres from you. Go now.'

'How do you know—'

The call disconnects before I can finish my question.

I sigh. 'Fine.'

I take my satchel from the passenger seat and place it behind my seat before getting out of the car. Taking just my phone, I head for the main gates. Felix is leaning against a pole. When he spots me, he immediately looks down at his phone, and I wonder if I should tell him that nonchalance is not his thing.

'Morning, Felix,' I say as I reach his position.

He looks up from his phone. 'Oh, hi Liberty,' he says, his cheeks the shade of overripe tomatoes.

'Message from Gemini,' I say. 'We need to meet him at his place.'

Felix clears his throat. 'When?'

'We need to leave now.'

He nods and gestures with his hand. 'Okay. After you.'

He follows me out of the school gates and I slow down so he can walk beside me. There's nothing creepier than someone walking behind you.

'Did he say anything about the portal? Or Elvira?' he says as I blip the remote to unlock the car doors.

'Nothing,' I say. 'The only message was that we leave immediately and go to the safe house.'

Felix frowns. 'Typical.'

'He probably didn't want to say too much – in case the message was intercepted.'

I don't see how his phone call could have been hacked though. If Gemini really is a spy and a genius, I assume he's got all the best tech. He's clearly got good surveillance equipment if he could tell that Felix was fifty metres from me when he called.

'Sure,' is Felix's only response.

Since we're going to be trapped in the car together for an hour, I consider making small talk, but decide against it. The last thing I need is him thinking I'm interested in him because nothing could be further from the truth. I don't need – or want – a boyfriend. Or a pair of crazy sub-seniors who want to be 'friends' with me.

I just want to get my mother back and finish Year 12 so I can focus on what's really important – going to the Lourdes Stunt Academy.

The hour-long journey passes without conversation for which I am grateful. Maybe he's realised he has zero conversation skills? Maybe I should give him some credit for that sliver of self-awareness.

When we pull up outside the safe house, Gemini is waiting outside. He's wearing black leather shoes, charcoal-coloured chinos and an open-neck blue business shirt. His dark hair has been tamed into a neat ponytail and he's wearing rimless glasses.

'You look like an optometrist,' I say through the open car window.

He opens the door behind me and slides into the back seat. 'Down to the shed,' he says.

'Really?' I say.

'You made us drive all the way out here because you needed a lift to the shed?' Felix asks.

Gemini snorts. 'I need you both at NSA,' he says, 'and there is only one way I can get the two of you onsite now, and it is beside the shed.'

'We're going to NSA?' Felix says. 'Did you find Elvira there?'

'Yes and yes,' Gemini says.

'Knew it,' Felix mutters. 'We're going to spring her?'

'*You're* going to spring her,' Gemini says.

Gravel crunches under my tyres as I negotiate my car down the winding driveway. My eyes flick between the road and the chopper beside the shed. The shiny, black aircraft has two pilot seats and a row of four seats in the rear cabin.

'Is that a helicopter?' Felix asks redundantly.

'It's an Airbus H125,' Gemini says.

Out of the corner of my eye, I see Felix's fists clench. 'And you're going to fly it?' he says.

'Yes,' Gemini replies. 'This is how I've been getting to work since I started at NSA – it's quicker than a car, which is a real advantage. *And* it means I don't have to go through all the checkpoints they now have for *wheeled* vehicles entering the site.'

'So that's how you're going to get us in?' I say, catching his eye in the rear-vision mirror.

Gemini nods. 'Correct. Drop me here, then park your car in the shed.'

'You can get out here too,' I say to Felix.

'Yep,' he says. 'Shotgun on the helicopter.'

'Negative,' Gemini says. 'There's only one pilot – and that's me. You're both riding in the back.'

I park my car alongside Gemini's van and allow myself a discreet fist-pump while there's no one watching. A helicopter ride! That's so cool. I was winched out of the ocean by helicopter once and it was brilliant! Admittedly, the floating around for two hours after my cousin's boat capsized – worrying about being eaten by a shark – was less than brilliant. But the helicopter rescue was the perfect ending to a crappy day on the water.

I decide I don't need anything other than my phone, so I leave my bag in the car and lock the shed before jogging out to the helicopter.

Gemini is in the front, headset on, and the rotors are slowly winding up. Even though I don't really need to, I stoop as I approach the rear door of the cabin. I slide onto the leather seat directly behind Gemini and pluck a headset from the hook above me. There are two spare seats between Felix and me, which maximises the space between us. I'm happy.

Felix's voice comes through my headset loud and clear. 'Is there a safety briefing?' he asks.

'Keep your seatbelt fastened,' Gemini says, 'and don't open the doors when we're off the ground.'

Felix mutters something as I say, 'How long have you been flying, Gemini?'

'Three days,' Gemini replies.

Felix and I trade a glance. Felix frowns.

'Three days?' I echo.

'Three days,' Gemini confirms. 'Only got this baby for the job at NSA.'

'They *gave* you a helicopter?' I ask, incredulous.

'Don't be ridiculous,' Gemini says. 'My *real* employer organised this for me when I got the job at NSA.'

Ignoring his complicated employment status for the moment, I say, 'Why would anyone give you a helicopter if you've never flown one before?'

'Well, I needed something faster than a car or a motorbike,' Gemini says, 'and a plane was out of the question because there is no runway. Hence – the helicopter.'

Felix folds his arms across his chest. 'I can't believe anyone would be stupid enough to give a helicopter to someone who has no idea how to fly one.'

'I never said I had "no idea how to fly one",' Gemini says. 'I read aircraft and flight manuals to relax – it's a hobby. I reckon I could fly any aircraft actually. Having a photographic memory and an IQ of 185 will do that for you.'

As we lift off, the helicopter drifts right before wobbling back left. Instinctively, I clutch my seat. I notice Felix is doing the same.

'All good!' Gemini announces as we gain altitude and plunge forward. 'Here we go!'

The rolling fields below us aren't enough of a distraction from the knowledge that there is a novice pilot at the controls of the helicopter I'm now trapped in, so I try another diversion.

'Who is your "real employer", Gemini?' I ask.

'That's classified information, I'm afraid,' he replies.

I inhale slowly, hoping some extra oxygen to my brain might help me find the right questions to ask. 'Didn't you say that your employer's objective is to ensure that my parents' portal works?' I say.

His answer is immediate. 'Yes.'

'And that Felix and Elvira and I are necessary to make that happen?'

'*Necessary* is a strong word,' Gemini says. 'Each of you is *connected* to the project, and each has some level of influence or usefulness.'

'Hmmm,' I say, pondering my 'influence'. 'Well, it seems that I'm kind of working for whoever you're working for, so I think it's only fair that I know who that is.'

'One thing you need to learn, Liberty,' Gemini says, 'is that life *isn't* fair. We all have a job to do. We just need to get on and do it.'

Felix's voice intrudes. 'I don't get what your job is exactly. You said you were a spy and an assassin and a dental hygienist. Then you were a doctor. Now you're an astrologer on some secret government project … and a helicopter pilot?'

Astrologer? Inwardly, I wince. My parents are definitely *not* astrologers.

'*Astrologers* write horoscopes for "lifestyle" websites,' Gemini says. 'I am currently working as an astrophysicist.'

'Quantum physicist,' I say. 'If you're *acting* in my mother's role, you're a *quantum* physicist.'

Gemini's sigh is clearly audible through my headset. 'Except that I'm having to pick up some of the slack for your father too, Liberty. Since your mother's accident, he's not as focused as we'd hoped.'

'That shouldn't be a surprise,' I say coolly. 'My father is devastated at what's happened.'

'And you're not?' Gemini says.

I feel Felix's gaze on me. If they think I'm going to crack, they've got another thing coming. Anger flashes through me but I contain it. It does spark an idea though.

'Your "employer" is obviously rich,' I say, steering the conversation in a different direction. 'Money is no object. But it's more than that. Not only does he or she give you all the toys you need for this role, my guess is they're priming you with all the intel you need as well. Any science you're contributing to this current project is actually coming from someone else, isn't it? You're just a glorified messenger boy, Gemini. You're probably working for some mining magnate who's desperate to get to Rhybor to corner the market when the new elenium trade starts. Someone who wants to hijack the portal or steal my parents' design for it.'

Felix sneers. 'He's just a thief then.'

Before Gemini can respond, I say, 'No … his *boss* is potentially a thief. Gemini is just a lapdog.'

Gemini's voice slithers out of my headset. 'That is a very plausible theory you've come up with there, Liberty, and I commend you on it. I would remind you, though, that regardless of any cover I happen to be operating under as a spy, I am primarily an *assassin*.'

'I know that's supposed to be a threat,' I say, 'but since your employer still needs me … until the portal is operational – I don't have anything to worry about.'

'You've got about seven more minutes to enjoy that feeling then, Liberty. So, make the most of it.'

'What do you mean?'

'We're about three minutes from NSA, so we'll be in Lab 17 in about seven minutes.'

Dread washes over me. 'The portal's already operational?'

'Yes,' he says.

My heart pounds inside my chest. 'And my mother?'

'The portal spat her out,' Gemini says. 'On Rhybor.'

Chapter 14

Felix

I visualise Gemini's map in my head as I wind my way through the corridors of the NSA establishment to where Elvira is chained up. I haven't passed any guards yet, but that doesn't mean I won't. Ignoring the CCTV cameras – Gemini promised he'd deal with them – I sneak a glance around the next corner. All clear. I jog to the next intersection. With my back against the wall, I listen for a moment before I peek up the next passageway.

This one is darker; fewer lights are on, but I don't hear anything so I proceed. This section of NSA's underground facility is relatively intact but has still been declared off-limits. It's the perfect place to hide a hostage. Only when I reach the room where Elvira is being held, do I find a guard. The woman is sitting in a director's chair with her back to me, scrolling through something on her phone.

I pull Gemini's red autoinjector from my jacket pocket and creep across the floor. When I'm in range, I don't hesitate. I shove her chair from behind, sending her sprawling face first onto the floor. She cries out but before she can roll onto her back, I wedge my knee against her shoulder and jam the injector against her neck. She tries to jerk away but I keep the pressure on her until her struggles cease. I roll her into the recovery position before proceeding to the bunk where Elvira lies, unmoving.

She is facing the wall, a rough woollen blanket draped over her. I put my hand on her shoulder and squeeze gently. She moans.

'Elvira,' I hiss, 'are you okay?'

'Moneypenny? Is that you?' she says, her words slurred.

I groan.

Elvira rolls onto her back. 'I told them nothing.'

'Just so we're clear,' I say, shocked to see a thick chain around her neck, 'who am I talking to right now?'

'The name's Bond,' Elvira says. 'James Bond.'

I pull back the blanket. 'You know James Bond is a man, right?'

'Please, Moneypenny, won't you join us in the 21st century?'

Her eyes are unfocused so she probably doesn't see me roll mine. 'Can you walk?' I ask.

'You're in a hurry,' she says, rolling to face me. 'Somewhere you need to be?'

'Yes,' I say, 'and you're coming with me. Sit up.'

Elvira complies amid the clinking of chains. I retrieve the laser cutter from my jacket. Gemini warned me about the wrist and ankle manacles. I'm not up for that though; I'll just cut the chains off them. The chain around her neck is tight and the trickiest to deal with. My hands sweat as I manipulate the laser cutter to focus on metal rather than flesh.

'Done,' I say at last. 'Can you stand?'

I watch her struggle to her feet.

'Check,' she says.

'Can you walk?'

'So many questions, Moneypenny,' Elvira says, patting me on the cheek.

I swat her hand away. 'You can stop calling me that.'

'But it suits you.'

'I think I'm more the "M" type,' I say, studying her eyes.

'No,' Elvira says flatly. 'You're definitely not.'

I sigh. 'You're clearly …' I'm about to say "fine" but I catch myself. 'You're clearly *you*,' I say at last.

She stumbles as she takes a step.

'Whoa!' I say, catching her awkwardly under her armpits. 'Steady on.'

'I'll be right,' Elvira insists. 'Just give me a minute. I'm a dragon, you know.'

I sigh. 'Yes. I am aware.'

Though she'll no doubt recover more quickly than a mortal might, I don't have time to wait now. I take the blue autoinjector from my pocket and jam it against her neck.

'Ouch!' she cries. 'What the hell?'

'Lithium dioxide,' I say, tossing the spent cartridge on the floor. 'It'll take the edge off.'

Elvira rubs her neck where I jabbed her. Her lips curl into a smile. 'You haven't seen my glasses around anywhere, have you?'

I shake my head. 'No.'

Elvira curses. 'Bitch must have taken them.'

I don't bother to ask who the 'bitch' is. I know it's Karina. It seems that the lithium dioxide has worked though. Elvira's eyes are focused, shining.

'So where are we going?' she asks. 'Please tell me "home for a shower".'

'Really?' I say. 'James Bond would rather go home for a shower than venture through a portal to the alien world of Rhybor?'

'Rhybor?' Elvira says. 'The portal is operational?'

'More or less.'

Elvira glares at me. 'That was a "yes" or "no" question.'

'Moneypenny doesn't have access to that information,' I say. 'You'll have to speak to Gemini.'

'Gemini is here?'

I nod. 'Liberty too. They're waiting for us.'

Elvira doesn't answer. She strides over to the unconscious guard, pulls the pistol from her shoulder holster and shoots her in the thigh. The gunshot reverberates around the small room as the smell of cordite reaches my nostrils.

'What the hell did you do that for?' I say as the guard groans.

'Whatever you sedated her with won't last long,' Elvira says. 'A bullet wound ought to slow her down a bit though.'

'How do you know I sedated her?' I ask.

'*That*,' Elvira says, pointing to the red injector on the floor, 'and the fact that I assume you wouldn't knock a woman out with your fist.'

'Fair enough.'

Elvira crunches the woman's phone under her boot on her way to the door. 'You coming?' she calls over her shoulder.

∞

'Finally!' Gemini says when we reach Lab 17. 'Good to see you, Elvira.'

Elvira, still channelling a British Secret Service agent, nods in his direction. 'Gemini.'

Lab 17 doesn't look a whole lot better than it did four days ago. The lighting has been restored and the gooey stalagmites have been pruned back but the floor is still a mess. The cables have been excavated from the congealed slime which has now hardened to a diamond-grade substance, making walking from the doorway to the portal like trekking across a rocky mountain pass strewn with electric snakes.

The portal looks stable though – a mesmerising, rippling mirror of magenta and silver. Parked at the end of the ramp leading to the portal are four quad bikes, with our supplies packed on the back. I'm glad we won't have to walk everywhere on Rhybor, but I reckon I'll ditch the helmet.

Liberty looks up from the screen she and her father are studying. 'Elvira? What's with the bracelets?'

'Oh, my goodness,' Caspian Fox says, sliding off his stool. He turns to Gemini. 'What's going on?'

'Long story, Boss,' Gemini says, 'but one that is less interesting than your portal. Shall we?'

Caspian glances at Elvira before returning his attention to Gemini. 'Are you serious? This girl needs help,' he says. 'She's got manacles around her wrists and ankles. Where the hell did she come from?'

'My stepmother's work,' I say, plucking a backpack from the tray of one of the quad bikes. 'Luckily though, Elvira is tough. She'll be fine.'

Caspian's eyes widen as he points to Elvira's bonds. 'Karina did that?'

'Yep,' Elvira says. 'Didn't do her any good though. She got nothing from me.'

I hand the bag to Elvira and nod towards a door behind her. 'There's a washdown facility through there,' I say. 'You can get changed in there. We leave in ten.'

'And what clothes am I supposed to change into?' she asks.

I point to her go-bag. 'Knock yourself out.'

Elvira eyes the bag through narrowed eyelids. 'Where did that come from?'

'You should be grateful,' I say. 'I spent most of the afternoon packing that stuff!'

Her spy persona implodes. Distress is etched on her face. 'What kind of stuff? I'm going to need underwear and—'

'I gave him a list, Elvira,' Gemini says. 'You should have everything you need.'

Elvira surveys all the bags as she gathers her composure. 'You ordered all this?'

Gemini nods. 'My employer is keen for this mission to be a success.'

'Well,' Elvira says as she lifts the bag, 'let's see what options I've got.'

Liberty rummages through a drawer at a workbench adjacent to the portal before plucking a tool from its depths. Waving a set of bolt-cutters, she says, 'Let's see if we can remove that silverware, Elvira.'

The girls disappear into the washroom and I turn to Gemini. 'Karina and her crew are on Rhybor?'

'Affirmative,' Gemini says, glancing away from his screen. 'They exited the portal in Rhybor two hours ago, headed south to the capital, Ilion.'

'We've opened the portal at the site of the original gate,' Caspian says. 'Karina and her team are heading to the capital to brief the Rhyborians on our efforts with the portal. Your mission is to the west. Gemini has the coordinates.' He pauses before adding, 'That's where my wife is.'

'You're going to hold the portal open?' I say.

'No,' Gemini says, without turning from the screen this time. 'We don't have enough juice to do that.'

'Meaning you don't have enough elenium?'

Gemini nods. 'The sooner we get the trade route up and running again, the better. Earth has a supreme shortage of elenium these days.'

I don't ask where the elenium they've used on the project has come from. My mind is on the next mission, which the Foxes don't know about – the one to stop Karina advancing the Crusaders' cause.

'By the time we arrive on Rhybor,' Gemini says, 'we'll be a comfortable distance behind Karina and her crew. FYI – it's a few hours until dawn on Rhybor. On your bike, Felix. Let's get moving.'

Caspian settles himself on his stool and his fingers are a blur across his keyboard. Concern defines every crease on his forehead.

As the two super brains tweak the portal controls, I climb aboard my quad bike. I fire it up and rev the throttle a few times before easing my transport up the ramp. I'm twitching to see what this machine can do, but I know better than to try any stunts in here. As I approach the portal, I study my reflection as it wavers in the ripples of the gateway. I try to imagine myself riding into the mouth of the portal, and then I wonder what the others will think about me going through first.

With her mother's life at stake, Liberty wouldn't hesitate to lead the way. But Rhybor is Elvira's true homeland so she might think she should have first dibs. Earth might be the only home she has known, but on Rhybor, she won't have to hide what she truly is. And Gemini? I don't know why he's going. He claims to work for Elvira's father, but what his true motivation is I couldn't guess. I don't know what he gets paid but surely it isn't enough to cover this gig.

And then, besides an unattainable perfect woman, a wehr, and a genius – is me. Why am I going? I'm leaving one world where I don't fit in, to go to another one where I won't be accepted. I'm a half-breed, a sub-species. An outcast. So why bother?

One word.

Revenge.

Karina needs to be put in her place and I'm up for that. It's all I've got.

By the time Elvira and Liberty return, I'm itching to get moving. Elvira has ditched the manacles and is now dressed for hiking. Hopefully, she's dredged up a new character to go with the outfit – one that won't call me 'Moneypenny'.

'Gear up, peeps,' Gemini says, rolling his chair a metre to his left to tap on a new screen. 'It's almost go-time.'

Elvira smiles. 'Or "showtime".'

I tighten my grip on the handlebars.

The silver curtain fades into a new scene. I see an elevated pad, about fifty metres in diameter, overlooking rolling fields. The moonlight reveals cows in the grassland, some grazing, some resting. Not too different from the landscape around the safe house we stayed at outside Indigo. Not what I expected. I was hoping for something more … alien.

'Felix,' Gemini says, 'go.'

I wind back the throttle. When I'm within two metres of the gateway, a wave of cold swamps me but I keep rolling. A chorus of engines echoes around the lab. Heart hammering inside my chest, I make my final approach, stopping when my front wheels are within centimetres of the gate.

Caspian's voice cuts across the lab. 'You're clear to proceed, Felix.'

Holding my breath, I roll the throttle again.

Once I'm through the portal opening and I've left enough room on the concrete pad for the others to follow behind me, I kill the engine and then scan the night sky as I wait for them to arrive. Three moons. That's more like it. That's more alien.

I remind myself that this is the actual location of the gateway that existed for the elenium trade. Weeds have infiltrated the platform now, but it's still easy to identify the portal landing zone.

Whatever structure existed previously for the gateway is gone. I wonder if we'll be here long enough to find out what really happened twenty years ago – what caused the portal to collapse. As a shiver races through me at the thought of solving the mystery, Elvira appears. I'm surprised she's actually wearing her helmet and goggles.

'What took you so long?' I ask as she brings her quad bike alongside mine.

'Get over yourself,' Elvira says, scanning the landscape.

She frowns.

'Not what you expected?' I ask.

'No,' Elvira says slowly.

Liberty and Gemini arrive, pulling up next to Elvira. They turn off their engines and remove their goggles but leave their helmets on. Dawn is still a couple of hours away and, in the absence of quad bike motors, the night is quiet.

The portal fades, taking only seconds to disappear completely.

'We're heading west,' Liberty says, 'about—'

'Ahoy!' an unfamiliar voice calls.

I spin round to see a golden-eyed man striding up the slope towards us, grey-flecked dreadlocks framing his dark face. He has no shoes and the robe he's wearing seems an odd choice – it doesn't seem to go with the blaster in the holster on his hip. I should be worried about the weapon but I remember where I am. Rhybor. Land of wehrdragons. I assume he is one of them. What's inside him is more deadly than his blaster.

Elvira steps forward. 'I am Elvira Elegand,' she says, 'and I have come here with a message for the king.'

The man closes the distance to stand well inside Elvira's personal space.

'Elvira Elegand, I am Alvin de Toit, and the bearer of bad news. The king is dead.'

'Since when?' Elvira asks.

'Since the Kauri invaded,' Alvin replies. 'Been twenty years now.'

Alvin studies Elvira. 'Crusader or Loyalist?' he says at last.

'Loyalist,' Elvira replies without hesitation.

Throughout this exchange, I watch Liberty's face which, as usual, betrays nothing. She *has* to surprised. How can she conceal that? *Her* mission is to rescue her mother; our focus is on Karina and the Crusaders. I didn't think we'd have to blow our cover quite so soon.

Alvin nods. 'We will talk. Follow me.'

Chapter 15

Elvira

Alvin unclasps his belt as he turns his back on us and Shifts. His robe slides from his shoulders. My blood heats up in response, but I control my own impulse to Shift. A dragon the colour of a sandstorm crouches in front of us, his golden eyes sparkling.

As I start my quad bike, I glance at Liberty who has both eyebrows arched. That's as much emotion as I've ever seen her show and I take some pleasure in it. I have to find some positives here.

Unless Alvin is lying, the king is dead. And Rhybor has been invaded by Kauri – whoever or whatever they are.

The king is dead. The Crusaders got their wish, but did they win? Are they in control now? Or did the Kauri crush them too?

Too many questions. The sooner I can talk to Alvin the better … unless he's leading us into a trap.

Alvin launches into the air, his holster dangling from one claw and his robe from another, and I guide my quad bike down the one-lane bitumen roadway after him. Twenty years ago, trucks would have driven along this roadway, transporting elenium from the railyard for export across the galaxies.

Liberty pulls up alongside me, interrupting my thoughts. 'What's going on?' she says, raising her voice to be heard over the engine noise. 'We're supposed to be heading west to find my mother.'

'And we will,' I assure her, 'just as soon as we've talked to Alvin. It sounds like we're going to need some local knowledge if we're going to succeed on this mission.'

'Sounds like there's more than one mission here,' she says.

I shrug. Now isn't the time for that conversation.

Liberty tries a different angle. 'You weren't surprised he turned into a dragon,' she says. 'You knew about that?'

I nod as I veer left onto a wider road.

'Is that because you can do that too?' Liberty says.

'Yes,' I call back.

Exhilaration rushes through me. I've just admitted the truth about my heritage for the second time. The admission might come back to bite me in the arse. But for now, I'm going to enjoy it.

I inhale deeply through my nose. The air here is so clear, I swear I can smell the moonlight.

We ride north for only a few minutes before Alvin lands on a ledge halfway up a steep hill within view of the portal landing site. Liberty, Felix and Gemini pull up around me as I switch off my bike and remove my goggles and helmet.

I frown at Felix. 'You really should wear your helmet,' I say. 'It's not much good to have it sitting on the back tray.'

He shrugs before his dismounts. 'I'm fine.'

'Yes, but—'

'We taking packs or leaving everything down here?' Felix says.

'Leave them,' Gemini says. 'There's enough tree cover that no one should see them. We won't be here long.'

'Good, let's get this over with,' Liberty says, turning towards a narrow walking track.

We clamber up the mountainside and find Alvin waiting for us. He's in human form again, robed and armed, still with no shoes.

'I hope you don't mind being underground,' he says, plucking a small torch from his belt. 'Follow me.'

Alvin takes three steps before disappearing into a cleft in the rock.

I fall in behind him to take advantage of the light, with Liberty beside me. Felix and Gemini bring up the rear.

'Is this your home?' I ask.

'Yes,' Alvin says. 'We are the Gyoma Lake clan. We used to live in houses by the lake, or in homesteads on the farmland, but when the Kauri came, we had to hide. These caves are the only reason any of us are still alive.'

We continue down the tunnel for several minutes before a hard-right spits us into a magnificent domed cavern.

'Whoa,' I say. 'It looks like a restaurant.'

'It is. In this environment, it makes sense to have a communal eating area for the clan,' Alvin says. 'Make yourselves comfortable. I will arrange for refreshments.'

Alvin strides across the room and, from behind a long bar, retrieves two jugs from a shelf.

'Nice place,' Gemini says, coming to stand alongside me. 'Don't let your guard down though.'

'Got it,' I say.

Liberty glances at Alvin as he fills the jugs with clear fluid before she turns to face me. 'I say we give this half an hour, then we get on with our mission.'

Gemini winks at me before leading the way to a table surrounded by five wooden armchairs with plush velvet cushions. We settle ourselves in our seats as Alvin places a tray of glasses and two jugs of water on the oak table.

'So, where you folks from?' Alvin asks, indicating that we should help ourselves to drinks.

'Earth,' Gemini says, leaning forward and extending his hand. 'I'm Gemini Holmes.'

Alvin accepts the handshake. 'Humans have managed to open a portal? That *is* a surprise.'

'Not really a surprise,' Liberty says coolly. 'They had the best scientists – my parents.' She too extends her hand. 'Liberty Fox.'

'I'm Felix,' Felix says, completing the introductions.

Alvin shakes his hand as Liberty says, 'How is it that you speak English?'

'Speak what?' Alvin says.

'English,' Liberty says again. 'We're from another planet. Surely we shouldn't be able to understand what you're saying.'

'Ah,' he says, tapping behind his ear. 'Universal translator. They are useful on any planet where there are multiple languages, but they're especially useful for interplanetary and intergalactic travel. Everyone on Rhybor has one. Most advanced races do.'

Liberty's eyes narrow. 'Advanced races?'

'You don't believe we're an advanced race?' Alvin says.

'I'm supposed to believe that reptiles living in caves are advanced?' Liberty says.

'We actually spend most of our time in human form,' Alvin says, folding his arms across his chest.

'Why is that?' Felix asks. 'I reckon it would be pretty cool to fly around and breathe fire.'

'It is,' Alvin agrees, 'and we mostly just use our dragon form for "fun" these days.'

'For fun?' I say.

Alvin turns his gaze to me. 'In the old days, in a world dominated by massive, vicious creatures, this evolutionary technique was essential to our survival. Now though, our predators are mostly gone and we enjoy the "lifestyle" our human form offers.'

'Lifestyle?' Gemini says.

'There are many wonderful hobbies that one can enjoy in human form,' Alvin says. 'Cooking for instance, or gardening, or singing. And everyday things are just easier – sleeping in a comfy bed, using a mobile phone.' He turns to Liberty. *Advanced race.*'

Liberty frowns. 'Fine.'

Alvin looks at me again. 'But you, Elvira Elegand,' he says, sipping from his glass, 'say you have a message for the king. Perhaps you can tell me about that?'

I pour myself a glass of water. 'You said the king is dead,' I say, 'so I guess the message doesn't really matter anymore.'

A black cat jumps onto Alvin's lap as the wehrdragon considers his next question. 'Who is the message from?' he asks, stroking the cat.

I sip my water. 'Who are the Kauri?'

Alvin sighs. 'Invaders,' he says at last. 'A superior race. They wanted our elenium and they're not the sort to negotiate. They came, they conquered, and they are now stripping our world of its most precious resource.'

'The Kauri must be pretty powerful,' I say, 'to overcome the might of the ... Rhyborians.'

'Yes,' Alvin says, eyes narrowing, 'they are cyborgs. They have a formula that makes them unstoppable.'

Gemini leans forward in his seat. 'A formula? What kind of formula?'

Alvin scoffs. 'They're not the sharing kind. All I know is that it's called the Prime Formula and it explains all existence – the relationship between matter, energy, space and time.'

'So, what do they want the elenium for?' Felix asks.

'To take over the universe.'

'Ambitious,' Gemini says.

'Indeed,' Alvin agrees. 'So, I've told you *my* story, Elvira. How about you tell me *yours*. Let's start with who your message for the king is from.'

'You're really fixated on that,' I say, as realisation strikes. 'You're a Crusader, aren't you?'

Alvin smiles and bows his head. 'I am.'

Alvin is a Crusader. That's a problem. But he's also a local and we need local knowledge. Especially with the added excitement of the Kauri which weren't on my radar.

I sweep my gaze across my companions. Felix's fists are clenched; he's ready for a fight. Gemini is smirking, like this is entertainment. And the Ice Queen is composed, as always. We could probably bust our way out but, if we make a ruckus, we'll make enemies of the whole clan. Tricky.

My father was a diplomat on that mission to Earth twenty years ago. I close my eyes, searching my biological schematic for any sign of those genes, but find nothing that will help. I don't have a character ready for this either. Though utterly preposterous, I might just have to be ... me.

I open my eyes. 'Guys, want to wait for me outside? I just—'

Before I can finish, Alvin is in dragon form again and hovering above us. He spurts a tongue of flame in our direction.

Liberty somersaults over the back of her chair, landing nimbly and striking a ninja pose. Felix and Gemini take similar action, but in a much less graceful manner. I stand slowly, feeling the blood ignite in my veins.

Alvin's robe is puddled on the floor. I don't have that luxury. Though I'm grateful to Gemini for his efforts in procuring me practical clothing options for this mission, I decide I can sacrifice one outfit for the cause.

I kick off my shoes and crouch down, closing my eyes as I give in to the rush of the Shift. Although I haven't had as many opportunities to take my dragon form as I would have liked, at least I've had enough practice that I'm not going to embarrass myself. Like I did the first time I Shifted.

Pushing thoughts of that excruciating experience aside, I inhale sharply as my ribs dislocate and my wings break the skin beneath my shoulder blades. It hurts less these days, but that bit always stings. My vertebrae swell, lengthening my spine to accommodate my tail and elongated neck. As my skin hardens into armoured scales, I wonder if the others can hear the soft clicking of my joints as tendons realign bones in my arms and legs. My skull and jaw morph, reshaping my hominid head into a reptilian snout. It's an odd sensation. I imagine it would be like having reconstructive surgery under local anaesthetic.

I leap into the air, fluttering in front of Alvin.

In my peripheral vision, I see Liberty turn to Felix. 'I suppose you can do that too?' she says.

'No,' Felix says. 'I can't.'

'It smells like … cloves … in here,' Liberty adds.

I blink a few times, willing my vision to clear. My pupils are slitted instead of round and the whole eyeball is a different shape from my human one. This plays merry hell with my balance and it always takes a few seconds for the vertigo to subside.

Are you the only one? Alvin says, his voice inside my head.

Of us, yes, I reply.

Why were you on Earth? he asks. *How did you get there?*

I was born on Earth, I say.

Alvin nods. *Tell me everything.*

I do tell him everything – about me. I tell him nothing of Karina though, or Felix either. That's not my place.

Alvin lands on the floor but doesn't relinquish his dragon form. I join him.

Felix, Liberty and Gemini are still behind their chairs, their eyes tracking the sandy dragon's every move. His lustrous scales, shielding a muscular body, gleam in the warm light of the cavern. The cat swats at the twitching, feathery end of Alvin's long tail. The dragon ignores his cat, his golden eyes on me.

And my eyes are on him. I've only seen one other dragon. I was so young that I just remember glimpses. My father and I were on a beach on a moonless night. The only light was our campfire on the sand. I remember the icy ocean breeze; the winter chill meant we had the beach to ourselves. My father's dragon was the colour of starlight, a lustrous, pearlescent silver. As beautiful as it was terrifying to a four-year-old.

The rumours are true, Alvin says. *There was a mission to Earth. Wehrs were stranded.*

Is this not known? I say. *Did no one try to rescue them?*

The Kauri destroyed every portal we had, Alvin says. *All our trading routes – gone. The Kauri wanted our elenium for themselves. They wouldn't risk anyone coming for it.*

You mean there might be other worlds where wehrs are stranded? I ask.

Alvin shrugs. *I don't know. I think it's unlikely. We were never much for intergalactic travel.*

And yet there were a couple of dozen on Earth … and no one bothered to try to—

Alvin roars and flames spurt from his mouth again. Demonstrative, not dangerous.

Felix hurdles a fallen chair to stand right in front of Alvin. He jabs a finger against the dragon's chest.

'Okay, we get it,' Felix says. 'You could roast us. We *get* it. You can change back now.'

Alvin turns his back and as his dragon form melts away, he collects his robe from the floor. He flicks it and it billows like a sail before settling over his shoulders. Once it is secured at his waist, Alvin strides to the wall and retrieves one of several robes from a row of iron hooks. He returns, tossing it to me.

'You still haven't told me your message for the king, Elvira,' Alvin says.

With my borrowed robe, I Shift back to my human form.

'I'll tell you the message … if you help us,' I say.

Alvin scoops his cat up into his arms. 'Help you do what?'

I hitch my thumb in Liberty's direction. 'Help us find her mother.'

'Deal,' Alvin says with a nod.

Chapter 16

Felix

While Liberty and Gemini discuss Operation Rose Recovery with Alvin, Elvira and I get some fresh air.

'Let's head north,' Elvira says once we've cleared the entrance to the cave.

I frown. 'Given that we haven't seen daylight here, how can you tell which way is north?'

'It's a gift,' she replies loftily.

'It's a dragon thing?'

'A gift,' Elvira says.

I scoff. 'You're all just glorified homing pigeons.'

I hear the rush of air an instant before I'm on my back, a scaly claw pressed against my chest. I have trouble sucking in enough breath to say, 'What the—'

Would you care to rephrase that? Elvira asks, her snarky tone evident even though she hasn't spoken aloud.

Her snout is millimetres from my face and I squeeze my eyes closed against the acrid smoke engulfing me. I try to apologise but a coughing fit consumes me. Elvira sits back on her haunches, eyeing me like prey.

As the smoke dissipates and my lungs find the oxygen they need, I say, 'Yeah, let's go north. Sounds great.'

'Excellent,' Elvira says, plucking her robe off the ground.

I close my eyes as her scales turn to skin again. When I open my eyes, she is standing over me, her hand outstretched to help me up.

'I'm fine,' I assure her, swatting her hand away.

'Mmm.'

Elvira swaggers away up the mountain path.

'Do you reckon we can trust Alvin?' I ask, following her at a distance that I hope gives me a sufficient buffer should she choose to switch to dragon-mode again.

'I don't think we have much choice,' Elvira says. 'We need local knowledge. Given what he said about the Kauri – and the king – there's clearly a lot going on here that we don't know about.'

Alvin doesn't really have much incentive to help us find Liberty's mother. Just the promise of a king's message.

'Do you really have a message for the king?' I ask.

Elvira's curls bounce up and down in response. 'Yes. All Loyalists know it.'

'What is it?'

She whirls round. 'Only Loyalists can know it.'

'Except that you promised to tell Alvin,' I say, 'and *he's* a Crusader. You're prepared to tell the enemy, but not me?'

Elvira cocks her head to one side and smiles. 'You think I'm actually going to tell him?' She pats my cheek. 'You're delightfully trusting, Felix.'

'I *do* value trust,' I say, 'and honesty.'

I let that hang between us for a moment. When she doesn't respond, I say, 'I want to know the message.'

'Only Loyalists can know it,' Elvira says again.

I fold my arms across my chest. 'How do I join, then?'

Elvira mirrors my pose. 'You really want to join?'

Suddenly, I feel pretty foolish. I'm rocketed back to Grade 1 when we were playing in the sandpit. We argued over who should get the toy grader and I ended up punching her in the nose. In hindsight, Elvira showed great restraint. She could have roasted me.

'Yes, I really want to join,' I say. 'As long as the initiation doesn't involve biting the head off a chicken.'

Elvira smirks. 'We can substitute a bat for the chicken – our charter allows for that.'

'Well, that's a relief.'

Elvira's smirk melts away. 'Do you hear that?'

'What?' I ask, instantly suspicious that she's trying to deflect me with another stunt.

But then I do hear something … whirring.

'Aircraft,' Elvira says. 'We should get out of sight.'

'The tree cover is pretty good here,' I say.

'Boulders … there,' Elvira says, pointing further along the path.

We duck behind the giant jagged rocks as a bird-shaped craft appears over the mountain at our backs, the dark vessel obscuring the stars as it passes.

Elvira whistles. 'That's cool.'

The aircraft veers left, away from us, before looping and heading back, skimming the farmlands and startling a few cows. High-powered horizontal turbines blast the ground as the vessel lands, flattening the long grass. Once on the ground, the craft's pearlescent mauve shell glistens in the moonlight as a ramp underneath the vessel descends.

Elvira places her hand on my forearm. 'If they capture us,' she says, keeping her attention on the aircraft, 'tell them nothing.'

I don't answer. My whole focus is on what is walking down the ramp. The five creatures are tall bipedal humanoids, clad in black and grey wetsuits. Their hairless heads reveal blue skin implanted with metal strips which glint in the moonlight. Blasters are strapped to their muscular thighs – for both males and females – and their weapons belts would be the envy of any soldier back on Earth.

When the group heads for the portal landing site, I release the breath I didn't realise I'd been holding.

'Wanna bet they are Kauri?' Elvira says.

'No bet,' I reply as the aliens stride effortlessly up the slope. 'We should warn the others.'

'Hold your position,' Elvira says.

I sigh. 'Yes, Mr Bond.'

'That's *Ms* Bond to you,' she retorts. 'We need to see what they're up to first.'

'We could steal their ship.'

Elvira turns to me, exasperation etched on her face. 'You could fly that?'

'Me?' I say. 'Don't be ridiculous. I assumed *you* could fly it though, being a master spy and all.'

'I'm not trained to fly *alien* aircraft,' she says haughtily.

'They couldn't be that different to the fighter jets you're trained for, surely?'

'Shut up, Felix.'

Her tone suggests that at this point she'd sell me out to the aliens. I'm tempted to push – there is a chance they would actually be better company than her.

'They're investigating the landing site,' Elvira says.

'That is not ideal.'

'No. It's not. We need to warn the others.'

'Excellent idea,' I say. 'Wish I'd thought of that.'

We retrace our steps and find Liberty, Gemini and Alvin in deep conversation in the hall. The cat appears to be asleep on a lounge, but I'd put money on the fact that it could reveal everything they'd talked about – if it could speak.

'We've got company,' Elvira announces. 'Blue creatures are checking out the portal landing site.'

'Kauri,' Alvin says. 'How many?'

'Five.'

'Could they have detected our portal?' I ask.

'Yes,' Alvin replies, nodding. 'They monitor stuff like that.'

Gemini stands up. 'We should steal their ship.'

I nudge Elvira, who pointedly ignores me.

'Could you fly it?' Elvira asks.

'Yep,' Gemini says.

'You don't even know what kind of aircraft it is,' Liberty points out.

Gemini shrugs. 'Doesn't matter. I can fly anything.'

'Don't know if it's confidence or cockiness,' Alvin says, 'but either way I like it. We don't have time to muck around. If we're to get that craft, we need to move fast.'

Alvin looks at me. 'You got any spare clothes in your kit?'

'Yeeees,' I say.

'Give me something.'

'Because?'

'If we get caught,' Alvin says, 'I want to look like an alien too. I don't want the Kauri to think there's a settlement here.'

'Sensible,' Gemini says. 'When we get to the quads, Felix gives Alvin some clothes and Elvira loses her robe too. Let's go.'

Alvin leads the way as Liberty says, 'What will the Kauri do to us if we're captured?'

'Interrogate you about the portal,' Alvin says, 'and then kill you.'

As we jog along the tunnel, something brushes my leg. 'What the hell is with that cat?'

'That's Grim,' Alvin says.

'I'll say,' I reply.

'No,' Alvin says, 'that's his *name*. Grim.'

Figures. I hope the cat doesn't turn into anything else. I decide it probably won't. Cats already think they are the epitome of evolution.

When we reach the mountain ledge, the Kauri aircraft is still visible. Its glossy shell reminds me of the carapace of a phosphorescent beetle. The ramp is still down, suggesting that the Kauri – though I can't see them – are still preoccupied with their investigation.

'OP-Razor,' Alvin says. 'Nimble little craft – a speedy shuttle and a decent fighter.'

Gemini rubs his hands together. 'Awesome.'

'Make a run for it?' Elvira says.

'We won't have time to run,' Alvin says. 'Change of plan. I'll take our pilot here to the Razor. When you hear the Razor's engines, start the bikes and barrel that way'—he points in the opposite direction of where the aircraft is parked—'and we'll pick you up along the way.'

Without waiting for a response, Alvin drops his belt and robe, and Shifts. He leaps into the air, snatching Gemini's wrists with his rear claws, and beats his wings to gain altitude.

Liberty swipes Alvin's blaster belt and robe from the ground before racing down the hill towards the quad bikes. I take off after her with Grim at my heals.

'Don't worry about the path,' Elvira says, panting. 'We need the fastest way to the bottom!'

I eye the steep slope and reset my course. Rather than running, I skid down the slope. Dunlop Volleys aren't the best option for down-hill skiing but I keep my balance, despite having to duck under tree branches. A glance to my right shows Alvin and Gemini silhouetted against one of the setting moons. They're close to the Razor now.

'There!'

The voice comes from the landing site.

'Damn it,' Elvira cries. 'They're blown.'

The Kauri race down the hill, their long, synchronised strides devouring the distance between them and the Razor. Their grace is mes-merising. As one, they draw blasters from their thigh holsters, training them on the airborne targets. Bullets of orange-tinged white light stream around Alvin and Gemini as they descend from the sky.

'Not very good shots are they,' Elvira says.

'Don't reckon they miss by accident,' I say, panting. 'They probably want to capture them, not kill them.'

As we climb aboard the quad bikes, Alvin and Gemini reach the ramp but the Kauri are closing in fast. Even if they make it up the ramp, I don't know how they'll close it before the Kauri get there – especially if there are any Kauri left onboard. Alvin drops Gemini before landing. They scramble up the incline and, within seconds of disappearing into the belly of the aircraft, the engines fire into life, ramp still down.

Liberty ditches Alvin's belongings into the back tray of her bike before pinching a leather rucksack from Gemini's bike. She straddles her bike and guns the engine.

'Who do you suppose is operating that thing?' I yell over the roar of the three quad bikes. 'Gemini – or one of them?'

Elvira yells back, 'My money's on Gemini.'

Grim lands behind me as I roll on the throttle. I look over my shoulder as I take off. The Razor wobbles left, then right – ramp still open, like the gaping maw of a metallic beast. A high-pitched squeal slices the night and the aircraft pitches forward.

Gemini's boast in the cavern comes back to me.

I can fly anything.

Yeah, sure. At least now I know it's Gemini at the controls. I'm sure no Kauri pilot would mishandle an aircraft that way.

After jittering left and right again, the Razor rights itself and spears towards us. Within seconds, it zooms over our heads as we dodge the trees at the foot of the hill and speed towards open ground. Blaster fire lights up the sky. The Kauri are in pursuit.

I wind open the throttle as far as it will go, glancing behind me to make sure Elvira and Liberty are still on course. Neither of them has a helmet on and Elvira's robe is flapping wildly in the wind. Didn't need to see that.

I break the tree line, crouching even lower so that my chin is almost resting on the handlebar rail. Ahead of us, the Razor slams onto the ground and skids. The ramp ploughs an impressive trench in the soil before the aircraft stops. When I'm within twenty metres of the aircraft, I test the brakes, slowing just enough so I can steer the quad bike up the ramp and into the aircraft. Once inside, I brake hard, pulling the bike around one-eighty degrees.

Grim hisses.

I spin round. The cat's claws are embedded in my kit bag and its ears are flat against its head. Alvin is still in dragon form and nods at me as Liberty and Elvira make it up the ramp.

Three rounds of blaster fire follow them through, one barely missing Elvira.

'Wheels up!' Liberty yells as she dismounts her bike and tosses Alvin's robe to him. 'Your belt's on the bike,' she adds, taking Gemini's rucksack from her quad and heading for the cockpit.

I catch Elvira's eye. 'You okay?'

'Just peachy,' she says, collapsing into a seat and buckling the harness.

'I'll look after her,' Alvin says, securing his belt around his waist. 'You go and keep Gemini company in the cockpit.'

I nod and head for the cockpit. Liberty is already in the co-pilot's seat, so I take a seat behind her. Grim lands on my lap as I reach for my harness.

Gemini presses a button from the dazzling array on the console. The Razor lurches as I try to secure the buckles on my harness and I grimace. Gemini might know the theory of flying, but he could have done with more time in the simulator. I try not to wince as Grim digs his claws into my legs.

The aircraft banks and light blazes past the main view screen. I crane my neck to look down. Blasters raised, the five stranded Kauri don't look like they are ready to concede defeat.

'Would they shoot down their own plane?' I ask as Grim snuggles into my lap.

'No,' Gemini says. 'They'll track it.'

'Not good,' I say.

'Can you jam the signal?' Liberty asks.

'Already doing it,' Gemini confirms, as he veers right and accelerates. 'Temporary for now, but once I have more time, I'll sort it out properly.'

'And in the meantime?' I say.

Gemini flicks a couple of switches. 'We resume our mission to find Liberty's mother,' he says. 'This baby will actually get us there faster.'

Chapter 17

Liberty

Dawn spills across the rocky ground as we approach the location where my mother would have exited the portal. The land is more mountainous and arid the further west we fly. We're approaching this northern continent's most famous mountain range – Belvedere's Bane – eight thousand kilometres of crumpled landscape stretching the entire length of the west coast. The countryside is breathtaking, but it is what's below the surface here that is most valuable.

Elenium.

If Earth's history books are accurate, the elenium within the mines scattered throughout the range could power ten thousand planets for ten thousand years. Elenium is ridiculously potent – the greatest source of clean energy in the known universe. Earth's uranium doesn't rate next to this stuff. Might as well be burning cow dung, my father says.

'Heading north now,' Gemini says. 'Two minutes.'

I nod as the Razor veers right, following a narrow canyon. Vegetation is sparse and scrubby here. Anything that lives in this desert – flora or fauna – would have to be tough.

Gemini flicks an overhead switch. 'Prepare for landing.'

With the memory of Gemini's last landing burned into my brain, I clutch the straps of my harness and take a deep breath.

I scan the desert floor, looking for any evidence of my mother's presence. A patch of disturbed ground ahead draws my gaze. Two circular depressions are evidence that an aircraft has landed here recently. Probably something like the Razor with rotating turbines on the wings, which blast the ground with air to cushion landings.

It could have been *this* Razor. Perhaps the Kauri we stole this ship from had come from this site a short while ago. I shudder.

Adjacent to the circles, something else catches my eye.

'There,' I say, pointing as I lean forward in my seat as far as my strap allows. 'Can you zoom in on that? Get it on the screen?'

Gemini's left hand glides over the console, caressing a selection of keys, and a magnified image of the globulous mass appears on the central display. It looks like a couple of large octopuses tangled together. My stomach clenches.

'Put us down here, Gemini,' I say.

'Yes, ma'am.'

The aircraft seesaws side to side as we descend and I clutch my harness tighter.

'Relax, Liberty,' Gemini says. 'I know what I'm doing.'

'Well, perhaps you could do it more gently this time?'

Gemini sighs. 'Everyone's a critic.'

Within seconds we've slammed down onto the desert floor. I'm out of my seat and, as I hit the button to release the door between the cockpit and the main cabin, Gemini presses the intercom for a cabin address. 'Welcome to terra firma,' he says, as Grim scoots ahead of me through the doorway. 'You will be exiting the aircraft today by the central ramp. Please take care when removing items from the storage lockers as bags may have moved during the flight.'

Felix is behind me and, when the ramp descends with a hiss, I almost miss his response.

'Moved?' he mutters. 'It'll be a miracle if anything is in one piece.'

'Yep,' Elvira agrees. 'I think I might have suffered spinal compression on landing. I reckon I'll be a few centimetres shorter.'

'Feel free to walk for the rest of your time on Rhybor,' Gemini says as he joins us. 'I've got better things to do than chauffeur you people around anyway.'

'Yeah?' Elvira says. 'Like what?'

I don't have time for their banter so I mount my quad bike and hit the ignition. Ignoring the others, I ease my transport down the ramp, my gut twisting painfully. Outside, with the veil of night slipping further westward, the air is still cool. I head for the organic mass. I know what it is and I want to run the other way, but I don't. I can't. My mother deserves better.

In my peripheral vision, I catch sight of Gemini jogging alongside me but I keep my gaze straight ahead. I park a few metres from the mass, kill the engine and dismount. Heart thudding in my chest, I crouch beside the tangle of elongated limbs.

'As Dad suspected,' I murmur. 'She *was* spaghettified.'

Gemini kneels beside me. 'I'm sorry,' he says.

I reach forward and touch her flesh. And it is just that. Flesh. My mother is gone.

Crunching gravel behind me tells me the others are approaching. I don't want their pity.

I turn to Gemini as the crunching sound grows louder. 'Can you get rid of them?'

'For a price,' he replies.

I flinch before realising what I've just said – to an assassin. 'This is no time for jokes,' I say.

'I understand that,' Gemini says. 'I'm not joking.'

I feel my composure unravelling and I fight to keep myself together. 'I'd like to be alone.'

'Make it quick,' he says. 'We shouldn't linger here.'

I push to my feet and return to the quad. Thankfully, the others won't see my hands trembling as I release the ratchet ties around the tough-box on the quad's back tray. Dad was more prepared for this eventuality than I was. I'd hoped to find Mum alive.

I lift the carbon-fibre chest off the quad and then return to my mother's remains. I kneel and shuffle as close as I can.

'Okay, Mum,' I say. 'Time to go.'

I slide my arms under her jumbled limbs and, as I lift, ribbons of flesh tumble down – it's like scooping long, delicate tendrils of pasta from a pot. Hot tears spill over my cheeks. I can afford to lose a few here … as long as I don't cry in front of the others.

Gemini told me to hurry, but I don't. I figure it will take the Kauri a little while to track us down. As I transfer Mum's remains into the Kevlar coffin, I can't help thinking that spaghettification is a truly appropriate description of her condition. I squeeze my eyes closed for a moment and steady my breathing. She was trapped in the portal for four days before it spat her out here. Was she in pain?

Once my task is complete, I close the lid and let a few more tears escape.

I collect stones and small rocks for a cairn. There should be something to mark the spot where my mother died. Dad will come here – once we've collected more elenium to ensure the portal remains stable and functional on an ongoing basis.

As I cradle a smooth stone in my hand, I think about Mum. She would have said that I am the same age as this stone. The matter we are all made from was created in the Big Bang. The matter in the stone, the matter that I am made of, the matter the dinosaurs were made of … all created in the Big Bang.

My mother had an unquenchable enthusiasm for discovering the origin of our universe, but I never really got my head around it, despite her many impassioned sermons on the subject. How an entire universe could be created by some weird bomb going off in some random place where nothing actually existed … is more than my brain could handle.

But it wasn't just one 'bomb', my mother would say. *The Big Bang didn't just happen in one place! It happened everywhere – all at once!*

Multiple 'bombs' going off 'everywhere, all at once' seems even more unlikely and incomprehensible to me than *one* bomb, but to my mother it made perfect sense.

I'm still trying to reconcile the universe's origins when Grim appears. He sniffs the case and goose bumps prickle my skin all over. I like cats but their manners are deplorable.

'Stop that!' I say, nudging him aside, then adding, 'I assume Gemini sent you?'

Meow.

I take that as 'yes' so I decide to return to the Razor. With a final glance at the small shrine, I squat in front of the tough-box and lift. It's heavy, though not as heavy as I'd anticipated. I place it gently on the tray of the quad and resecure it with the tiedown straps.

I look at Grim. 'Ready?'

He rubs against my leg. *Meow.*

I scoop him up and plop him on top of my backpack before taking my seat for the short ride back to the Razor. On my approach, I notice the word *Allegro* painted on the side of the ship. I don't know if it's the model or the name of this particular aircraft but I decide I don't really care. I just want to get my mother home now.

Once I'm back inside the Razor, I take the seat closest to my quad and strap myself in while Grim retains his place on my pack.

I look at Gemini. 'Let's go,' I say.

He salutes. 'We'll swing by one of the abandoned mines to procure ourselves some elenium,' Gemini says, 'so we can open a temporary portal to deliver you home.'

Without waiting for a response, he turns and stalks towards the cockpit.

Felix glances at the case on my quad. 'I could help you take that back if you—'

'No,' I say, raising my hand in the universal sign for 'stop'. 'I'll be just fine escorting my mother's remains home by myself.'

I'm not entirely sure this is true, but I don't need *his* help.

Gemini's voice comes over the intercom. 'Buckle up, folks.'

'So,' Elvira says, taking the vacant seat beside me and placing her hand on mine, squeezing gently. 'I'm sorry about your mum, Liberty. Glad you found her … before anything else did.'

A picture explodes in my mind of scavengers feasting on my mother's remains. I inhale deeply and exhale slowly as the Razor wobbles into the air.

'Sure,' I say, extracting my hand from Elvira's grasp. 'Thanks.'

Alvin says, 'I don't reckon I'd count on that, Elvira.'

'What do you mean?' Elvira says.

'Someone beat us here,' Felix replies. 'Someone with an aircraft like this one.'

Alvin catches my eye and holds my gaze. 'You saw the ground before we landed?'

I nod.

'The Kauri,' Felix clarifies, brow creased in concentration. 'That can't be good.'

'They'd have picked up the energy signature of the portal opening,' Alvin says, 'and come to investigate.'

'Like they did when we arrived,' Felix says.

Alvin nods, his gold eyes glinting in the low light of the cabin.

'Well, whoever might have been there didn't disturb her,' I say. 'For which I'm grateful.'

'Lucky they didn't take her away for research purposes,' Felix says.

I glare at him as Elvira shakes her head.

Felix's face and neck flush red. 'Sorry,' he mumbles. 'I was thinking about science because your mum is a scientist – *was* a scientist. I mean—'

'My mother was a *quantum physicist*,' I say, enunciating each word slowly, as if to a child, 'not a forensic pathologist – so she was never into corpse mutilation.'

Even to my own ears that sounds harsh. Not Karina-Warhurst-harsh, but harsh, nonetheless.

'Beth was a forensic pathologist,' Elvira says.

When Felix groans, Elvira shoots him a withering look.

I don't ask who Beth is because I don't care, but Elvira doesn't seem to register that.

'Beth O'Brien is a character I played in *Bones of a Clown*,' she says, turning her gaze on me. 'She was super intelligent—'

'We're at cruising altitude,' Gemini says via the intercom. 'Feel free to move about the cabin, but in case of turbulence I recommend you keep your safety belts fastened while you are seated.'

'Turbulence?' Felix mutters. 'That'll be the least of our problems with Wile E Coyote at the controls.'

'Who?' Alvin says.

'He's a character from the Roadrunner cartoon,' Felix says.

'Alvin won't know Roadrunner, Felix,' Elvira says. 'He's never been to Earth.'

Felix's shoulders sag. 'Yeah, right.'

As Felix and Elvira reminisce about cartoons they watched as kids, I catch Alvin staring at me.

'What?' I say.

'You're tough,' he says, 'for a human.'

If he's waiting for me to crack, I'm going to take great pleasure in disappointing him. 'For a human?' I echo. 'What do you know about humans?'

'Rhybor was a massive intergalactic trade port,' Alvin says, 'so we know plenty about lots of species – humans amongst them.'

'And how many of those species know what you guys really are?'

Alvin grimaces. 'None – just the way the Loyalists like it,' he says. 'Now if were up to the Crusaders, *everyone* would know.' His gaze drifts to Elvira. 'We Crusaders are proud of our heritage.'

'And what about the Kauri?' I say. 'Did they know?'

'What they knew about wehrdragons before they came here, I don't know.' Alvin sighs. 'Whether they did or not wouldn't have made a difference anyway. The Kauri are apex predators in this galaxy. They fear nothing because they can trample everything in their path.'

'They haven't met my stepmother,' Felix says. 'I'd love to introduce them.'

'What we need now,' Elvira says, slamming her fist into the open palm of her other hand, 'is an army – to fight the Kauri.'

I scoff. 'If all the Ryborians here haven't been able to defeat them in twenty years, what makes you think *you* – of all people – can do anything?'

Elvira's eyes narrow. 'Maybe because I'm not a heartless, self-absorbed bitch, I have the capacity to care for a cause – *and* for other people outside my own tiny bubble. Unlike some other people I could name ...'

Anger flares inside me but I contain it. *I'm* heartless? If giving a spray like that – to someone who's just scooped their mother's spaghettified remains off the desert floor – isn't heartless, I don't know what is. What a hypocrite!

I'm glad they're staying here. And the sooner I get back to Earth, the better.

Chapter 18

Elvira

We touch down – or more correctly *slam* down – at the abandoned elenium mine three hours after escaping the Kauri at the landing site, and I am itching to get outside for some fresh air.

Alvin is frowning.

'What's wrong?' I ask as we unbuckle our harnesses.

'I don't know how many of Gemini's landings the *Allegro* can take,' Alvin says.

To be honest, I don't know how many of Gemini's landings *I* can take.

The cockpit door slides across into its recess and Gemini breezes through the doorway, tablet in hand and leather rucksack on his back.

'Welcome to the economy section of the aircraft, Captain,' I say, bowing to him.

'You up for the next shift in the cockpit are you, Elvira?' he asks.

I nod. 'Sure thing. I'm sick of serving the drinks back here.'

Gemini shakes his head. 'Right,' he says, 'Elvira, Alvin … you're with me. We're going to find the elenium we need to power the portal to send Liberty home. Liberty, make sure you've got all your stuff packed and it's outside ready to go; then help Felix guard the ship.' He fixes his gaze on Felix. '*You* don't touch *anything* in the cockpit.'

'If we're under attack,' Felix says, 'I'll do whatever it takes to save the ship – even if it means having a crack at flying it. Anyway,' he adds, 'I don't reckon I could do any worse than you.'

Gemini snorts. 'Just take your toys outside – and make sure no one gets in here.'

Felix had used a chunk of time during the flight to trawl the weapons compartments onboard. He now wears a handheld blaster at each hip, a portable rocket launcher on his back, and he's nursing a blaster that looks like it's straight from a science-fiction movie. Alvin assures us all the weapons – Rhyborian military tech stolen by the Kauri – are fully functional.

I really hope he doesn't have to use them while Gemini, Alvin and I are in the mine.

Grim saunters down the ramp.

'Follow the cat, people,' Gemini says.

I don't need a second invitation. I'd rather be down a mine than stuck in here with the Ice Queen. The sooner we can send her back to Earth, the better.

The *Allegro* is perched precariously on the edge of what looks like a dry riverbed. To my right, a carpet of red rolls away to the horizon, dotted with knee-high clumps of spiky grass, and the sun has the sky all to itself – there's not a cloud in sight.

Across the ditch are the decaying remains of a village. The scattered brick buildings are crumbling into the prickly grass, like they are being devoured. Few of the buildings have roofs. Perhaps the roofing material was valuable enough to take away when the inhabitants abandoned their homes. Behind the buildings, rusted steel machinery languishes in the desert silence.

It's so quiet here I think I can hear my fingernails growing.

Felix appears beside me and offers me a blaster.

I raise an eyebrow. 'You do remember that I can turn into a dragon, right?'

'Just take it, okay,' he says, 'and be careful down there.'

Accepting the weapon, I say, 'Okay. Thanks. We'll be back as soon as we can.' I glance at Liberty, who is making her way down the ramp on her quad bike. So much for the silence. 'If the Kauri do turn up, she'll probably make them look like good company.'

He frowns but says nothing as I set off after Grim, who is slinking between the spiky tufts down towards the riverbed.

The path is steeper than I'd originally thought, but the plugs of grass stop my feet slipping on the slope. By the time I reach the bottom, Grim has turned left, heading westward. Sweat is trickling down my forehead, stinging my eyes. But through the sweat I can see this isn't a riverbed as I had thought. It's a dirt roadway, leading to a barricaded tunnel.

A mine.

When I reach the roadway, Gemini and Alvin flank me.

'Let's get this done,' Gemini says, striding towards the gate.

The steel grill barring the tunnel is about a hundred metres away. Grim has wriggled his way between the bars and is enjoying the shade beyond. Envy grips me. Shade. The sun has had only a couple of hours of sky time today and already it is baking hot out here. Enclosed spaces are not my favourite thing but the promise of shade outweighs being underground.

'Want me to deal with the lock?' I ask, waving my blaster.

Alvin strides forward and wrenches the gate open. 'Not locked.'

'Isn't that kind of pointless?' I say.

'The old mines are rarely locked these days,' Alvin replies. 'They've all been raided by scavengers.'

'You two wait here in the shade while I get the elenium,' Gemini says, pulling a headlamp from his leather rucksack. 'If anyone comes calling – deal with them.'

'Scavengers?' I say as Gemini is swallowed by the darkness.

'Wehrs,' Alvin says. 'Those of us who are left raid old mine sites for whatever elenium we can get our hands on. So, the danger here is two-fold. We could run into wehrs who are super-protective of their loot or we could encounter Kauri who monitor these sites because they know we come here.'

The Kauri, I expected. Gemini says he's jammed the tracking signal on the *Allegro* but if the Kauri are as advanced as Alvin says, they'll probably find us. I hadn't anticipated scavengers though. Fighting my own kind wasn't on my to-do list.

I sit on the floor with my back against the rock wall, enjoying the relative cool of the tunnel. Grim crawls onto my lap and curls up like a croissant. He purrs as I stroke his soft fur, the rumbling vibrations providing a pleasant distraction from my current predicament.

My thoughts turn to Felix and the potential damage he might suffer from Liberty in my absence. With any luck, whatever she says or does will make him come to his senses, and he'll see past the cool ninja warrior to the prickly, stuck-up cow that she truly is. He's been fixated on her for a year now. It's time he moved on.

Grim hisses an instant before I hear a voice outside.

'Hey, fellas,' the voice says, 'looks like we got some trespassers here.'

Grim jumps off my lap and I'm on my feet instantly.

Three teenagers leap down onto the roadway just beyond the steel grill, joining the one leering at us through the gate. Three males, one female – all wearing robes and sandals, and all armed with blasters. They're not blue so they're not Kauri. The robes mark them as wehrs.

'We don't want trouble,' Alvin says. 'We're just cooling off in the shade.'

'Right,' says the girl wehr, aiming her blaster at my head, 'like you couldn't cool off in your spaceship?'

One of the males, who is completely bald and looks to have been carved out of caramel, levels his blaster at Alvin's chest. 'Place your weapons on the ground, then kick them over here – slowly. Do it now!'

Gemini's words bounce around in my head. *If anyone comes calling – deal with them.*

'We come in peace,' I say.

The male wehrs laugh as they mimic me. 'We come in *peace!*'

Alvin catches my eye and the message in his golden orbs is clear. Silence.

'Do as Tobi says,' the female wehr says. 'Weapons. Now!'

Alvin and I comply. Tobi picks up my weapon and tucks it under his belt. Another of the males, one with blonde dreadlocks sprouting from a leather band on top of his head, collects Alvin's blaster.

'Thank you,' the female wehr says. 'Now, where is the other one?'

'Other one?' Alvin echoes.

'Two of your crew stayed with the ship and three of you came in here,' she says. 'Where is the other one who came in here?'

'He had to take a leak,' Alvin says, 'and he needs privacy.'

The female wehr scoffs as she flicks her long dark braid over her shoulder. 'As if.' She turns to her companions. 'Mannion and I will stay here and wait for the other intruder to return. Tobi, Jace … you escort these two,' she points her thumb over her shoulder at Alvin and me, 'back to the ship.'

The male wehr with blonde dreadlocks salutes. 'You got it, Shebah.' Turning to his bald companion, he adds, 'You can have the girl, Tobi.'

Tobi grins. 'Thanks, Jace. You're too kind.'

Jace points his blaster at Alvin. 'Hands behind your head. Walk to the ship. Do it now.'

Alvin follows the instructions as Tobi waves his blaster at me. 'You know what to do,' he says.

I put my hands behind my head and follow Alvin out onto the dirt roadway. Once outside, the sunlight dazzles me and I squeeze my eyes closed. I take a sharp breath before opening my eyelids a fraction to peer down the roadway to where the *Allegro* is parked.

Two more wehrs have Felix and Liberty pinned to the ground, facedown. A third is astride Liberty's quad bike with Felix's rocket launcher in her hands.

'Bugger,' I mutter.

As I watch Grim saunter along at Alvin's side, I assess options. This wehr pack must have been hiding in the abandoned buildings and seen us land. There are seven that I know about; hopefully, there aren't any more. Gemini is underground, unaware that he will be walking into a trap when he returns to the surface, and the four of us who are left, have been disarmed. Not awesome.

'There were three,' the female astride the quad bike calls out as we scramble up the slope. 'Where is the other one?'

'Shebah and Mannion are waiting for him,' Tobi replies.

The female wehr relinquishes her seat on the quad and strolls towards us, still nursing the rocket launcher. Instead of a robe, she's wearing a bright floral sarong that has been fashioned into a short dress, tied at her shoulder and waist.

Tobi shoves me to the ground beside Felix, who has a black eye and blood smeared across his chin from a split lip. His hands, secured behind his back with a thick zip tie, are turning blue.

'This isn't quite going to plan,' he whispers.

'Yep,' I say. 'Noticed.'

'Shut it!' Jace says as he kicks at Alvin's ankles, sending him sprawling in the dirt. 'You're all going to lie nice and quiet and still.'

'Or we'll use our blasters to *persuade* you,' Tobi adds as he lashes my wrists together.

Once my hands are tied, a weight slams across my back, winding me. As I struggle to refill my shocked lungs, I see Jace knee Alvin in the back, pinning him to the ground like Felix and Liberty have been. Stars dance across my vision but through the light show, I see Grim crouch beside Alvin and lick his face.

Zrip! Zrip!

'Jace!' the sarong-wearing female wehr says. 'What are you doing?'

Jace sneers. 'I hate cats, Ruby,' he says, swivelling on Alvin's back and waving his blaster. 'Where'd it go?'

'It's hiding under the quad bike,' Tobi says, 'so hold your fire. We need that machine.'

Alvin grunts as Jace shifts his weight again.

'So, in case it's not clear,' Ruby says, 'we are going to take all your stuff – the Razor and everything in it.'

'You reckon you can … fly it?' Felix wheezes.

'Oh, we can *fly*,' she says. Ruby pauses as her companions snicker. 'But we will take whoever is the pilot amongst you because we'd much rather have a chauffeur.'

'We should take their clothes too,' Tobi says. 'They're neat.'

The wehr guarding Liberty says, 'There are other packs onboard full of clothes. I say we bury these aliens in what they're wearing and just take the clean stuff.'

Aliens. How do they know?

Probably because we're not wearing robes – even Alvin is wearing something he borrowed from Felix – and because none of us has Shifted. When Ruby said they could *fly*, the others laughed. That must have been a test. Wehrs would have got it. Perhaps there is an expected response that wehrs give to distinguish themselves from aliens here.

Twenty Rhyborians were trapped on Earth when the Kauri invaded. I wonder how many aliens were trapped here. Probably plenty. Rhybor was a major intergalactic trading port.

'So,' Ruby says, 'who is the pilot here?'

No one answers.

'Looks like they aren't up for talking,' Jace says, pressing his blaster against Alvin's neck.

'Relax,' Ruby says. 'We have time. We'll at least wait until Shebah and Mannion bring the other intruder. Once we find the pilot, we can kill the rest then.'

'We could take turns trying out the quads in the meantime,' Tobi suggests.

Ruby shakes her head. 'We can't afford to waste fuel. We'll wait for the others, locate our pilot, and then we can find ourselves a new mine.'

'At last,' the wehr restraining Felix says.

'Won't the Kauri be able to track the ship?' Tobi says. 'They'll find us.'

'Well, they haven't found these bozos,' Jace points out, 'so *we* should be fine.'

'We wait,' Ruby says again.

For several minutes no one speaks. I try to ignore the jagged stones that are digging into my torso and legs through my cotton shirt and cargo pants, so I can concentrate on a plan. As I check my inventory of characters for one that might have something to offer, a buzzing sound distracts me.

'Hey,' Jace says. 'What's with all those flies?'

I turn my head, scraping my chin on a rock in the process, to see what Jace is looking at. Flies are swarming around the tough-box on the back of Liberty's quad bike.

'What's in the chest?' Tobi asks.

Ruby strolls around the back of the quad and rests the rocket launcher against her left shoulder as she releases the straps on the case.

'Don't touch that!' Liberty yells. 'Don't you *dare* touch that!'

'Sounds like this is important, fellas,' Ruby says.

'Treasure?' Jace says.

Tobi answers. 'What kind of treasure attracts flies?'

'I dunno,' Jace says. 'Maybe—'

'Bally hell!' Ruby shrieks. 'What the hell is …?'

'Close the lid!' Liberty screams.

Liberty is on the other side of Felix so I can't see her, but her voice clearly betrays her distress.

'They're … spaghettified … human re—mains,' Alvin wheezes. 'Nev—er seen … those before?'

Pain shoots down my neck as I turn back to face Alvin. I really need to get this wehr off my back – literally – before I suffer some permanent damage. Alvin winks at me like he's got a plan.

'Black holes spaghettify things,' Ruby says, swatting the box closed and backing away from it.

'Wormholes too,' Tobi adds.

A moment of silence follows before Jace says, 'Wormholes? … A portal? Someone's opened *a portal?*'

'Is there a portal?' Ruby demands, recovering her composure and stomping towards us.

Alvin's playing with fire. I'm pretty sure sharing information about the portal would not be in Gemini's game plan.

'I need answers!' Ruby says. 'Roll them over, sit them up. If anyone tries anything cute – the Persuasion Protocol is in effect.'

Tobi removes his knee from my back to roll me over and I wince as my tightly bound wrists are crushed under me. The wehr hooks his forearm under my armpit before wrenching me into a sitting position. As I cross my legs so I can sit more comfortably, I feel the tip of Tobi's blaster behind my ear. He leans close. I feel his breath against my other ear.

'Misbehave,' he whispers, 'and I'll blast an ear off first.'

'That's the Persuasion Protocol?' I say.

'Yep. It's all about maiming – until we get what we want.'

Before I can ask what happens once they get what they want, Ruby spins round towards the mine entrance. I jerk my head in that direction to see Gemini running towards us, clutching his rucksack in one hand and a blaster in the other. The two wehrs left to capture him are nowhere to be seen.

Ruby strides forward and grabs a handful of Liberty's shirt. 'Hold the launcher,' she says to the wehr closest, 'and give me your blaster.'

Once the wehrs have traded weapons, Ruby drags Liberty to the edge of the slope – never taking her eyes off Gemini. Liberty rolls onto her side to save her bound hands being shredded on the rocky ground.

'Drop the blaster!' Ruby yells. 'Or I'll start shooting bits off your friend here!'

Gemini raises his weapon and fires, sending Ruby's blaster flying through the air. Ruby screams as she wrenches the tie at her waist and steps out of her sandals. She Shifts before her sarong hits the ground.

'Elvira,' Alvin hisses. 'It's time.'

'I'm really not dressed for the occasion,' I say.

'Just do it, Elvira!' Felix yells as he kicks out at the wehr nearest him.

Gemini reaches us, knife in hand, and then there are five dragons before us. Shades of burgundy, brown and beige … it's like they've all come from a painter's autumn palette. On all fours, they slink into position, surrounding us.

I flick my gaze towards Felix. Gemini has cut the ties on his wrists and is now working on Liberty's.

Okay. It's time.

Alvin's borrowed clothes shred as his body morphs to its new form. I'm slower to Shift so Alvin slashes at Tobi with his tail to shield me while I complete my transformation.

Ruby, with her dazzling red scales that shine like the gem she is named for, has her eyes on Liberty. A red blur is all I see as Ruby springs and slams Liberty against the ground. The dragon's claws close around Liberty's throat. Sandwiched between the dragon's armoured body and the rocky ground, Liberty writhes helplessly.

'Let her go!' Felix roars.

Felix dashes towards me, but his eyes are on the blaster on the ground – the one Gemini shot out of Ruby's grasp. I kick it, sending it skidding towards him. He snatches it off the ground and spins in one fluid movement. I've seen him do that on the cricket field, many times.

I spin round again in time to see a gleaming mahogany dragon leap at me. I'm pinned on the ground again but this time my scales protect me from the jagged rocks.

Suddenly, his voice is in my head. *You're full of surprises, sweetheart,* Tobi says, as I try to wriggle free, *but you're not going anywhere until we've got your portal and your spaceship.*

Go to hell, I say. *You're getting nothing from us.*

A reptilian shriek rips the air and I twist my neck around, hoping it's not Alvin. Relief floods through me as I see Ruby stumble backwards, a smouldering hole in her side. Felix's blaster is still pointed at her and Liberty is scrambling towards Gemini, who is extracting a knife from the skull of another dragon. A rust-coloured dragon is lying a few metres away, a trail of crimson leaking from a large wound in its side.

Alvin spears into Tobi, knocking him off me. They somersault across the ground as I flip onto my front and scramble across the ground towards Felix.

The next sound takes everyone by surprise. The Razor's engines.

Alvin bounds over to me. *It's Grim, wouldn't you say?*

That depends on who's in the cockpit. Five against two out here is in our favour.

Hopeless, Alvin says, snorting smoke.

Maybe we should check—

Forget it, Alvin says. *Let's just finish up out here. Oh wait …*

He looks skyward and I follow his gaze to find the two remaining dragons flying back towards the city.

Looks like we're done here, I say.

Stay alert, Alvin replies. *They could be going for backup. We should see what Gemini is doing.*

Gemini is on the roadway with Liberty, who's astride her quad bike. Felix is skidding down the slope towards them. I'm about to follow him when Alvin launches into the air.

I can do that!

I take off and glide onto the roadway in time to see Gemini draw what appears to be a mini pistol from his rucksack. The gleaming silver weapon looks to be the perfect prop for a high-society murderess in a 1920s mystery thriller but looks totally out of place here. From another pocket on his pack, he extracts a silver sphere about the size of a golf ball.

'What's the ball for?' Felix asks.

Gemini screws it onto the barrel of the pistol. 'I have fashioned an elenium bullet,' he explains, 'which is already in the chamber. I will fire it into the PPG – portable portal gateway here,' he points to the ball, 'and that will give us a temporary gateway back to Lab 17 at the NSA.'

He beckons to Liberty. 'Get ready. We could have more wehrs here any minute!'

With a complete lack of ceremony, Gemini lifts his arm and fires. The ball rockets through the air and lands about fifty metres down the roadway. It rolls a few more metres before coming to a stop. It then sits, glinting in the sunlight.

'Now what?' Liberty says.

'Wait for it,' Gemini says without taking his gaze from the ball.

I count seventeen heartbeats before it happens. A cloud of black erupts from the sphere. It swirls soundlessly for several moments before streaks of colour appear. When the colours stabilise, I recognise the scene. It's Lab 17 at the NSA. Just as Gemini said.

'More wehrs incoming,' Felix says. 'A dozen.'

Gemini tosses another blaster to him. 'Hold them off.' To Liberty, he says, 'A bit of hustle, Liberty.'

Armed with a blaster in each hand, Felix turns to Alvin and me. 'You heard the man. Let's go.'

Without a backward look, Felix races towards the far embankment to intercept the incoming wave of wehrs. I notice Liberty's raised eyebrows before I spring into the air after him.

She'd better be grateful.

I bank slightly, drifting into Alvin's slipstream. I need to conserve some energy; I'm not conditioned for this. I roar, hoping I sound terrifying rather than terrified but the incoming wehrs don't flinch. Of course, they don't. It's twelve against two.

We're flying right at them. It's like a game of chicken. I'll hold right until the last moment then …

Zrip! Zrip! Zrip! Zrip! Zrip!

Bolts of white-hot energy stream past me and the resonant hum of the blaster fills the air. I curl up instinctively and, unsurprisingly, plummet towards the ground like a stone. I have only seconds to decide what presents the greatest threat to my life – the wehrs, my imminent impact with the ground, or Felix's blaster.

Zrip! Zrip! Zrip!

I stretch out, unfurling my wings – pulling up just short of the rocky roadway. In desperation, and before I've stabilised my glide, I twist my neck to scan for the wehrs. Bad idea. I veer right and crash into the slope adjacent to the roadway, rolling several times before I come to rest at the bottom.

Ouch!

Zrip! Zrip! Zrip! Zrip! Zrip!

My right wing is tucked painfully under my torso and I really need to flip myself over. Alvin lands next to me, giving me a solid nudge with his snout, which does the trick. I crouch on all fours, trembling.

'Elvira!' Felix says, spraying dirt in my face as he skids to a stop in front of me. 'Are you okay?'

I'd probably be better if my friend didn't try to shoot me out of the sky! I say, hoping my voice in his head is loaded with snark.

Felix laughs. 'I wasn't aiming for you.'

And yet—

'Come on,' Gemini says. 'Liberty's gone home. We need to get on the ship before these wehrs regroup.'

I scan the landscape. A couple of dragons are lying still but many are crawling, some are testing their wings.

Gemini turns to Alvin. 'I assume Grim started the engines?'

Alvin nods.

'Well, I suggest we get aboard before he figures out how to fly that thing,' Gemini says, 'and he leaves us all here.'

Chapter 19

Elvira

We are halfway up the Razor's ramp when Gemini stops so suddenly that I run into the back of him. 'Your reflexes aren't as quick in dragon form, Elvira,' he says. 'You should work on that.'

Thanks, I send to him. *I really appreciate the unsolicited feedback.*

Gemini points to the carnage closest to the ship. 'That floral robe there,' he says. 'Get it. You're going to need it.'

My stomach rolls. It's not a robe. It's Ruby's sarong.

'I'll get it,' Felix offers.

Alvin waves a robe dangling from his claws.

Gemini nods. 'Yep. You go change. We're wheels up pronto.'

Alvin follows Gemini up the ramp as I wait for Felix. At least the sarong won't have any blood on it. Felix shot Ruby while she was in dragon form, and she'd shed the sarong before she Shifted.

Felix hands me the floral material. 'Knock yourself out.'

Thanks, I say. *And shotgun, by the way.*

'We'll see,' he says, turning his back on me and strolling up the ramp.

I follow him, my claws tapping the metal ramp with every step. Felix heads for the cockpit so I'm left alone in the main cabin. Alvin must have Shifted already and be in the cockpit too. I Shift and then wrestle with the sarong before slipping on some sandals and joining the others.

By the time I reach the cockpit, everyone else is strapped in. Except Grim, who is unrestrained, curled up on Felix's lap. Felix and Alvin are seated in the second row so the co-pilot's seat is empty.

Gemini indicates the empty seat. 'Come on.'

I'm careful as I ease myself into the seat. I'm not sure the knots on the sarong will hold since I haven't had much experience with sarong styling.

Gemini turns to me. 'You injured?'

I thought I'd be sore after my spectacular crash landing. But one of the benefits of being wehr – rapid recovery.

'No,' I say. 'Just trying to keep this oversized handkerchief in place.'

'Please do,' Gemini says.

He adjusts the stick and flicks at a few switches on the control panel with his spare hand. Seemingly satisfied with the dazzling array of lights, he turns to me. 'Next stop is Topaz Forest – home of Aedonis and Eva Elegand. Ready to meet your grandparents, Elvira? Begin the Crusade against the Kauri?'

'I'd be more ready if I wasn't turning up in *this*,' I say, pointing to the sarong. 'First impressions count, you know.'

'Indeed,' Gemini says.

Alvin rests his head against the seatback. 'Great. Topaz Forest is miles from here. I can nap.'

'You can,' Gemini says. 'Flight time is four hours, eighteen minutes.'

'Further west?' Felix asks.

'East this time,' Gemini says. 'If we went four hours to the west, we'd be over the ocean.'

My stomach churns. Gemini knows where my grandparents live. He's not family. He shouldn't know that stuff.

'Aeon's on his way,' Gemini says.

My head snaps round. '*What?* How … When?'

'He left Russia as soon as the portal was operational,' Gemini says. 'I'd say he'll be here within the next twenty-four hours – as long as he can convince Caspian Fox to let him use the portal.'

Jealousy slithers through my veins. Gemini has spent a lot of time with my father over the last ten years, while I've been banished on the other side of the Earth.

'You're like a sister to me, you know,' Gemini says, his gaze fixed on the displays.

'What!' I say. 'You barely *know* me.'

'Aeon's told me a lot about you. He talks about you all the time.'

I snort. 'Well,' I say, 'he never mentioned you.'

It's supposed to be hurtful but Gemini smirks.

'Assets are never identified,' he says.

'Assets?' I echo. 'Don't you mean assassins?'

Gemini presses a button which beeps at his touch. 'I'm fine with either.'

I don't know what bothers me more – that my father employs an assassin or that the two of them have become so close. The drone of the engines nibbles away at the awkward silence that follows. Eventually, Gemini tries again.

'I reckon you'd be a lot of fun to be around,' he says.

'I didn't know assassins were allowed to have fun.'

'How much do you know about assassins?'

I sniff and return my gaze to the landscape beyond the cockpit view screen. 'Thankfully, very little.'

'Anyway,' Felix says, 'how much longer?'

Gemini glances at him. 'Seriously? Did you just do the old "are we there yet?"? How old are you?'

'At this moment, I'm not exactly sure,' Felix says. 'I've just been through a wormhole and I don't know how time flows on this planet.'

I twist in my seat and gaze at him. Felix doesn't often surprise me, but not only was that retort quick, it was intelligent as well. That one would have impressed Liberty. I bet he's cursing that she missed it.

'If you gave me your date – and time – of birth on Earth,' Gemini says, 'I could calculate it for you … in my head.'

I sense an impending escalation of hostilities as these two scrap for the position of alpha male in our dwindling pack. What they've missed, though, is that they are both outranked. As wehrdragons – the superior species – Alvin and I would have to duke it out to be the leader of this pack. With his local knowledge, Alvin would probably edge me out but I'd be a close second. In any case, I can't stomach their petty rivalry.

'If you two behave like this when we get to my grandparents' home,' I say, 'you'll probably end up being roasted.'

Felix rolls his eyes. 'Maybe I'll wait in the car.'

'Good idea,' I say. Glancing at the feline on his lap, I add, 'Grim will look after you.'

Felix grunts. 'He's better company than you, anyway.'

I smile and return my attention to the landscape. As we speed towards my paternal grandparents' home, I wonder if my father will contact me or Gemini first when he arrives.

∞

'And we're here,' Gemini says as we touch down, more gently this time, in a clearing in the sprawling forest.

We're on the eastern side of the continent now, a region renowned for its forests. In this southern landscape, sequoias dominate, but it's the mountain in front of us that is the main show. It looks like a colossal stone spear lodged in the ground. Perhaps it had been rocketing through space – a god's weapon gone astray in some celestial war – and Rhybor had been the lump of rock that stopped it. Or maybe it is simply the result of natural geological forces here. Clear water cascades down its slopes, several streams pooling into a lake to our left.

'Wow,' Alvin says. 'It's beautiful.'

'Never been here?' I ask.

Alvin shakes his head as he unbuckles his harness.

'Should we cover the Razor with branches or something?' Felix asks. 'In case any Kauri fly over?'

Gemini scoffs. 'In the very unlikely event that they do fly over, I don't think they'll be fooled by such a primitive charade.'

'Gemini is right,' Alvin agrees. 'Our best strategy is just to keep moving. Let's just get what we came for and then move on.'

Get what we came for. The words bounce around inside my head. Before I can build a network – an army – to fight the Kauri, I need to connect with my family. My grandparents don't even know that I exist. Will they believe my story?

'You're right, Alvin,' I say, climbing out of my seat. 'We need to go.'

'You boys behave while Elvira and I are gone,' Alvin says.

'What are we supposed to do?' Felix asks.

'Guard the Razor,' I say, adjusting my sarong.

'And Grim,' Alvin adds.

Felix and Gemini frown simultaneously.

As Alvin and I pass through the main cabin of the ship, Alvin says, 'Lose the shoes.'

'What?'

'We're flying, so we need to Shift. Shoes are a problem.'

'Fine.'

I kick off my sandals and follow him down the ramp.

Outside, birdsong fills my ears as fresh air fills my lungs.

'You ready for this?' Alvin asks.

'No. But we should go anyway,' I say. 'Do you think you can find the entrance from Gemini's directions?'

'Yes,' he says.

I nod. 'Turn around then. Time to suit up.'

Alvin turns away from me and I undo the knots in my sarong. I shiver in anticipation as I crouch down, ready to Shift. I push aside that resentment that courses through me – that my father shared the location of his parents' home with Gemini and not with me – to complete my transformation.

I flick my tail and flutter my wings. Everything appears to be in working order. I drag one of my talons over a slab of rock. The white trail I leave is not unexpected, but the sparks are.

So cool!

Alvin's voice is in my head. *Elvira, follow me.*

Alvin takes to the air without waiting for my response. I ball my sarong into one of my claws before springing after him. Exhilaration infuses every cell in my scaly body as I beat my wings to gain altitude, exalting in a freedom I haven't experienced before. I try to follow Alvin, who makes flying look effortless. I feel clumsy in comparison, but I don't care. Here on Rhybor, I'll have the opportunity to practise.

The ease with which Alvin finds an entrance to the mountain takes the edge off my excitement. Can I really trust him? He's a Crusader after all, and my only backup is back on the ground.

Once on the ledge, Alvin Shifts and slips into his robe, then waits for me to do the same.

'After you,' he says once my sarong is in place.

'Any rules of etiquette I should know about?' I ask. 'I don't want to get roasted.'

Alvin hands me a small torch from his robe pocket. 'Calling out your folks' names as we go down the tunnel might be a good idea.'

I nod as I test the torch.

'Hello?' I call as I take my first steps down the passageway. 'Eva Elegand? Aedonis Elegand? Is anyone home?'

Sweat drips down my back, partly from excitement but also fear.

'Eva?' I call again. 'Aedonis? I'm here on behalf of your son, Aeon!'

The echoes of my voice bounce around me as the darkness draws me deeper into the mountain.

'I am your granddaughter, Elvira!' I say. 'I was born on Earth, but I have come home.'

There is no answer but I push on. If I were in hiding from the Kauri, I wouldn't be rushing to the entrance to greet guests. I'm hoping that's what my grandparents are thinking – if they're even here.

As we wind our way deeper into the mountain, Alvin says, 'This doesn't feel right. We're too deep.'

I remember the first chamber in Alvin's hillside home was only about twenty metres from the entrance.

'Maybe it's safer further inside?' I say.

Alvin grunts. 'If the Kauri were to find this place … this deep down – you're trapped.'

'Maybe they're stocked for a …' I struggle to find the right words, 'prolonged siege?'

'If the Kauri come,' Alvin says, 'this place is not defensible. It's a tomb.'

The tunnel's darkness seems to swallow my torchlight. I suck my tongue, attempting to manufacture some saliva, so I can try again to make contact with my grandparents.

'Aedonis! Eva! I'm here on behalf of your son, Aeon.'

'Yes!' a male voice replies. 'We hear you!'

I stop, holding my breath, listening.

Light suddenly explodes in the tunnel and I whip my arm to my face to shield my eyes.

'Now,' the voice says softly, 'explain yourself.'

I can't see the owner of the voice for the dazzling light.

With my eyes closed, I say, 'Aeon Elegand is my father. He was stranded on Earth twenty years ago when the portal between Rhybor and Earth collapsed. I am Elvira – his daughter.'

'Who is your mother?'

'Rhianna Lindstrom,' I answer.

'Where is Aeon now?'

'Hopefully, on his way here,' I say.

'Hopefully?' the voice says.

'It's complicated,' I say. 'Could we sit and talk about it? I'll do my best to explain.'

'Who is your companion?'

Alvin answers for himself. 'I am Alvin de Toit, a Gyoma Lake dragon. I am Elvira's guide.'

'Curious,' the voice murmurs. 'Very curious.'

'May we come in?' I say.

The light drops. 'Follow me.'

I blink my eyes, trying to clear the lingering bright splotches from my retinas and, by the time I can see again, the tunnel is clear. Whoever owns the voice is gone but there is only one path, so I follow it until I find two people in an opulently furnished chamber.

The couple looks to be in their early forties, not old enough to be my grandparents. The man, who I assume is the owner of the voice, shares my father's dark hair and widow's peak – his chocolate-coloured eyes too. His companion has dazzling emerald eyes and looks to have been carved from ivory. A river of wavy auburn hair cascades over her shoulders, pooling in her lap. Her lacy, pastel-pink robe could well have come from a royal wardrobe.

'So,' the man says, 'you claim to be Elvira Elegand, daughter of Aeon Elegand?'

I shiver. On Earth I am Elvira Bergesten. I'm not used to hearing my true name.

'Yes, I arrived this morning – through a portal,' I say.

The woman stands up and walks towards me, arms outstretched. 'I am Eva Elegand,' she says, folding me in her embrace. 'Tell me everything.'

'You're my grandmother?' I ask, inhaling the scent of lavender. 'You don't look old enough.'

Eva laughs and it sounds like crystal bells. 'Bless you,' she says as she pulls back and holds me at arms' length to inspect me. 'Elvira. My son named you after me.'

I smile. 'Yes.'

Eva turns to her partner. 'Aedonis,' she says. 'Give our granddaughter a hug.'

I haven't hugged my father in over ten years, so when Aedonis embraces me, a tear slides over my cheek. I've missed having family.

'What should I call you?' I ask.

'Naina and Pop?' Eva says.

'I can do that.'

'Take a seat, Elvira,' Pop says, 'and tell us how you came to be here and what has become of our son.'

Naina gestures for me to sit next to her on the lounge. 'I am interested to hear your story too, Alvin,' she says, 'when Elvira is done.'

'Would anyone care for tea?' Pop says.

Naina scoffs. 'No one wants tea, Aedonis! We need brandy – the good stuff. In our best glasses.'

Pop smiles broadly, revealing perfect teeth.

I bet he's a handsome dragon.

Starting with my first memory of my father and images from my mother's funeral, I pour out my life story as my grandfather pours four glasses of brandy. I recount my isolation from when my father placed me in Winona's care, so I could monitor Karina Warhurst's involvement in a portal project while he took up a position in Russia working on a similar project.

'It was a race to see who could get back first,' I explained.

'Well, you're here,' Pop says, 'so Aeon won?'

I down the last of my brandy and shake my head. 'No,' I whisper as the alcohol scours my throat on its way to my stomach. 'Karina made it first.'

Naina drains her glass. 'Which is why you're here? You were spying on Karina and you followed her through?'

My chest tightens; my heart feels like it's in a vice. 'More or less.'

'Let's go with "more",' Pop says.

I nod, pushing my empty glass towards him for a refill. I'm not a drinker but the brandy is delicious. Alvin sits forward in his seat, waiting for the next chapter of the story.

'The portal didn't work the first time,' I say, accepting my refill.

I take a sip before detailing the aftermath of the collapse of Karina's portal. My grandparents hear about all the major players – Karina, Felix, Liberty, Caspian, and Rose Fox – and I'm almost at our arrival on Rhybor when a soft beeping interrupts me.

Pop's eyes flick up over my head. 'We've got more company.'

I spin round, see the screen mounted high on the wall showing five figures on an infrared display.

'Where is that?' I ask.

Transfixed by the image, Naina says, 'Start of the entrance tunnel.'

'You saw *us* coming?' I say.

Naina nods. 'Wehrs glow brighter on the screen. We did not think you two would be a threat.'

'So, these are …?' I say.

Alvin growls. 'Kauri.'

'No!' I say. 'How could they find us? We weren't followed.'

'No?' Alvin says, pushing to his feet and looking directly at Pop. 'You expecting any other visitors?'

'We weren't expecting *any* visitors,' Pop says.

'Do you have a back door?' Alvin asks.

Naina gulps the last of her brandy. 'Follow me.'

Chapter 20

Felix

My blood boils inside my veins – fuelled by anger, envy and jealousy – as I watch Elvira fly away with Alvin. If Karina had been my mother instead of my stepmother, I'd be able to fly too. *And* on Rhybor, I'd be home.

'That's rude,' Gemini says, pointing to the retreating dragons, 'just taking off like that and leaving us here.'

Rude? Gemini's an assassin. Kills people for a living. And yet he thinks being left to guard the *Allegro* is rude? It's ridiculous that someone whose moral compass is so defective should worry about something like that.

'I don't reckon we need to worry about the cat,' I say. 'Grim can look after himself.'

'Yep,' Gemini says. 'Just watch the ship.'

'What?'

Gemini rubs his hands together. 'You can take the first shift here. I'm on recon.'

I glare at him, but it's wasted. He's turned away, already intent on his mission.

'Jerk,' I mutter under my breath.

I head back up the Razor's ramp. Might as well take advantage of having the ship to myself. I can do my own recon. Once inside, I'm about to head to the artillery compartment when I notice the cockpit door is open. I detour past the cockpit, eyeing the empty pilot's chair. Change of plan.

I settle myself into the moulded leather seat. I smile. Even if Grim does see me sitting in it, it's not like he can tell anyone. Adrenaline surges through me – energising me – making my fingers tingle. Without thinking about it, my left hand is hovering over the controls, while my right clutches the steering rod.

No one will ever know.

I swipe my hand over the control board, illuminating a dizzying array of lights on the transparent display to my left. Three lights start flashing in time with the syncopated beeping coming through the speakers.

Nothing to worry about. The beeping is faint. It's not like it is blaring throughout the ship.

'Good morning, all,' I say, 'this is Captain Dangerfield in the flight deck, welcoming you onboard today's flight to Never Never Land. I'm just finalising the safety checks so we'll be on our way shortly. Weather conditions are perfect for flying today and our expected flight time is seven and a half hours. Once the seatbelt signed is switched off, you are free to move about the cabin but, while seated, I suggest you keep your belt fastened in case of unexpected turbulence. I wouldn't worry too much about that today though – your biggest danger on this flight is probably the cat who is lurking somewhere on the ship. He's always looking for a lap to lie on.'

I press a couple of innocuous looking switches, avoiding any that are red, or say 'start' or 'on', before continuing my cabin address.

'As you probably gathered from the seven and a half-hour flight time I mentioned, we'll be utilising our hyper-drive engines today. For those onboard who might not be fans of hyper-drive, you have two options. One, disembark immediately and find yourself a reputable cryo-freeze company who will prepare your body for the ten-thousand-year non-hyper-drive journey. Two, remain onboard, resisting the urge to visit me in the cockpit to whinge about your rumbly tummy. And finally, I remind passengers that smoking and vomiting on the ship are strictly prohibited.'

I'm enjoying my current role as airship commander more than I should be. Maybe Elvira has influenced me more than I'd realised. I scan the control board and adjust a couple of the gauges – not too far, I don't want Gemini to notice.

A hissing sound behind me makes me jump. I swivel round.

'Grim!' I say. 'Don't *do* that. I thought a pressure valve had come loose or something.'

The cat hisses again, baring his gruesome teeth.

'Yeah,' I say, taking a deep breath to slow my heartrate. 'I love you, too.'

When Grim hisses a third time, I decide to move. I've got better things to do than to be hissed at by a cat. I find the artillery store and spend the next hour rifling through all the equipment. I've been through them all before but it's still cool.

Footsteps on the ramp startle me. I curse. I'm supposed to be guarding the ship. Obviously, Gemini's trying to make a point about the lack of surveillance on the perimeter.

But when I reach the midsection of the aircraft, I don't find Gemini.

Two tall, blue bipedal humanoids with blasters block the ship's entrance.

'Let me guess,' I say. 'Kauri, right?'

A band of green light blasts from the eyes of the female Kauri and a luminous cold sweeps over me.

'You're scanning me?' I say.

'Hybrid,' the Kauri says at last. 'Human-wehrdragon cross. No threat.'

Her voice is like crystal – clear and sweet with a sharp, dangerous undercurrent.

Her companion nods. 'A viable sample then.'

'Yes,' the female agrees.

'I don't give permission for you to take any samples from me,' I say, hoping that Elvira and Alvin are on their way back. Even Gemini would be welcome right now.

'I'll secure the cargo,' the male Kauri says in an inflectionless voice. 'You can pilot.'

The female gives a curt nod before she heads to the cockpit. I study the male Kauri as the engines whir into action. A shiny metal strip runs from just above his left eye-ridge – he has no eyebrows – tracing a crescent shape on the left side of his head and ending behind his ear. The right side of his head is a canvas for delicate silver tattoos. I'm tempted to think the pattern is ornamental, but it does have a distinct computer circuit-board look to it.

'I didn't know taking hostages was your thing,' I say.

'It isn't,' he says. 'You're not a hostage – you're a sample.'

My heart races, firing a surge of adrenaline through my system. I launch myself at the Kauri, leading with my fist, but the male catches my fist in his vice-like grip and rotates his forearm like he's checking the time on his wristwatch. Pain flares in my arm as tendons and ligaments are stretched beyond their limits.

I grunt, teeth clenched tightly. 'Well, you'd better hurry up …'

The Kauri cocks his head to one side. 'Because?'

I'm about to threaten him with, 'because my backup is on its way', but reality hits me. Saying that will put Elvira in danger. I can't think of a convincing lie and no witty wisecrack springs to mind either. It's the pain. My hand, wrist and forearm are ablaze with it. It's unlike anything I've felt before.

The Kauri's grip on my fist tightens. 'Because?' he says again.

The agony intensifies and tentacles of delirium swarm through my mind, strangling my consciousness. As reality ebbs away, I regret my decision to tamper with the ship's controls. I might have led the Kauri here.

Chapter 21

Elvira

My grandfather shoves me from behind and I almost trip over my grand-mother's heels as we race out through the rear door of their chambers. The Kauri's sudden appearance, so close behind us, doesn't seem like a coincidence. They have followed us. I'm responsible for bringing this menace into my family's home.

The echoes from our footfalls as we scamper through the winding tunnels, fill my ears and rattle my brain. My grandparents' torches create a strobe-like effect in the vacuous darkness and I pray that whatever pursues us, should they catch up to us, is sensitive to flickering light. An epileptic seizure would surely slow them down.

My leg muscles are tiring and my breathing is becoming more laboured by the second. I'm built for speed not endurance. It would be helpful to know how much further so I could pace myself, but I don't dare ask.

The rumble of rapid footsteps intensifies. There are certainly more than four of us now. I pump my arms harder, spurring myself on. I'm keeping pace with Naina but only just.

'Hurry!' Alvin urges from the rear. 'They're gaining on us!'

Pop grunts. 'We're close to an exit,' he says, panting. 'Be ready to Shift.'

Shift? Inside the tunnel? While dragons would easily *fit* in the tunnels, *flying* would present a definite challenge.

I'm about to ask if he'll tell me when to Shift but, as if he can read my thoughts, Pop says, 'You'll know when.'

The tunnel seems to be narrowing, though I can't tell for sure with the inconsistent light.

'Left!' Naina calls.

She disappears from sight and I interpret her instruction a second too late. I skid and twist but not quick enough. I shoulder-charge the tunnel wall. The pain is explosive and the crunching sound in my shoulder turns my stomach.

'Right turn!' Naina yells. 'Then a sharp left!'

Crap! Why all the chicanes? I wouldn't have thought they'd need traffic-calming here.

I make the turns in good time, but my grandfather makes better time – and crashes into me. His arm snakes around my waist as I pitch forward. He wrenches me back. I fall against him.

'Run, Elvira!' Pop hisses, his breath hot against my ear. 'They are upon us!'

His words are barely out when a scream rips through the tunnel.

'NOOOOOOOOOO!' Alvin cries.

Pop thumps me so hard in the back that he winds me.

'Fly, Elvira!' he yells.

Suddenly, the ground disappears and I'm tumbling in … air! Hot air.

Fly, Elvira.

Cocooned in heat, I fumble the knots of my sarong as the Shift takes me. When they don't cooperate, I slice through the fabric with my talons. If I survive this, I'll want to cover myself when I Shift back to human form.

Fly, Elvira.

My grandfather's words reverberate inside my head. My shoulder is bad, and though it will heal relatively quickly, it's not instant. And I've had limited flying experience. I somersault over and over, wings flailing impotently. The boiling lava is speeding towards me.

Naina's voice infiltrates my brain.

Elvira! Pretend you're a dolphin. Dive, push up, dive, push up.

I do as she says.

It's working, I send back.

Good. Now follow me down.

Down?

Elvira!

I look down. Naina is an exquisite reptilian silhouette against a canvas of … lava.

Tunnel entrance ahead, Eva says. *About ten metres above the river. Be ready.*

My heart almost seizes in my chest. I don't have much experience in landing, let alone precision landing. But swan-diving into a river of lava isn't on my bucket list, so a bit of focus is needed.

I extend my wings to wash off some speed, but the heat threatens to incinerate them, like a naked flame to paper. Retracting my wings, I'm thankful to have my scaly armour rather than my human skin at this moment. Being hairless in this form is a bonus too. All my hair would have been singed clean off by now.

I train my eyes on my grandmother, tracking her elevation and trying to emulate her trajectory.

I hold my breath.

Glide.

Point my nose up slightly.

Glide.

Veer right.

Glide.

Naina alights on the lip of the tunnel then scurries out of sight. But as I adjust my leg positioning ready to land, something wrenches on my tail. I spin through a triple somersault before levelling out.

Pull up now! Pop cries.

Instinctively, I lift my legs and, stupidly, I close my eyes. I tumble into the tunnel with zombie-like grace and land, a quivering mess, at my grandmother's feet. She's in human form again. Her pink robe is singed and tatty, but it covers her from shoulder to knee.

'That was a novel take on landing, Elvira,' Naina says, smiling.

I groan. *I'm sure it was.*

Pop lands behind me. *That was like watching a bowl of trifle being spilt across the floor,* he says.

Yeah, well – thanks for your 'help', I say irritably. *Did you not consider that wrenching on my tail at the last moment might impact on my artistic expression score?*

Pop Shifts back to human form, donning his robe quickly. 'If I hadn't intervened,' he says, 'you'd be a mural baked on the wall out there, rather than a pudding on the floor in here.'

'You made it,' Naina says. 'That's the main thing.'

'Shift, Elvira,' Pop says.

Without caring who's watching, I let my dragon melt away and wrap what's left of my sarong around me as best I can. The heat clearly wasn't kind to it. Slicing it didn't help either. I struggle to my feet, my shoulder aching.

'Where's Alvin?' I say.

Pop grunts. 'Kauri got him.'

I shake my head as my legs fail me and I crash to my knees. 'No … no. They … He can't be …'

'He's gone,' Naina says. 'The Kauri can't fly down here, but we should keep moving nonetheless.' She takes my hand. 'Come on, Elvira. We've a bit of a walk ahead to get outside.'

I let her help me to my feet again. 'Should we warn the others?'

'Others?' Pop says.

'Whoever else lives in the mountain?' I say.

Naina shakes her head. 'Only us here now. Come on.'

My grandmother turns, aims her torch into the darkness and sets off. I follow her with Pop behind me, trekking in silence as I try to absorb my new reality.

The Kauri are here.

Alvin is gone.

My grandparents are safe for now, but what will happen once we get to the end of this tunnel?

Another thought sends shards of ice through my heart. *Felix.*

'The boys,' I murmur. 'Not the boys.'

'Pardon?' Naina says, looking over her shoulder at me.

'Felix and Gemini are back at the ship,' I say. 'Grim, too.'

Pop appears at my side and wraps his arm around my shoulders. 'I think you should brace yourself for the worst,' he says. 'The Kauri wouldn't have missed them.'

We trudge through the near darkness. Somehow, Naina still has her torch. The ache in my heart eclipses the pain in my shoulder as I imagine what I will find when I am finally free of the underground. Part of me doesn't want to surface again. I don't think I can face what's out there; what has happened to Felix. But I can't not know either. I can't ignore his fate.

'We're here,' Naina says at last. 'This is the door to the outside world.'

Before us is a ladder. Overhead are two wooden doors secured from the inside with four thick metal bolts.

'Ready?' Naina asks.

'No,' I say, 'but let's go anyway.'

Naina climbs, releases the bolts and pushes one of the doors open. Sunlight pours in through the breach, blinding me.

When she gasps, I freeze.

What now? More Kauri?

'Eva?' a familiar voice says.

'Depends who is asking,' my grandmother replies.

Pop brushes past me as I fight to clear my vision. 'Who's there?' he says.

'Allow me to introduce myself,' the voice says. 'I am Gemini Holmes. I know your son, Aeon.'

'Elvira?' Naina says.

I nod. 'Yep.' As I climb the ladder, I add, 'Where's Felix?'

'Guarding the Razor,' Gemini replies, holding his hand out to help me.

I swat it away and clamber out under my own steam.

'I hope you don't mean *that* Razor,' Pop says, pointing skyward.

I crane my neck and with a sinking heart, witness my worst fear. The Razor – our Razor – sails away towards the north.

'We have to go and find Felix,' I say.

'Elvira,' Gemini says, 'you should wait here. I'll go and look for him.'

'Kauri would have killed or captured him,' Pop says.

I'm not sure I will cope if the Kauri have killed Felix but I can't let Gemini do my dirty work for me. It's bad enough he does my father's dirty work. And besides, I don't know that I trust him to tell me the truth.

'I'm going,' I say. 'The Kauri who got Alvin maybe haven't got—'

'Alvin's gone?' Gemini says.

I nod. 'So, if they haven't made it back to their own craft yet, they're still here. We need to be careful.'

'Agreed,' Naina says. 'Let's go.'

Considering how far we seemed to venture through the tunnels inside the mountain, it's not as far from my grandparents' 'back door' to our landing site as I'd imagined. When we arrive at the clearing, I catch Gemini's eye.

'You knew where the back door was?'

Gemini nods. 'Aeon described where it was. I didn't know if your grandparents would still be here, but I thought it would be a good idea to be close – just in case.'

Again, I feel the cold knot of jealousy in my gut. Surely if I'd been living with my father, he'd have shared all this stuff with me. Gemini was just in the right place at the right time. Just convenient.

'So much for jamming the tracking signal,' I say.

Gemini's expression doesn't change. 'I can't say how the Kauri found us,' he says, 'but my program had two fail-safes. *Someone* would have had to actively dismantle both of them for the program to stop working.'

Anger now consumes the jealousy. 'Are you implying that Felix dismantled the fail-safes, since he was the only one here?'

'Certainly not,' Gemini says. 'Felix wouldn't have the brains to do it. My money would actually be on Grim.'

'Well, whatever happened,' Naina says, 'the Kauri *have* been here, and they've taken the Razor.'

'And all our stuff,' Gemini adds.

'Except your rucksack,' I say, eyeing his leather bag.

'Yes,' Gemini says. 'The Kauri got all our stuff *except* my rucksack.'

'And they've got Felix and Grim,' I say.

'The cat would have been smart enough to get away,' Gemini says, 'and to be honest, I don't know why the Kauri would take Felix. They are an apex predator, the most advanced species in the known universe – what could they possibly want with Felix?'

Pop raises his hand like he's in a classroom. 'The Kauri are cyborgs – AI brains with fabricated organic bodies. They are fixated on emotions, something that organic lifeforms are born with but that Kauri have to program. Consequently, they have a keen interest in studying emotions and hormones of different species. It's possible that they took your friend as a test animal – to study his emotional responses.'

'Before we jump to any conclusions,' Naina says, 'we should look around first. Felix might have gone for a walk.'

'Agreed,' I say. 'We'll split up, take a compass point and scout around. Be careful – there might still be Kauri about. One hour.'

Gemini salutes. 'One hour.'

I spend the hour traipsing east through the open woodland at the base of the mountain with only the occasional birdcall for company. It's as if the forest itself is holding its breath, watching and waiting. There's no evidence that Felix, or anyone else, has been here recently. Short of finding a body though, it's not like I'd know. Tracking isn't one of my skillsets.

I return to the landing site a few minutes late and find three people. No Felix.

'Nothing?' I say.

Naina, Pop and Gemini all shake their heads.

I let out a shuddering sigh. 'Some way to start building an army,' I mumble. 'I've already lost two soldiers.'

'Army?' Naina says. 'What are you talking about?'

'She wants to raise an army to fight the Kauri,' Gemini explains. 'She wants to unite the Crusaders and Loyalists under one banner.'

I nod. 'I wanted to have made progress before Father arrives.'

'So, what's your plan now, Major General?' Gemini asks.

I've got two immediate priorities. Saving Felix and locating Karina. My head says that Karina is the strategic priority; my heart wants to look for Felix.

This is war. War isn't won by sentiment. It's won by soldiers.

'We need to find Karina,' I say.

Gemini sniffs. 'Then we need to steal another ship.'

I stand up and stab my index finger into his chest. 'That's your first job, *Lieutenant*.'

Chapter 22

Felix

I'm woken by someone tapping on my forehead. I try to open my eyes but they remain stubbornly closed.

Tap. Tap. Tap.

What?

Tap. Tap. Tap.

That's going to get old *real* quick.

Tap. Tap. Tap.

'Okay!' I say. 'I'm awake. Just stop that already.'

'Open your eyes,' a voice says.

'Yep, working on it. Just give me a second.'

I invest a bit more effort and finally pry my eyelids apart.

A lone Kauri stands over me. He looks about my age, but that doesn't mean anything since cyborgs can engineer their appearance. I reckon he's probably a few centimetres taller than me but has the physique of a stick insect. The ceiling light glints off the metal strip on his head, as well as the silvery web of tattoos. His eyes are rounded and hypnotically luminous – the irises are vibrant amethyst with silver highlights and his pupils are wells of impenetrable darkness.

The Kauri's purple lips twitch into a smile. 'Felix Dangerfield,' he says.

I grunt. 'Where am I?'

'You are in our research facility.'

I glance around the stark, white room. 'What kind of research are you doing?' I say. 'There is zero equipment in here.'

He smiles, white teeth appearing from behind his lips. 'There is equipment,' he says. 'You just can't see it.'

'Is it all white?' I say. 'It's camouflaged? Like a polar bear in a snow storm?'

The Kauri's eyelids flutter. 'A joke?' he says finally. 'Or sarcasm? We have come across both in our journey across the universe, but it is still difficult to tell the difference between them in some species.'

I glance down. 'What the hell?'

'Allow me to explain,' the Kauri says.

'I'm *naked* and strapped to a crazy dentist chair,' I snap. 'The only explanation I need is "why".'

'You are a hybrid, Felix Dangerfield. A human-wehrdragon cross. We've not seen this before. We need to study it.'

'I'm supposed to believe that you're a scientist?'

'Yes.'

I tug at the metal restraints around my wrists but they don't budge. Neither do the bands around my ankles. The chair divides where my crotch begins, so each leg has a padded length of cushion supporting it. Midway between my ankles, a cylinder protrudes from the floor with several buttons on its surface.

Dozens of slender silver tubes sprout from my arms, legs and torso. The tubes are long – I can't see the ends of them. They disappear under the chair somewhere.

'I didn't authorise anyone to do any tests on me,' I say.

'Your authorisation is not required.'

Nudity doesn't usually bother me, but it does today. The Kauri's loose white t-shirt looks like finely spun wool – if they have wool here. In any case, I could probably squeeze into it. The trousers might be a problem though. The shiny, burgundy leather trousers, zippered at the side rather than the front, are a snug fit on his slim frame. But it's worth a shot. If I could get out of this chair, I reckon I could take him.

'You got a name?' I say.

'Okita.'

'How long am I here for?'

'Until we've collected the data we need.'

'And then I'm free to go?'

'No,' Okita says. 'You will be stored – along with the rest.'

'Stored? What do you mean?'

'We will eliminate all the excess space in your body and store you in our Seed. It is possible that you'll be recalled at some point in the future, Felix Dangerfield.'

Again, I tug at my restraints. 'What the hell are you talking about?'

When Okita sighs, it's a teacher's sigh. 'This universe is flawed,' he says. 'We Kauri – as the supreme beings in the universe – are cataloguing and classifying all the lifeforms we encounter in our travels and, once we're done, we'll analyse our data and map out a plan for who and what goes where. If you are worthy, you will be recalled.'

My chest constricts so tightly, I'm worried that my heart will be squeezed into my abdomen. 'So essentially, you are sweeping galaxies and wiping out whatever lifeforms you find there. Then, once you're done, you're going to go back and regrow what you think should be there?'

'We're not "wiping them out",' Okita says. 'We are storing them for potential future use.'

A shudder rakes through me. They haven't been to Earth yet but, by opening the portal, we've probably handed them a free pass.

'But you've slaughtered most of the wehrs here,' I say. 'Are they not worthy of a place in Kauri utopia?'

'Firstly,' Okita says, holding up the index finger on his left hand, 'we haven't slaughtered "most" of the wehrdragons here. Certainly, some died opposing us, but the ones we have captured have been stored. Many of them will be reintroduced in a new environment.'

'Why a new environment?' I ask. 'Why not this one?'

'Wehrdragons cannot be trusted to manage the resource that is abundant here. Elenium is a hugely powerful element and one that, in the wrong hands, is incredibly dangerous.'

'What have they done with it that is so dangerous?'

'Sold it *indiscriminately*,' Okita says. 'The wehrdragons are materialistic and motivated by greed. They don't care who they sell to – and they should. There are plenty of species out there who would use elenium for evil. On Earth, for example, humans use it to make weapons.'

So, the Kauri know about Earth. It's only a matter of time before they invade there too.

'That's why we destroyed all the portals when we arrived here,' Okita says, 'to preserve what elenium is left.'

I don't believe that the Kauri are preserving elenium. It's more likely they are using it for their own purposes. Fuelling those spaceships to take them all over the universe would require something pretty powerful.

My head pounds with the effort of sifting through Okita's story to sort fact from fiction.

I study the gleaming silver tubes snaking from my body and they look a whole lot more menacing now. 'What are the tubes for?'

'The tubes have various functions,' Okita says. 'Some are supplying nutrients, some are removing waste, while others are testing your blood and organ functions.'

'You're not going to harvest my organs, are you?'

Okita grimaces. 'I think not!' he says. 'What a repulsive thought! We Kauri have no need of such primitive techniques.'

I snort. 'And strapping prisoners to chairs isn't primitive? I would have thought a truly "supreme" species could have come up with something more sophisticated than that!'

Okita smirks. 'You're not a prisoner,' he says. 'You're a *sample*. Just be thankful you're not hanging from your ankles.'

Movement behind Okita snags my attention – another Kauri – striding across the grey archway. A doorway. An *open* doorway. My heart beats faster.

'Your heartrate is accelerating,' Okita says. 'What are you thinking about?'

I frown. 'What I'm going to order for my last meal. Do you do pepperoni pizzas here?'

'I should tell you, Felix Dangerfield,' Okita says, tapping his temple, 'that I can access the data on your vitals whenever I wish. You are being monitored constantly.'

'You can't read my mind though?'

'We are working on that,' he says. 'We have the capacity to remove a lifeform's consciousness and transplant it into another host body. It will not be long before we can monitor thoughts.'

I shiver. I really hope he's lying about harvesting and transplanting a person's consciousness. I do *not* want to wake up in someone else's body.

'You said you're storing all the … lifeforms you encounter after you take all the "space" out of them?' I say.

Okita nods. 'We have a device called a "squidger" that eliminates space in objects down to the subatomic level. Did you know that if you took four billion wehrdragons and squeezed out all the space inside them, the amount of physical matter left would take up about the same volume as a sugar cube?'

'Sure,' I say. 'Everyone knows that.'

'We've done it, Felix Dangerfield,' Okita says. 'We have four billion wehrdragons stored in our Seed. It has taken us longer to round them up than we would have liked – but we almost have them all.'

'And did you steal all their consciousness … consciousness*es* … before you stored them?'

'No,' Okita says, shaking his head. 'We harvested a few for testing purposes, but the rest of the wehrdragons are essentially in stasis until we finish our review.'

'They're alive?'

'In a manner of speaking. We can sustain lifeforms this way indefinitely.'

I close my eyes. Stored lifeforms. Subatomic spaces. Stolen souls. I never signed up for this.

'I will leave you to rest,' Okita says. 'I will return when it is time for you to be stored in the Seed.'

'Don't hurry,' I say without opening my eyes.

After a few seconds, I crack open my eyelids to make sure he's gone. He is.

I let out a long breath. If I can get out of this seat, I've got a chance to escape and warn the others. My brain spits out a list of problems that I'd encounter if I *did* manage to make it out of this room, but I ignore that. Instead, I cling to the idea that I could actually make it into the corridor.

Chapter 23

Elvira

I don't know why people like riding motorcycles. My legs are cramped, my butt aches and I've inhaled too many bugs. I'm riding pillion with my grandmother and although I had a bandana covering my mouth and nose when we left my grandparents' home eight hours ago, clearly I didn't secure it well enough. The wind managed to whip it away within the first hour of our trip.

Naina isn't afraid of speed; we're chewing up the miles faster than I'd like. At the speed we're going, I can't even make myself heard when I yell. The wind steals my words the instant I utter them. I'd have preferred the quad bikes but my grandparents' trail bikes are faster.

Gemini appears alongside us. Show off. Gemini gets to ride solo since my grandfather stayed behind to await my father's arrival.

After hours of this relentless torture, the hillside home of the Gyoma Lake wehrs looms before us and Eva rolls off the throttle. My relief that the ride is finally over is short-lived; anxiety steals in as the task at hand becomes a reality.

I have to tell Alvin's family that he's dead.

And then I need to find Karina. The tracker Gemini had hidden in her vehicle died an hour after she exited the portal here, so we've got no idea where she is now. With any luck, some of the Gyoma Lake wehrs might have seen her and be able to give us a lead. Though, it'll be tricky to ask 'have you seen this woman?' just after we've delivered news of a clan member's death.

I manage to get off the bike without falling over or burning my leg on the exhaust, which is a blessing. I stretch my aching muscles as my grandmother dismounts.

Gemini extends his hand towards me, my borrowed green and orange paisley bandana pinched between his fingers. 'Lose something?'

'Thanks,' I say, accepting it from him. 'I can't believe you stopped to pick it up.'

'I didn't,' he says with a shrug. 'I caught it.'

Of course he did!

Naina tucks her bandana into the pocket of her trousers. 'Job to do. Let's get inside.' She nods towards Gemini's bike. 'We can leave them out here. The Kauri shouldn't see them under the tree cover.'

We climb the hillside to Alvin's home for the second time in two days. I wish we'd at least been able to bring Grim back.

When we make it to the entranceway, my grandmother calls out. 'Hello? I am Eva Elegand, a wehr from Topaz Forest. My granddaughter is with me, along with another friend. May we enter?'

A female voice rings out in the dimly lit tunnel. 'What is your business here?'

'We bring news of Alvin de Toit,' I say.

Karina's face appears out of the gloom. Her gaze grazes Naina before landing on me.

'Elvira,' she says with a smile, 'did you not like the accommodation I had arranged for you at the NSA?'

I stare at her open-mouthed as Gemini stands at my side.

'Karina,' Gemini says, 'you didn't make it far from the landing site. Trouble with your vehicle?'

Karina smiles. 'The vehicle is fine. Your tracker broke though. Shame.'

'And the team of SEALS that accompanied you?' Gemini says.

'I thought you said you brought news of Alvin?' Karina says.

'You know him?' I ask.

Karina nods. 'He's my uncle.'

'He's dead,' Gemini says without ceremony.

Karina's expression doesn't alter. 'How?'

'Kauri,' my grandmother says. 'They found our home. Alvin didn't make it out.'

'But *you* did,' Karina muses. 'That's convenient.'

Suddenly anger displaces my guilt at Alvin's death. 'What are you trying to say?'

Gemini speaks before Karina can answer. 'You wanted the portal opened here because it's close to your home, Karina?'

'Yes.'

'And let me guess,' he continues, 'you killed the SEALS when you arrived because they would get in the way of your real mission?'

'Yes,' Karina says. 'Their mission was to "escort me safely to the capital so I could report to the Rhyborians how clever the Earthlings were in reopening the portal". That didn't align with *my* mission though. I just wanted to get home to see how the rebellion was going. To see how much progress had been made in the *twenty years* I'd been gone.'

'And once you found out how much things had *really* changed,' Naina says, 'you revised your plan?'

Karina nods. 'Yes. Alvin was to be your guide, Elvira.'

I glare at her. 'He was meant to spy on me, I think you mean.'

'Guide,' Karina says again. 'When I realised what had happened here, the new mission was obvious. Defeat the Kauri. I knew you'd come. Alvin's job was to assess your usefulness for the mission.'

I recoil. 'You had me kidnapped and chained up for two days! And now you expect me to work for you?'

'Kidnapped?' Naina says. 'Chained up? What are you talking about?'

'Ladies,' Gemini says, 'time to discuss that later – like after we've dealt with the Kauri.'

'Is Aeon here yet?' Karina says.

'On his way,' I reply.

Karina scoffs. 'If he doesn't hurry, he'll miss all the fun.'

'He's probably already assisting my husband in recruiting the forest wehrs as we speak,' my grandmother says.

'Right. And where is Felix?' Karina asks. 'Is he dead?'

'He was captured by the Kauri,' I reply.

Karina sighs. 'Thank goodness for small mercies.'

I truly despise this woman and I don't know how I'm going to work with her.

Gemini runs a hand through his dark hair. 'It's great that you have identified the mission, Karina,' he says, 'but *we* have a plan.'

Karina's eyebrows arch. 'Really? And what is it?'

'The Kauri are cyborgs,' Gemini says, 'running on highly sophisticated software. If I can download a sample of their operating system, I can write a virus to destroy them.'

Karina strides forward and stops when she is toe-to-toe with Gemini. 'Can you? I wasn't aware that's what physicists did.'

'I have done some hacking in my time – misspent youth,' Gemini says. 'And besides, I haven't found anything yet that I *can't* do.'

'You're cocky,' she says. 'I like that.'

Unflinching, he says, 'So, you in?'

'Yes,' Karina says, smiling. 'You reckon you're a hacker?'

Gemini nods.

'According to my family here,' Karina say, 'the Kauri have a Star of Truth. It's some kind of AI/supercomputer that is the central repository of all Kauri knowledge.'

'Do you know what access protocols there are between that and the individual Kauri?'

Karina frowns. 'Our intelligence suggests that the Kauri can access it – to deposit or draw on information – but that it's more than just a database. It is a learning intelligence. If you could release a virus to destroy that …'

'Right. I'll need all the intel you've got on that.'

Karina extends her hand. 'Deal.'

'Deal,' Gemini echoes, accepting her handshake.

Volcanic anger gurgles inside me. Gemini is supposed to be loyal to my father and, by extension, to me. And he's just made a deal with the devil.

Karina turns to me. 'In the meantime, you can continue your recruiting drive. A virus is only part of the solution. We might actually need to steal the Star of Truth from the city to deploy the virus so we'll need all the bodies we can get. We'll use this as our staging point – bring everyone you can here.' She reaches out and caresses my cheek with one hand. 'I'll give you a week.'

'We will return in a week,' I say, slapping her hand away, 'with whoever we can rally. We can plan our assault in detail then.'

'Gemini,' Karina says, turning to him. 'Let's get to work.'

Gemini pats his rucksack. 'I've got everything I need.'

'Gemini,' I say, 'can I have a word with you – in private – before we go?'

'Sure,' he says. 'I'll walk you back to your bike.' To Karina, he adds, 'I'll join you shortly.'

'I'll assemble the others,' Karina says before turning and heading back inside the mountain.

My grandmother slips her arm around mine as we exit the tunnel. 'You've got a lot more to tell us, I think.'

'It'll wait till we get home,' I say, patting her hand.

As we make our way down the hillside, Gemini says, 'So what's on your mind, Elvira?'

'Felix,' I say. 'Is there any way you can track him?'

'I know how far away his phone is and in what direction – and I know it's still with the *Allegro*.'

I gasp. 'Why didn't you tell me before? Where is he?'

Gemini puts his hand on my shoulder. 'I don't know where *he* is. The signal keeps moving. I assume because the Kauri are flying around in the Razor. I think his phone is in the Razor, but I can't imagine they'd keep him in there.'

'I need to find him.'

'It's not safe for me to hack the Kauri satellites, Elvira,' Gemini says, taking his hand from my shoulder to rummage in his rucksack, 'but I'll give you this.'

He hands me what looks like an old pager.

'Our mobiles won't work here,' he says, 'but you can contact me on this. It's old tech but it'll work. I'll let you know if I make any progress on finding Felix.'

'Please try to find him – don't listen to Karina.'

'I'll do what I can,' he says.

I frown.

'What now?' he says.

'If our phones won't work here, how do you know where his phone is?'

Gemini smiles. 'I've got a tracker in his phone – yours and Liberty's too – linked to a receiver in my tablet. It's like my own personal surveillance network. Works okay over short distances, but it's less perfect the further away you get.'

I shudder. 'You're creepy.'

'I love you, too.'

I glare at him and he winks in return.

My grandmother clears her throat. 'In case you hadn't noticed, I'm still here.'

'It's not what it sounds like,' I say as we reach the trail bikes. 'He's just messing with me.'

'Key is in the ignition,' Gemini says, gesturing towards my grandfather's bike.

I wasn't anticipating such a quick turnaround on this trip and I shudder at the thought of another eight hours in the saddle. At least I don't have to ride pillion this time. I've got my own wheels.

I tuck Gemini's pager into my jacket pocket as I throw my leg over the seat. 'Don't let Karina—'

'Relax, Elvira,' Gemini says. 'I've read or listened to every report you sent your father on her. I know what she's like. And I know what I'm doing.'

As my grandmother kickstarts her bike, I wonder what Gemini really *is* doing – and who he's doing it for.

Chapter 24

Liberty

The intercom beeps three times.

'*Dr Fox?*'

My father's gaze doesn't shift from his screen. 'Yes.'

'*I have Aeon Elegand in reception, insisting on speaking with you. Are you available?*'

'I've heard that name somewhere before,' my father mutters.

I wave to get his attention. He looks up at me, brow furrowed.

'Elvira's father,' I say.

'Ah,' he says, nodding. 'I remember now.'

'*Dr Fox?*'

'Yes, yes. I'll send Liberty up to fetch him.'

'*I'm sorry,*' the receptionist says, '*do you mean you'll see him down there?*'

'Yes, that's right. Liberty will come for him.'

'*That is highly irregular, Dr Fox.*'

My father scans his lab. 'I don't know if you've been down here lately, David,' he says, 'but my walls have melted. There's nothing *regular* about NSA at the moment. Out.'

'*Noted, Dr Fox. Out.*'

I slide off my stool. 'I'll go fetch our guest.'

'Try not to interrogate him too much on the way back, Liberty,' my father says. 'I don't want to miss anything.'

'Got it,' I say, smiling.

I almost break into a run once I'm outside Lab 17 but I force myself to walk. Need to be calm and controlled. I take the stairs up to the lobby – the lifts are still out of order – and by the time I get there, my legs are burning with lactic acid.

I'm out of condition. I need to get back into training.

I've been back for about forty-eight hours and, during that time, my parents have been my focus. No time for training. I'm desperate for a workout though. I need to burn off some energy – and channel my grief. My martial arts training strengthens my body and my mind – which is something I need right now.

I reach the lobby and find the sole visitor there standing near the lifts.

'Aeon Elegand?' I say, walking towards him.

The man nods and extends his hand. 'Miss Fox.'

Aeon's charcoal suit has an expensive look to it – tailored fit, no creases – and his blue, open-necked shirt is perfectly pressed too. The black leather belt encircling his slim hips has a gleaming silver buckle, which he must polish after putting it on because there isn't even a finger-print smudge on it. His complexion is a few shades lighter than Elvira's but their eyes are the same. Yet, while Elvira's hair is a mass of corkscrew curls, even if Aeon grew out his short back and sides, I don't reckon his dark locks would show a kink anywhere.

'Call me Liberty,' I say, accepting his handshake. 'Please, come with me. My father is waiting.'

Aeon keeps pace at my side as we venture into the bowels of NSA's underground warren of labs.

'So, you want to go through my parents' portal?' I say.

Aeon smiles. 'You don't do small talk, huh?'

'Waste of time.'

'Agreed,' he says. 'So – yes. I do want to go through your parents' portal.'

'Couldn't get yours working?'

His stride falters but he recovers quickly. 'No.'

'You're surprised I know about that,' I say, a statement rather than a question.

'A little. There are only two people who could have shared that information with you, but I'm guessing my daughter told you. Gemini would never divulge such information.'

My daughter. Gemini.

I already dislike this man. Aeon abandoned his young daughter while he moved to the other side of the world to work on a project. In ten years, he's never visited her nor had her to visit him. He expected her to spy for him and feed him information about Karina. And when he refers to her, he doesn't even use her name. Gemini, on the other hand, is apparently deserving of a name. And why? Because being an assassin is somehow cooler than just being a spy?

Prick.

It takes all my focus to not drop him with a jab to the solar plexus. Suddenly, I am very grateful to not have wehr parents. Elvira's and Felix's families are really messed up.

'I won't reveal my sources,' I say. 'What's your plan once you get to Rhybor?'

'Do you really think I'm going to tell you that?'

I shrug. 'You can choose not to, I suppose, but I will hear your plan when you tell my father. You do realise you will have to convince him to let you through the portal?'

Aeon chuckles. 'I can be very convincing.'

Dread washes through me. Is he armed? Perhaps he plans to take the portal by force. I'm revising all my martial arts moves when another, more terrifying, prospect presents itself. Aeon doesn't need a weapon. Aeon *is* a weapon. If he Shifts, I don't know that any of my moves will work.

So, if punching my way out isn't an option, I need to think my way clear here.

'Your king is dead,' I say.

Aeon stops. 'What did you say?'

'King Helion is dead and Rhybor has been taken over by a more advanced species – the Kauri.'

'You've been there?' he says.

I nod. 'I went to find my mother.'

'My daughter and Gemini are still there?'

'Her name is Elvira, in case you've forgotten,' I say. 'And yes, they are both still there.'

Aeon starts walking again but his frown suggests he's having difficulty digesting this new information.

'Gemini hasn't contacted you?' I say.

'Our technology doesn't work over that distance,' Aeon murmurs. After a few moments he adds, 'You're back though, so can I assume you found your mother?'

I glance at him before throwing his owns words back in his face. 'Do you really think I'm going to tell you that?'

I feel his gaze on me but I keep my eyes directly ahead.

'Let's try this question then,' Aeon says. 'What was Elvira's plan when you left?'

'To raise an army to defeat the Kauri.'

'Elvira? Raise an army?'

'Starting with your parents, I believe.'

Aeon rubs his chin. 'I did give Gemini their location. Hopefully, they're still there.'

'I don't know what preparations you've made for your return, but I'd suggest you start getting used to the idea that you and Karina are going to be teammates.'

I want to believe he shuddered at that suggestion, but it could just be wishful thinking.

And then, in the blink of an eye, he's standing in front of me with his hands on my shoulders. Instinctively, I balance my weight over the balls of my feet. Aeon nods and lowers his hands.

'You'd be a formidable enemy, Liberty Fox,' he says, 'which, conversely, would also make you a powerful ally. You have strength and, no doubt, have inherited some of your parents' intelligence. It's little wonder that Elvira is intimidated by you and that Felix lusts after you. If what you have said about Rhybor is true, my daughter will need you. Will you accompany me to Rhybor?'

'A minute ago, you weren't going to tell me your plan. But now you want me to come with you?'

Aeon clasps his hands in front of him. 'I believe you speak the truth about Rhybor,' he says, 'so I've had to revise my plan, and my *new* plan involves you.'

'We're almost at the lab,' I say. 'You can share your plan with us when we get there.'

'Okay.'

Once we reach Lab 17, I introduce Aeon to my father.

'Is your mother here?' Aeon asks. 'I'd like to meet her.'

Without turning, I gesture to the large, sealed glass jar on the bench behind me.

Aeon cocks his head to one side. 'Are you pointing to the bottle of – is that tapeworms?'

'That,' my father says, 'is my wife, Rose Fox. What remains of her, anyway.'

Aeon's eyes widen momentarily. 'I'm sorry.'

My father nods. 'When the portal imploded – I'm sure you heard about it – Rose was trapped inside it. It finally spat her out on Rhybor, but she was spaghettified in the process. Liberty brought her remains home.'

'When's the funeral?' Aeon asks.

'We had it this morning,' my father says, picking at his fingernails. 'We decided that Rose would be comfortable resting in a jar of formaldehyde in a lab.'

Aeon shows no surprise at the unusual interment. 'Well, again, I offer my condolences, and I'm sorry to impose on you at such a difficult time.'

'Liberty and I are trying to keep busy, so visitors are a good distraction.'

Aeon nods. 'In that case, perhaps I can be of service.'

Goose bumps prickle all down my arms. Aeon is too smooth, false. I'm liking him less and less by the minute.

'What service are you offering?' my father asks.

'I'd like to test your portal with some specific Rhyborian coordinates,' Aeon says, 'as well as some communications equipment.'

My father drums his fingers on his workbench. 'Okay. And?'

'I'd like your daughter to—'

'I have a name,' I say. 'Remember?'

Aeon frowns. 'Of course. Dr Fox, I'd like Liberty to accompany me to Rhybor.'

My father sits upright on his stool. 'Because?'

'Can I assume that you know that I am from Rhybor originally?'

'Yes, I do know that.'

'Good. According to your—' Aeon stops and clears his throat before correcting himself. 'According to *Liberty*, Rhybor is not as it was when the portal collapsed twenty years ago. An alien race has invaded; my people are under siege. We – my people – are going to need help to rid Rhybor of the invaders.'

My father takes a deep breath then exhales slowly. 'And you think Liberty is a soldier?'

'No,' Aeon admits, 'but I sense in her qualities that could easily be developed, that would aid us in this matter.'

'In this *war*, you mean?' my father says, getting to his feet. 'Let's not mince words.'

Aeon shrugs. 'Fine. I sense in her qualities that could easily be developed, that would aid us in this *war*.'

My father turns to me.

'Liberty, do you want to go?' he asks.

From what I've learned about wehrdragons so far, they are not my favourite species and I'm not sure they are worth risking my life for. But I don't know that I can picture myself returning to school knowing that two of my fellow students – even though they are really weird – are fighting a war on a far-away world while I am running laps of the oval in preparation for the Cross Country Carnival.

I should probably stay and complete my senior year. The finish line is in sight. Even though I don't need the final piece of paper because

Lourdes Stunt Academy has already accepted me, Mum would have wanted me to complete my studies.

'If you go,' my father says, 'I'll come with you.'

I peer at him through narrowed eyelids. 'Really? Why?'

My father opens his hands and starts his checklist. 'One,' he says, 'I want to try out this portal that Rose and I made. Two, I want to see the place where she died – maybe I'll leave a little marker there in her honour. Three, if you go to help your friends, I'll be there to support you.'

I don't actually count Felix and Elvira as friends. They are school acquaintances but I keep that to myself.

'Even if it means not finishing my senior studies?' I ask.

'Wars don't wait,' my father says, 'but your studies will. You could complete your senior certificate anytime. You're a smart cookie.'

I hope Aeon is paying attention to this. Unlike him, *my* father wouldn't ditch his daughter in some weird place, abandoning her to fight alone.

'Righto,' I say, turning to Aeon. 'We're in. When do we leave?'

'My stuff is in my van outside,' Aeon replies. 'I'm ready when you are.'

I check my watch. 14:00.

'Come home with us,' I say. 'You can wait while we pack and we'll leave tonight.'

'I could just meet you here at a certain time,' Aeon suggests.

I don't bloody think so. I wouldn't trust this guy as far as I could spit.

'If we really are a *team*,' I say, 'then we start acting like one. And we start now.'

Aeon nods once. 'Fine.'

∞

It has just gone midnight and my father is making the final tweaks to the portal for our journey to Rhybor. The poor sucker who ends up reviewing the security footage for Lab 17 won't believe their eyes. I test the throttle of my quad bike and it responds with a gratifying rumble. We each have a quad bike – me, my father and Aeon – loaded up like we'll be camping in the wilderness for a month.

Despite the danger this trip represents, or maybe because of it, my stomach is a flurry of butterflies. This will be no ordinary trip through the portal. I cast a glance over my shoulder at the glass jar on the bench containing my mother's remains.

'Wish us luck, Mum,' I murmur. 'We are gonna need it.'

'Are you ready, Aeon?' my father calls.

'I am,' Aeon replies, holding an apple in the air.

My father nods. 'First portal opening in three … two … one!'

A bright flash in the belly of the portal is quickly followed by a new scene. A desert landscape in the evening. Aeon pitches the apple through the portal opening, followed by three more in quick succession.

Aeon cups his hands around his mouth and yells, 'How do you like them apples?' He turns to my father. 'Next!'

My father nods. 'Second portal opening in three … two … one!'

Aeon fires a handful of apples through this portal as well, this time on the banks of a forest stream. The portal opening and apple throwing routine will repeat twice more before we get to the main event.

Aeon is still a prat in my books but he's not stupid. When I told him of the Kauri's ability to identify locations where portals had opened, he came up with an idea which is so ridiculous it almost has to work. Four openings, where all they'll find is apples. And while the Kauri race from site to site investigating each opening, they will hopefully be blind to the one we actually use – the one in the sky.

Like on Earth, Rhybor's polar regions glow with shimmering auroras. Aeon's theory is that if we open a portal in the middle of the Northern Lights, the magnetic interference generated by the aurora will make our portal opening impossible to detect. That does leave us with the slight problem of arriving on Rhybor in mid-air – riding quad bikes. Nothing a good parachute can't fix though.

'I think we're ready for our turn now, Dr Fox,' Aeon says.

My father salutes. 'Start your engines, folks.'

'Remember, medium revs when we hit the ground,' I say. 'We don't want to spin out on the rocky ground.'

My father winks at me and I hope my mother is watching over us. I flick on my Go-Pro. When I get to Lourdes Stunt Academy – assuming I survive this crazy escapade – they are going to want to see this.

The portal springs to life again, this time revealing an eerie, hypnotic pool of glowing green and yellow.

Aeon barks an order. 'Liberty, go!'

I snap my goggles in place over my eyes before twisting the throttle and aiming my quad bike at the heart of the portal. I barely suppress a squeal of excitement as I rocket into the opening. The transition from Lab 17 to the frigid sky of Rhybor is instantaneous and, before I can blink, I'm plummeting towards the ground.

I jam my left thumb on the recently installed button on the handlebar to deploy the chute. With the chute open so soon we have more hangtime, which increases the risk of being seen from below; however, delaying opening the chute means the bike might tip over – a decidedly worse alternative.

Clumps of snow cling to the patches of hardy grasses that sprout defiantly from the rocky ground. But instead of white, the snow is a vibrant green thanks to the iridescent glow overhead. There isn't time to admire the view though. I twist the throttle and brace for impact – making sure I clench my jaws tight so I don't bite off any of my tongue.

I slam down so hard I feel like the asteroid that wiped out the dinosaurs on Earth, although, the drag of the parachute helps as I brake, bringing my quad bike to a skidding halt. Panting hard, I turn to see if my father has landed safely.

My father roars up beside me, spinning almost a full revolution as he brings his quad bike to a stop. Icy gravel sprays over me. I shield my face with my hands.

'Did you see that, Lib?' my father cries. 'Nailed it!'

I smile, partly because his enthusiasm is infectious, but mostly because I'm relieved I didn't just lose my remaining parent.

'Yeah, Dad,' I say. 'You totally nailed it.'

'You were pretty good, too,' he says, winking at me.

I raise one eyebrow. 'Is that so?'

My father reaches over and claps me on the shoulder. 'Just kidding – you were amazing, Lourdes won't have much to teach you, I'd say.'

Aeon joins us and I endure another gravel shower.

'I'm glad there's no one else coming,' I mutter.

'You'd better hope there *isn't* anyone else coming,' Aeon says, scanning our surroundings. 'We need to ditch these parachutes somewhere out of sight though, just in case.'

'Yep,' I agree. 'ASAP.'

We dismount, detach the chutes and roll them up.

'Hand them over,' Aeon says, holding out his hands. 'I'll stash them under those boulders down the hill there.'

Happy to be relieved of that duty, I hand over my chute and climb back aboard my quad bike.

My father settles himself back into his seat. 'This ought to be good,' he says, watching Aeon. 'How's he going to shift those rocks? They are huge.'

'Wehrs are stronger than humans,' I say, 'and they really like to show off about it.'

Once Aeon has disposed of the parachutes, he jogs back up the slope.

'We need to move,' he says. 'My parents' home is about three thousand kilometres south.'

'Lead the way,' I say.

Three thousand kilometres is the best part of two days riding. This continent is massive. We're almost as far north as one can get, and when we reach the Elegand's home, we'll have driven less than half its length. It's freezing here, but Aeon assures us his forest home never sees snow.

Chapter 25

Liberty

Aeon parks his quad bike under a stand of sequoias at the edge of a mountain trail and signals for us to kill our engines.

'We're here,' he says.

My father dismounts and stretches. 'Please tell me we're on foot from here.'

'Rest here,' Aeon says in a hushed voice. 'I will go inside for recon. It's been twenty years since I was last here. I can't assume that my parents are still here – or that this area is safe.'

Inside my head, a warning bell tinkles. 'I'll join you.'

'The entrance is over a hundred metres up,' Aeon says, 'so I'm flying up there. I'll be back before you get half way up the trail.'

'But you're so strong,' I say. 'You could surely take a passenger.'

Aeon's eyes narrow. 'You don't want to stay here with your father?'

'I can take care of myself,' my father says, puffing out his chest. 'The bikes and I are undercover. It'll be fine.'

'You'll be more of a hindrance than a help, Liberty,' Aeon says.

I glare at him, arms folded across my chest. 'I have a jetpack in my kit,' I say. 'Would you prefer I used that?'

Aeon's eyes bulge momentarily. 'No! Okay, fine. I'll take you.'

He kicks off his shoes and without another word he walks a short distance away, disappearing into the gloom of the forest. Moments later, a magnificent silver dragon slinks back towards us, his robe draped over his neck. Muscles ripple under scales that look like they've been fashioned from pearl shells, their gleaming lustre breathtaking, even in the low forest light. Ribbons of smoke curl from his nostrils and frame his glowing brown eyes.

As I consider how to mount a dragon, Aeon springs into the air – the downdraft from his leathery wings nearly knocking me off my feet. I raise my arms to shield my face and his claws snatch at my wrists.

'Liberty!' my father cries as my feet leave the ground.

The ligaments securing my arms to the rest of my skeleton stretch to their limits as Aeon beats his way skyward. This is absolutely not how I pictured this ride, although I shouldn't be surprised. Alvin carried Gemini off this way when we stole the Kauri's Razor. My hands grasp uselessly at thin air. My wrists are turned outwards so my hands can't latch onto his ankles. Stomach churning, I realise I am completely at his mercy. He could let go at any moment and I'd have no chance to save myself.

I insisted on joining him because I didn't trust him to return to us after his recon. But I trusted him to fly me safely to the mountain entrance? Stupid. In my defence though, I hadn't envisaged this method of flying. I was thinking horseback style rather than flying fox.

Aeon dumps me on a ledge in front of a narrow opening in the mountain, then lands next to me. I rub my aching wrists as he transforms back into human form.

When he is robed, he crouches beside me. 'Enjoy the ride?' he asks.

He's such an arse.

'Not so much,' I reply.

'Well, let's not hang about out here,' he says.

Damn right. It's cold up here.

Aeon strides towards the entrance with me on his heels. I unhook my torch from my belt as we enter the tunnel and flick the switch for the highest setting. Aeon has no torch so I assume mine is giving enough light or he has supercharged dragon eyesight.

'Doesn't smell right in here,' he mutters, jogging ahead.

I quicken my pace to keep up with him, but soon the jogging becomes a sprint.

'Hey!' I say. 'Wait up.'

'If you can't keep up, you shouldn't have come.'

'I get that you're keen to see if your parents are here but we should be careful,' I say, panting. '*Especially* if it doesn't smell right.'

Aeon grunts but dials back to a jog. For the next few minutes, I follow him without speaking, my focus on trying to keep the torch light steady so I don't trip over.

'Door ahead,' Aeon says. 'Lower your torch.'

I do as he says. I can make out thin streaks of light ahead; light leaking out through the gaps around a door.

Click.

The sound of a sliding bolt echoes up the tunnel. Is that someone locking a door or unlocking it?

The shower of light answers my question. The door is open and the silhouette of a man appears.

'Aeon?' the man whispers. 'Is it really you?'

'Father!' Aeon cries, embracing the man tightly and slapping him on the back.

'Come inside,' the man says. 'You must tell us everything.'

'Us?' Aeon says. 'Mother is here too?'

'No, she's off on an errand. Elvira is here though.'

The man stands aside and Aeon walks inside.

I approach the door and extend my hand. 'I'm Liberty Fox,' I say. 'I go to school with Elvira.'

'Aedonis Elegand,' he says, shaking my hand firmly. 'Welcome.'

'Nice to meet you.'

Aedonis nods before turning to his son. 'I should warn you, Aeon,' he says, 'that your daughter has been through a lot. Her friend, Felix, has been captured by the Kauri, and a wehr ally she met here has also fallen victim to the invaders when they breached our home the day before yesterday. Your mother and I only just got her out. It was a harrowing experience for her. And if that wasn't enough, she has visited Karina too.'

I keep my position just inside the doorway as Elvira – as if summonsed – enters from a side room. She is barely recognisable. It's mostly the bald head, but also the grey trackpants and sweatshirt – a far cry from the fashion she wears at school.

'Daughter,' Aeon whispers as he approaches her. 'Is Gemini here too?'

I thought he'd ask after her well-being, or why her head is shaven – because I'm keen for an answer on that one.

When he reaches out to caress her cheek, Elvira swats his hand away.

She glares at him. 'I have a *name!*'

Aeon opens his mouth, but Elvira cuts him off.

'I don't want to hear it,' she snaps, pushing past him and dashing out the door beside me.

Aeon shakes his head. 'That's not how I thought our reunion would go.'

'Did you actually give it any thought?' I say.

Both Aeon and Aedonis look at me – Aeon's eyes are narrow slits, while his father's are almost bulging out of their sockets.

'And you'd have done it differently?' Aeon says through gritted teeth.

'Certainly would have,' I say. 'I reckon I'd have started with a big hug, and then added "Elvira, it's so good to see you. I have missed you terribly, beloved daughter. I am sorry it has been so long".'

Aeon takes two steps towards the door. 'I'll just go and—'

I step left, barring his exit. 'I'll go and talk to her.' I look past him to Aedonis. 'While I'm gone, how about you give your son some parenting tips – he could clearly use some.'

Without waiting for a response, I flick on my torch and head back up the tunnel, eventually finding Elvira sitting on the ledge at the tunnel entrance with her legs dangling over the side. I sit beside her.

For a minute, the only sound is the whine of the frigid breeze, but then I say, 'Want to talk about it?'

Elvira stares straight ahead. 'What is "it", exactly?'

'Whatever you want "it" to be,' I reply. 'Felix, your father, Karina, Alvin, Gemini …'

Elvira snorts. 'What? We're suddenly best friends? Why should I talk to you? Why should I *trust* you?'

'I'm not asking for trust,' I say, 'but you might consider that of everyone around you, I'm the only one who's not a threat to you.'

Elvira turns to me. 'Really? You think that?'

I meet her gaze. 'Yes.'

'You're a cold fish, Liberty,' Elvira says. 'I have no idea what Felix sees in you.'

I can't think of a constructive response to that comment, so I let it slide.

Eventually, Elvira says, 'What are you doing back here anyway?'

'My father wanted to see where my mother died,' I say, not prepared to admit that her father requested my presence here.

'Uh-huh.'

I sigh. 'And, I would have felt weird sitting in English class knowing that two of my fellow students were on another planet fighting off a race of cyborg aliens.'

'So, you want to be a soldier now?'

'Not really. Mostly I'm here for my dad; I haven't totally figured out the rest yet.'

Elvira scoffs, running her hand over her recently shaved head. 'Could it be true? The amazing Liberty Fox really *doesn't* have everything figured out? Is she human after all?'

I swivel, swing my legs back onto solid ground and roll onto one knee ready to stand. 'I'll give you some space, Elvira,' I say.

Her hand latches onto my forearm, but her eyes are on the horizon.

'I'm going to find him,' she murmurs.

'Felix?'

Elvira nods.

If the Kauri captured him he's probably dead, but I say, 'Do you know where he is?'

'In the city … somewhere.'

She has no clue. But since it's not helpful for me to point this out to her, I sift through my brain for something positive to offer her. An idea finally swirls into focus.

'You're planning on a disguise to get you into the city?'

The corners of her mouth twitch, hinting at a smile. 'Yes. I am transitioning to a hairless being, and my grandmother is preparing the dyes as we speak.'

'You're going to turn blue?'

Elvira nods. 'And I'll have silver tattoos on my scalp as well.'

I wince. 'Sounds painful.'

'I expect it will be,' she says. 'It's going to be an intricate design.'

I run my eyes over her. 'Are you planning to get taller?'

'Not all Kauri are tall,' she says. 'The soldiers are, but many who reside in the city are not. Depends on their function.'

'Sounds like *you've* got it all figured out.'

'Far from it,' Elvira says. 'It's going to be tricky with no contacts on the inside.'

My next question tumbles from my lips before my brain QAs it. 'Do you want help on this mission?'

She glances at me, lips pursed. 'Are you for real?'

Timing could be an issue. My priority is really my family, taking Dad to visit the site where I found my mother's remains. But I did kind of want to help out my school friends – acquaintances – otherwise I'd be sitting cramming for my final exams.

'Yes,' I say at last.

'Are you sure you wouldn't rather fight the cyborgs? You being the adrenaline-junkie-kung-fu-panda-stunt-double person and all?'

'Open warfare – not really my thing,' I say. 'A covert rescue mission sounds more my style. And besides, if you and Felix, who have actual wehr heritage, aren't *actually* on the frontline, fighting to save your species … why should I be?'

'Fair enough,' Elvira says.

I hold out my hand and we shake to seal the deal.

'Plan?' I ask.

Elvira crinkles up her nose. 'To be honest, I haven't got much past the disguise at this stage.'

Typical actor, I think, *stuck in wardrobe.*

I keep a neutral expression. 'Tell me what you know about Kauri culture. Maybe I can help flesh out your plan.'

Elvira inhales deeply and the crease lines on her forehead fade. Her back straightens, opening her diaphragm. I sense what's coming – a performance rather than a factual presentation, which is what I'd prefer. I did ask though, so I settle back to enjoy the show.

∞

The stones are where I left them, huddling on the sand, marking the spot where my mother died. In the predawn light a cool breeze whips around us, stirring the sand at our feet. The shifting sands have already cast a fine veil over the cairn. In time they will blanket the stones completely. I'm lucky I've found them today.

'I thought I was prepared for this, Liberty,' my father says, 'but I'm really not.'

Tears prick the corners of my eyes but I don't let them go. 'Me neither.'

'My Rose died, alone, on an alien planet,' my father whispers. 'I sent her to her death.'

I snort. 'Don't say that. You were both equally committed to that portal. It could have been either of you – or both of you – who ended up here.'

My father wipes his nose with a handkerchief. 'I wish I could trade places with her.'

I don't respond to that. Instead, I say, 'Mum would be happy you got it working.'

'Yeah. But now I wonder if it was the right thing to do. Opening the portal has opened up something much bigger – much scarier.'

He's right, but this isn't the place to talk about it. There'll be time for that when we get to Gyoma Lake. I try to push that distraction – as well as all the other ones – aside so I can focus on my mother. Karina and the portal, Felix and Elvira, Aeon and his parents, Gemini, Alvin and Grim, the Kauri … I picture all of them in a steel box and then me slamming the lid closed and sitting on it.

I wanted to leave something permanent here to mark the place where my mother died. Something more fitting than a random pile of stones. Mum would have hated a plaque, and here in the desert, there's nothing to attach it to anyway. Sparse shrubs and prickly grasses don't lend themselves to lasting memorials.

I reach for my pendant, pinching my Liberty coin between my fingers. I'd thought about leaving this here, but the thought of the desert swallowing it and leaving no trace was enough to make me throw that idea out too.

In the end, I realised there was nothing I could leave here that would last for long – let alone forever. The best my father and I can do is visit here together and try to imagine what my mother's final thoughts and feelings might have been. I want to believe her end was peaceful, but that seems unlikely. My mother had a good heart and I am nowhere near ready to be without her. She'd allow me a few tears, but then she'd expect me to get on with things.

Life is for living.

'Life is for living,' I murmur.

My father hooks his arm around mine. 'Life is for living,' he echoes. 'I'm glad you brought her home, Liberty.'

We stand in silence as the sun peeks over the horizon, and when the golden disc is fully visible, my father says, 'We should go.'

I nod. If we stay much longer, Aeon will probably come and interrupt us anyway. He's keen to get to Gyoma Lake to see Gemini. And I need to prepare for my trip to Ilion with Elvira so she can try to save Felix. I'm still not totally sure why I volunteered for this crazy mission, but I can't back out now.

Chapter 26

Felix

My eyes have been closed so long, I wonder if the skin of my eyelids has grown together, fusing them shut permanently. I can't stand to look at the leech-like silver tubes that snake from my body, so keeping my eyes closed has been my sole focus. There isn't anything else in the room to look at anyway.

It seems like I've been here for days. I've dozed off several times but it's difficult to tell how long I've slept. Or even how long I'm awake in between. Okita hasn't visited again. I really didn't expect him to since he said his fond farewell, but any company – even Kauri – would be welcome.

A soft rumbling sound intrudes on my thoughts, alerting me to something that might be interesting or entertaining. My eyelids resist momentarily but then surrender. My pupils aren't as quick to adjust though. All I can make out is a dark, blurry blob against the doorframe. I blink a few times to coax my pupils into action. Finally, they cooperate.

'Grim?'

The cat rubs his face against the doorframe, marking his territory. I'm not sure that marking the perimeter with cat pheromones will stop the Kauri, or their pets if they have them, but Grim's appearance is welcome despite his redundant defence strategy.

'Grim, where did you come from?' I say, wriggling in my chair.

The cat saunters over towards me, tail waving hypnotically in the air. At the foot of the chair, he crouches and springs, landing on my lap. His paws are velvety but his claws are not.

I wince.

Grim puts a testing paw on my abdomen and I tense instinctively. He climbs until his hindlegs are on my abdomen and his front paws on my pecs. Staring into my eyes, he puts his wet nose against mine. I hold my breath until my head starts to spin.

Grim purrs and rubs his face against my cheek, breaking the spell. I release the air in my lungs and gulp in more. When my breathing stabilises, I move onto my next task which is avoiding the cat's sneeze-inducing whiskers tickling my nose.

'Yeah, it's great to see you, Grim,' I say, flicking my head from side to side, 'but do you reckon we could save this until *after* I've escaped?'

Grim digs his claws into my chest, which I interpret as 'no'. He does stop rubbing his face against mine, at least, but moves onto his next trick which is even less desirable.

'Cut that out!' I say, thrashing in my seat now. 'You lick your butt with that tongue. I don't want you licking my face with it.'

Eventually, he relents and sits back, resting on his haunches.

Meow.

'*Meow* to you, too,' I say. 'Now, do you have a plan to get me out of here by any chance?'

Grim flicks one ear before twisting his body and slinking along my left leg. When he gets to my ankle, he teeters before pouncing on the narrow cylinder protruding from the floor between my feet.

Click.

The metal bracelets around my wrists and ankles retract.

'Grim,' I say, rubbing my chaffed wrists, 'you're a genius.'

The cat leaps to the floor and saunters towards the doorway as I ease myself off the chair.

My next problem is the tubes. For a moment I'm routed to the spot. Can I just pull the tubes out? I study the ones on my hands and forearms but can't tell how they are connected. They're like silver veins on the outside of my body, grafted to my skin.

I pinch one between my fingers and pull, expecting to see a patch of skin on the back of my hand tear away with it. It doesn't though. A couple of drops of pale-yellow fluid dribble from the end of the tube before it seals over, and there is no mark on my hand. It's as if the tube was never there.

I rip all the tubes from my arms before starting on my torso. It takes half a minute to remove all the tubes and by the time I'm done, the floor looks like the morning after a snake rave party.

No alarms have sounded yet, but I know I'm on the clock. Getting out of the chair was probably the easy part.

I creep to the doorway where Grim is waiting. As I arrive, he looks up, his eyes tracking the last part of my masculine anatomy to stop moving.

'Don't even think about taking a swipe at that,' I say, holding up a warning finger.

Grim's baleful glare suggests that it would be beneath him to do such a thing but I'm not fooled.

I glance left and right to find that the grey corridor is curved. Entranceways like the one I'm standing in are the only features. There are no visible cameras, signs or other markings.

'No good reason to choose one way over the other,' I murmur.

Meow.

Grim is to my left, halfway to the next entranceway.

'Do you want to keep it down?' I whisper.

Meow. Meow.

Maybe if I pick him up, he'll be quiet? I take a couple of steps towards him and he scampers out of arms' reach.

'Fine,' I say. 'Be like that then.'

Grim purrs as he saunters off along the corridor. After half a dozen steps, he looks back over his shoulder.

Meow!

I don't speak cat but I'm getting the idea that he wants me to follow him, and it's probably not a bad strategy since he's managed to avoid the

Kauri this long. We pass four arched entranceways as we creep along the corridor, but I keep my eyes on Grim. If there is anyone in the rooms, I hope they've got their eyes closed. Anyone who sees a naked man walking past is bound to alert security.

When Grim reaches an open fire door, he disappears through the opening. I follow him, hoping we're heading for a basement where there's a getaway car and maybe some clothes.

But when I make it into the fire escape, I find Grim heading upstairs.

'Really?' I say. 'If your getaway plan is a helicopter on the roof, I hope you can fly it.'

I follow the cat up fifteen floors before he slinks out of the fire escape. A quick glance up and down the corridor here reveals something more like a hotel than a research facility. The gold-edged blue carpet looks brand new and the walls are painted pale grey. At least it is Kauri-free.

The rooms on this floor have doors rather than open archways, and Grim is sitting in front of one to my right, his dark tail swishing back and forth.

I join him in front of the door. 'I hope there are clothes in here,' I say as I push the handle.

The door opens into a spacious room. The silver curtains are drawn back, giving a panoramic view of the city through the floor-to-ceiling glass that runs the length of the room. We must be over a hundred storeys up, maybe two hundred.

Small aerial vehicles stream between the sleek skyscrapers of the sprawling city. There are no lane markings at altitude but the traffic flow is orderly despite its hectic pace.

'Well, this is unexpected,' a voice says.

My gaze flicks from the view outside to the wall to my left. A Kauri woman is strapped to a chair similar to the one I escaped from. Unlike me, she has clothes on. And she doesn't appear to have any tubes attached to her. Some people get special treatment here it seems. *Kauri*, I remind myself. Not people.

But what is a Kauri doing here like this?

'There are clothes in the drawers,' she says. 'Help yourself. *Please.*'

I feel the heat in my cheeks as I open a drawer and pull out a sleeve-less shirt and cotton pyjama pants. With my back to her, I dress quickly. When I turn around again, Grim is perched on her lap.

'That's better,' she says. 'Is this your cat?'

'No,' I mumble. 'He belongs to a … friend.'

'What's his name?'

'Alvin.'

The Kauri looks at the cat. 'Nice to meet you, Alvin.'

'N-no,' I say. 'My *friend* is Alvin. Well, he's kind of a friend; I haven't actually known him that long but … you don't need to know that, do you? The cat's name is Grim.'

The Kauri frowns. 'Okay. And what's *your* name?'

'Steve Rogers,' I say. 'What's your name?'

Her frown deepens. 'I … I'm not sure.'

'Really?' I say. 'How can you not know your name?'

'I didn't say I *don't* know it,' she says, shaking her head. 'The problem is that I have a name in my head, but when I look at this body,' she glances down, 'they don't match. This body isn't right. And my brain feels weird too, like it's got empty spaces … I remember some things but I feel like there's a lot missing.'

'Okay,' I say. 'I'm not sure—'

'You're human, aren't you?' she says.

I shrug. 'Um, sort of.'

'Sort of?'

'Long story,' I say. 'How about we go with "yes"?'

She nods. 'I think I should look like you. I *think* I'm human.'

Okita's face flashes in my mind. *We have the capacity to remove a lifeform's consciousness and transplant it into another host body. It will not be long before we can monitor thoughts.*

I take a few steps towards her. 'What do you *think* your name is?'

'Rose,' she says softly. 'Rose Fox.'

Awkward. Liberty's mother has just seen me naked. But I guess that isn't the most important thing right now.

'Everyone thinks you're dead,' I say.

Her eyes widen. 'You know who I am?'

'I know who you *were*,' I say.

'You're from Earth?'

I nod. 'My name isn't Steve Rogers. It's Felix Dangerfield. I go to school with Liberty.'

'Liberty,' she murmurs. 'Is she here?'

'She was,' I say, 'but she went back to Earth. She took your ... body back home.'

'My body ... spaghettified?'

I nod. 'Yep. That.'

'Tell me everything,' she says. When I hesitate, she smiles. 'It's okay. I can take it.'

I tell her as much as I know about her demise and her expression barely changes.

'Interesting,' she murmurs when I'm done. 'The Kauri must have captured my consciousness somehow and implanted it into this synthetic structure. I *have* to know how they did that!'

Her eyes are sparkling. Well, not *her* eyes. The Kauri's eyes. This isn't Liberty's mother. This isn't really Rose Fox. She's a Kauri version of Rose. Kauri-Rose.

'I need to get out of here,' Kauri-Rose says. 'Help me?'

Liberty would have to be impressed if I rescued her mother – her mother's consciousness anyway. I can't afford to screw this up.

I stride to the raised panel at the foot of her chair and study the array of buttons. Grim managed to find the right one to release me so it couldn't be that difficult. I press one button and the backrest reclines. I choose another and raise the left armrest.

'Sorry,' I say. 'The symbols are confusing ... they—'

Grim leaps onto the panel and the wrist and ankle restraints snap open instantly.

Bloody cat.

Kauri-Rose rubs her wrists as she swings her legs over the side of the chair. 'Okay. Where to now?'

'Basement to find a getaway car?' I suggest.

Kauri-Rose looks out the window. 'Car? Maybe they have something we could fly?'

'*You* can fly?'

She shrugs. 'How hard could it be?'

'Righto,' I say, scooping Grim up off the chair and handing him to Kauri-Rose. 'You're the Kauri escorting test subjects to new accommodation. Pity you don't have a blaster or something.'

'Blasters,' she says, eyelids fluttering. 'Basement Level 10 in this wing.'

'How do you know that?'

Kauri-Rose taps the side of her head. 'Building specs are in this brain.'

We reach the weapons' store without being intercepted by Kauri.

I whistle softly into the gloom as we exit the elevator. 'This whole floor is weapons?'

Kauri-Rose nods. 'This one and thirty-nine others,' she says.

'Forty floors of weapons? That is a *lot* of weapons.'

'Agreed. But let's just get what we need and get out of here.'

'Can you find out where the "squidgers" are?' I ask.

'Squidgers?' Kauri-Rose closes her eyes. 'Devices that remove the space down to the subatomic level within lifeforms so they can be stored in the Seed.'

'Yep. Can you tell me where they are?'

'Blasters first,' Kauri-Rose says, 'and I'll search my database for the location of the squidgers on the way.'

I nod as I follow her to the blasters section where we find at least a dozen different types.

'Take what you can easily carry,' she says. 'And by the way, your squidgers – ten floors down.' Her eyes narrow. 'How do you know about them … and what do you want them for?'

I quickly explain to her what Okita told me about how the Kauri capture lifeforms.

Her frown deepens. 'This is troubling.'

'The Rhyborians are planning to fight back,' I say, 'and they're going to need all the help they can get – weapons, intel … everything. Whatever we can get.'

'A war?'

I nod.

'I really just want to get home to my family,' Kauri-Rose says.

'Looking like that?' I say. 'I don't reckon it's a good idea for you to turn up on Earth looking so … blue.'

'Okay, fair point,' she says, 'but I don't know how much use I'll be in a war.'

I don't know how much use I'll be either but I'm not admitting that to her. 'Look, for now let's get a couple of squidgers and then find somewhere in the city to lie low while we make a plan.'

Kauri-Rose grips my forearm. 'If you're from Earth, why are you so invested in this?'

'A good friend of mine – her family comes from here.'

She holds my gaze. Finally, she says, 'There's more, which you'll tell me once we're out of here.'

I nod. 'Sure.'

'We should hurry. The Kauri don't patrol the building – they assume it is impossible for prisoners to escape – but if their data reads are off they'll come and investigate.'

'You're talking about the tubes and stuff I had in me?'

'Yes.'

'Okay. Let's move.'

Chapter 27

Elvira

I hold my breath as the gyrocopter swerves right to merge into a north-bound traffic stream. I'm purely ornamental in the cockpit. This flight is all Gemini. He stole the gyrocopter, modified it and is now remotely flying it so Liberty and I can attempt our rescue mission. Best guess is that Felix is being held in the palace – what used to be the wehrdragon king's residence but is now Kauri HQ. It's in the middle of the city, so we have a lot of traffic to negotiate to get there.

'Elvira, what can you see?' Liberty calls from behind me.

'The sun setting on a crazy big city,' I call back from the pilot's seat.

Ilion is the shiniest city I've ever seen and my heart swells with pride. *My* people built this. The Kauri have taken it over, but this remarkable city remains a testament to wehrdragon innovation. Massive gleaming skyscrapers sprout from an ordered framework of city blocks interspersed with sprawling parks and gardens. Smooth, wide, multi-level roadways allow traffic to move at speed – though from up here it looks like a cross between a racetrack and a bowling alley.

'Can you see the palace?' Liberty asks.

'Yes,' I say. 'It's hard to miss.'

The palace isn't so much a building as a complex. It's two hundred and ten storeys high and its penthouse soars almost a kilometre above ground level. My grandmother told me that if all the pieces of the complex were laid end to end, they would stretch over a quarter of the way around the planet.

A light on the display flashes red.

'We're making our approach,' I say, 'landing in less than a minute.'

'Hold on,' Liberty says. 'I can't imagine Gemini's remote landings are any better than his actual landings.'

I smile to myself. Part of me hopes he does screw this up because it's heartening to be reminded that he's not perfect. Another part of me knows that will be a problem though. I'm a Kauri pilot escorting a prisoner to the research facility. And a Kauri pilot wouldn't stuff up a landing.

I hold my breath as the building looms larger and I can see our landing pad, which is on Level 100 on the north wing.

10 … 9 … 8 … the numbers on the display tick down as we pass into the building's shadow.

'Five seconds,' I call.

The gyrocopter glides onto the landing platform like a swan landing on a lake.

'Thanks, Gemini,' I whisper, flicking the switch he'd described that puts the remote access system into sleep mode.

I release my harness and the catch on the door before clambering out. Three other vehicles are parked in this hangar but I can't see any Kauri present. We'd hoped an evening mission would mean fewer Kauri on the premises. I draw my blaster from its holster, open the back door and drag my handcuffed prisoner out.

'Let's go,' I say.

The metal door to the main building slides silently aside as we approach. With my blaster pressed against Liberty's ribs, we walk along the carpeted corridor to the elevator. When we are only metres away, a female Kauri rounds the corner ahead and walks directly towards us.

I nod at her as I press the 'up' button. The Kauri nods in return and stands beside me, looking me up and down. Aware that my eyes aren't as round as Kauri eyes, I open mine wider hoping to fool the Kauri with illusion.

The lift doors open and the Kauri walks in, turns around and stands looking straight ahead with her hands clasped behind her back. A shiver runs down my spine. The Kauri hasn't pressed any of the floor number buttons. She doesn't need to. Cyborgs are wireless computers. *That explains the look she gave me when I pressed the 'up' button.*

I press the tip of my blaster against Liberty's back. 'In,' I say.

Liberty glares at the Kauri as she enters the lift.

I mirror the Kauri's pose, hoping that she isn't going to the top floor.

The Kauri nods at Liberty before turning her gaze on me. 'New sample?'

'Yes,' I say.

'Species?' she asks.

'Human,' I say.

'Interesting.'

When the lift doors open on Level 124, the Kauri turns to me and winks.

'Be seeing you,' she says as she exits the lift.

Not if I see you first.

I punch the button for Level 150 – Gemini's best guess at where captives might be held. We exit the lift into a curved corridor. No carpet here – the floor is polished concrete – and the walls are stark white with arched open entranceways at even intervals on the opposite wall.

'Come on,' I say. 'Let's take a look.'

With my hand grasping her elbow, I guide her along the corridor. A peek in each room reveals a range of containment devices. After checking out a dozen rooms, I've seen a large wire cage with a furry six-legged creature sleeping in it; two massive fish tanks – one containing a cat-sized scorpion and the other, iridescent lizards; two cylindrical, liquid-filled tanks containing exotic aquatic creatures I can't identify; a mound of glowing spiky mushrooms; and six empty dentist chairs.

'I reckon we're in the right place,' I murmur.

'Agreed,' Liberty says. 'How about I sit in one of those dentist chairs while you take a poke around?'

'Yep.'

I follow her into a room and take off her handcuffs. Once she's settled in the chair, I hand her my spare blaster.

'Tuck that behind your back,' I say. 'Just in case.'

Liberty nods as I place the restraints over her wrists and ankles, careful not to lock them.

'Comfy?' I say.

'Just get on with it, Elvira,' she mutters.

I nod and stride from the room as I imagine an arrogant Kauri would. A lap of the floor reveals no Felix so I take the fire escape up to the next level. This one is similar to the last, as are the next two. Most rooms are empty except for a few alien creatures I've never seen before. I complete a circuit of five levels before I encounter another Kauri.

In the second room on Level 155, I find a Kauri checking on a prisoner.

The Kauri looks up and his purple lips curl into a smile. 'You're the impostor Tiang saw in the elevator.'

I curse. Pressing the 'up' button was definitely a mistake.

I spin round and sprint for the fire escape. I leap down the stairs two or three at a time – praying I don't faceplant – expecting an alarm to sound any second. By the time I reach Level 150 where I left Liberty, there is still no alarm but, in my mind, I can imagine the Kauri marshalling and ready to nab me.

I bolt from the fire escape into the corridor, turning right but throwing a glance behind me to check for pursuit. Two Kauri break into a run when they see me.

Pumping my arms, I race for the room where I left Liberty.

'Gotta go!' I yell as I skid round the entranceway.

Liberty leaps from her seat, blaster in hand.

She's only a step behind me as we make it back into the corridor.

I snatch at her wrist and grab hold. 'Come on!'

Liberty stumbles but quickly regains her balance. 'What's your plan?'

I scan the entranceways on the curved wall and spy a tantalising glimpse of glass panels through one of them.

I grunt. 'We're going to break the emergency glass.'

'With what?'

The glass wall looms larger as I drag Liberty towards it. 'Your department,' I say.

'Oh, great!'

I glance behind me again. The Kauri are closing on us.

'Blaster!' I say. 'Now!'

The hum of blaster fire is followed by the shattering of glass.

'You're welcome,' Liberty says, waving her blaster. 'But tell me you're not going to—'

'Totally am!' I say, snatching her wrist as I leap through the vacant space where the window used to be.

Together we plunge from the hundred-and-fiftieth floor through the gloom of dusk.

Liberty screams. I smile.

'Trust me,' I yell.

Metres from the concrete, I complete my Shift, relishing the feeling of wind against my wing membranes. With Liberty's wrist firmly in my claws, I beat down hard to slow our landing, which doesn't work as well as I'd hoped. My wings aren't strong enough. They aren't conditioned for this.

We slam down hard and Liberty somersaults several times once I release my hold on her. When she finally comes to a stop, she lies motionless on the roadway. Motorbikes and scooters on the street swerve to avoid us and the sound of screeching tyres fills the air. My sensitive nostrils detect the smell of burning rubber an instant before I'm illuminated by a shaft of light from above.

I freeze.

The Kauri are assembling, intent on my capture. I spin a three-sixty, scanning the terrain while whipping my tail defensively. I can't stay here.

Pouncing on Liberty, I clutch her upper arms in my hind claws before leaping into the air again. Tiny comets – laser fire – whiz past me as I beat my wings frantically to gain altitude. I raise my left wing to sweep towards an alleyway. Though off the main street now, I'm still not safe. Bars and restaurants line the pedestrian mall and hundreds of Kauri are enjoying an evening out. I glide over them with my unconscious comrade dangling from my grasp. Shouts echo down the strip as I pass.

I beat my wings again, desperate for altitude, while my eyes scan for an escape route. I need a secluded space. The buildings here are densely packed but the limited lighting suggests they are sparsely populated. If I can find an empty alleyway, I might be able to find a hiding place. Somewhere I can revise my plan.

I'd like to think I'm weaving a graceful path between the buildings but I'm not. I'm desperately swerving – every twist and turn inspired by sheer panic – to avoid splattering myself on concrete or glass.

Eventually, I find an alleyway devoid of Kauri. I flutter my tired wings, depositing Liberty as gently as I can on the concrete before landing. The sound of aircraft engines sharpens my focus. I scan the alleyway. The buildings lining the narrow roadway here present many possible options in terms of doors.

Assess all *options. Look up. Look down.*

I glance upwards. I *could* fly up onto a balcony. Drawing my gaze down, I flick my eyes along the roadway where drainage grates punctuate the gutters at regular intervals. I shudder. Crawling through drains sounds really unappealing but it is probably the safer option.

Drains often have rats though.

'Balcony it is,' I whisper. 'Fingers crossed I pick one that doesn't have a tenant.'

Decision made, I collect my unconscious cargo. I sail up several storeys before choosing a balcony with a unlit living space beyond it. Landing in a confined space is challenging enough, but having a lifeless body in my grasp increases the difficulty rating significantly. Glad my grandparents can't see me, I tumble onto the tiled floor of the balcony.

Regaining my human form, I inspect my companion more closely, hoping I haven't been carrying a corpse around with me. I put my ear to her chest to see if I can detect a heartbeat. I close my eyes to focus my attention, trying to ignore the sounds of the pursuit from the street below.

And I'm rewarded with a faint echo from inside her chest cavity.

'Okay,' I whisper to her. 'Once I've found some clothes, you'll need to wake up.'

Chapter 28

Felix

Kauri-Rose clutches her head. 'What the …'

'What's wrong?' I ask, placing the squidger on the bar.

Our temporary hideout is an abandoned nightclub six blocks from the palace. Very little of the furniture – or the bottles on the shelves behind the bar – is intact. The Kauri must have blasted it with heavy fire when they invaded here. I've cleared the bar of broken glass and spilled spirits so I have somewhere to study my new weapons while Kauri-Rose comes to terms with her new body and brain. The torchlight is feeble, making my task challenging, but we can't risk anything more.

'There's a transmission,' Kauri-Rose says, eyes closed. 'The cyborgs can broadcast to every individual.'

I shudder. How do they communicate? Are they all connected? Can they track Kauri-Rose?

'Impostors gained access to the research facility but they've escaped,' she says. 'This is unprecedented.'

My heart races. 'Any details about the impostors?'

'Both female,' Kauri-Rose says. 'One, disguised as a Kauri, is confirmed as a wehrdragon; the other is a pale-skinned humanoid.' She cocks her head. 'Wehrdragon? Wehrdragons – shapeshifters. Humanoid default form with the ability to transform into a winged reptile.'

'You sound like a dictionary.'

'Shapeshifters,' she says, ignoring my comment. 'Really?'

I slide off my stool. 'Really,' I say, 'and we have to find that one.'

'Why?'

'Because she's my friend.'

'What? How?'

'Twenty years ago,' I say, 'when the portal between Rhybor and Earth collapsed, there was a secret delegation of Rhyborians stranded on Earth. The indigenous Rhyborians are wehrdragons – shapeshifters. My friend, Elvira, is the daughter of two of those stranded Rhyborians. She's a wehrdragon.'

'How do you know her?'

'I've known her since I was six. We go to school together.'

'You still go to school together?'

I nod. 'Same school that Liberty goes to.'

'You're all friends?'

I clear my throat. 'Not exactly. Elvira and I are a grade behind Liberty.'

'Right,' Kauri-Rose says. 'How can you be sure it's her?'

'I guarantee you, Elvira is the only one crazy enough to come into a city full of Kauri.'

'She came for you?' Kauri-Rose says.

I nod. 'I reckon so.'

'And what about the pale-skinned humanoid?'

'I dunno – and there's only one way to find out.'

'How are we going to find them before the Kauri do?'

I sigh. 'I'm not sure we will. You've got the intel though,' I tap my head with my index finger, 'so where do we start?'

'Maybe,' Kauri-Rose says, 'the question isn't where do *we* start, but where did *they* start their mission? How did they get into the city?'

I shrug. 'They couldn't walk in – riding a motorbike or quad bike would be too obvious … which really only leaves flying.'

'Can your friend fly?'

'When she's a dragon she can,' I say, 'but aircraft … no.'

'Her friend could have?'

Gemini could fly but he couldn't be the female companion. Could the 'friend' be Liberty? I know she went home, but could she have come back? I don't want to say anything to Kauri-Rose in case I'm wrong, so I just say, 'I don't know. It's possible.'

'Let me see if I can find how many aircraft landed at the palace today,' Kauri-Rose says, closing her eyes. 'Fifteen,' she says at last.

'Can you narrow it down? They couldn't have been inside for long. What about within the hour before the broadcast about the wehr?'

'Two,' Kauri-Rose says after a brief pause. 'One on the east tower, one to the north. The one on the north had a single female pilot.'

My pulse quickens. 'That one. Where did it land?'

'A PATV-39 gyrocopter landed on Level 100.'

'Can you tell if it's still there?'

'Um … there's no record of it leaving, so I'm going to say it's still there.'

I drum my fingers on the bar as Grim jumps onto the stool beside me. Elvira has to get out of the city somehow, so she's got to go back for her transport. If I could get there before her … no, too risky. I couldn't get in there.

'I have an idea,' I say.

'Yes?'

'Can you deliver a note? Leave it onboard the gyrocopter?'

Kauri-Rose flinches. 'You want me to go back there?'

'I'd do it – but they'd spot me easily. You *look* like one of them. *You* could get in and out without anyone noticing.'

Grim steps onto the bar and lies down, purring softly. I stroke his dark fur as Kauri-Rose considers her response.

'Okay,' she says. 'Write your note.'

I scrounge around the dingy nightclub for something to write a message on and find a pencil and a pad of sticky notes.

E,
Go to Archie's Café.
I'll be waiting.
F.

I hand the note to Kauri-Rose. Her brow creases as she reads.

'Where is Archie's Café?'

'A few doors down across the street,' I say. 'I can keep watch from here.'

'So, if the Kauri intercept the note, you're not leading them straight to us?'

I nod. 'That's the idea.'

Kauri-Rose smiles. 'I wonder why Liberty never mentioned you. You seem like a smart lad.'

I feel the heat in my cheeks and hope the low light in here means she can't see them going red.

As she tucks a blaster into the waistband of her trousers, I say, 'Be careful. Hurry back.'

Kauri-Rose salutes. 'Roger that.'

∞

While Kauri-Rose is gone, I know I have to come up with a plan. Now that it's just us boys – Grim and me – I feel like I can think more clearly.

I eye the bottles on the wall behind the bar, the few that are still intact anyway. In the movies, the hero would pour himself a shot and knock it back in one go. Then he'd pour himself another, and then probably one more for good luck. Then, he'd come up with the plan to save the world.

On impulse, I round the bar and find myself a glass, then peruse the bottles. I can't read any of the labels. I'd have to choose by colour first and then resort to the sniff test. I unplug a few and the fumes make my eyes water, so I put them back on the shelf. Having the occasional beer with Harry is fine, but drinking unidentified spirits on an alien world when lives are at stake … is probably not the best idea.

Meow.

'Yeah,' I say, taking a larger glass from under the bar and filling it with tap water, 'I'm on it.'

I fill a second glass and place it on the bar in front of Grim. 'Cheers,' I say.

221

Meow.

Grim laps from his glass as my stomach rumbles. I'd give my right arm for a burger and chips right now, but I'll have to settle for water. I need a plan by the time Kauri-Rose returns.

If she returns.

I finish my first glass of water and refill it. 'So, Grim,' I say, 'do *you* have a plan?'

Meow.

'Good. Care to share?'

Meow. Meow.

'Okay. Can't understand what you're saying. I wonder if one of the universal translator things Alvin talked about would help?'

Grim returns his attention to his water glass and I'm left to come up with the plan.

If Elvira wants to defeat the Kauri, she's going to need a lot of soldiers and a lot of firepower. I don't know how many wehrs have avoided capture over the last twenty years, but I can't imagine it'll be enough to threaten the Kauri, who have a huge stash of highly sophisticated weapons.

Not only can the Kauri kill with blasters and rocket launchers, they can also capture their enemies with the squidgers. And then there's whatever device they used to extract Rose's consciousness from her mangled remains and implant it into a synthetic body. Someone definitely needs to destroy that one.

Maybe not just that one. Destroying *all* their weapons would have to put a massive dent in their mission. Blowing up the forty floors of weapons Kauri-Rose and I found would be a good start.

And then there's the Seed that Okita talked about. Where all the lifeforms they've captured so far on their quest are stored. I should steal that. If we could release the wehrs that are in there … it would at least start to even up the teams.

'Hey, Grim,' I say, hurdling the bar. 'You up for a secret mission in the palace?'

Meow.

'Yes? Good. We're gonna steal the Kauri's most precious jewel and then fly away with it.'

Meow. Meow.

I slap my palm on the bar. 'Yep! Brilliant plan! Kauri-Rose is gonna love it. With any luck she'll put in a good word for me with Liberty … when they're finally reunited.'

Chapter 29

Elvira

Liberty is still unresponsive. She's currently in the recovery position on the balcony of the apartment I've broken into. She's breathing. But for how long? She's suffered a brutal concussion. She needs treatment. Professional treatment.

But I need to find Felix too.

First things first though … I need clothes.

I head for the bedrooms, hopeful I'll find something to wear. A film of dust coats everything. I'm guessing that no one has lived here since the Kauri invaded. In a walk-in robe, I find a selection of robes and dresses. The fabrics are hideous and as I pull a blue and yellow striped dress from a rusted metal hanger, a puff of dust wafts into my face. I wrinkle my nose and turn my head, shaking the dress to get rid of the worst of the dust.

When I've decontaminated it as best I can, I slip the wraparound dress over my shoulders, ignoring the musty smell, and tie the sash around my waist. In the full-length mirror, I study my reflection. I look ridiculous. The tie dress is totally at odds with my Kauri visage. Can't be helped. I might need to Shift again so I need to wear something practical. A pair of black slip-on flats completes my outfit.

I've been expecting a crack team of Kauri to smash down the door at any moment but, so far, nothing. Nor have I heard sirens or any sounds of pursuit. Are they toying with me? Like a cat with a lizard? Or maybe immortal creatures don't feel the need to rush anything. Perhaps urgency is a foreign concept to them.

'I'm just one wehr,' I murmur. 'Hardly a threat to them. Maybe I've got a bit of breathing space.' I sit on my backside and cross my legs. 'Think.'

Maybe I should just fly and see how far I get. But what about Felix? I have no leads on his location. I didn't find him at the research facility, but that doesn't mean he isn't there. And even if he isn't there, I have no idea where to start looking.

I need to get the gyrocopter out of the palace. If I could get it back here and load Liberty into it, I'd be ready to make a fast escape if I find Felix. Correction … *when* I find Felix. I have to find him. Failure is not an option. I need to prove to my father that I can do this.

'Gyrocopter it is,' I say aloud.

I can't leave Liberty outside though, so I retrieve her from the balcony and lay her down in the bedroom.

I rummage through the dresser drawer until I find an old lipstick and scrawl a note on the mirror in case she wakes up while I'm gone.

Gone for gyro.
Back soon.
Elvira

I exit the apartment and find the elevator, glancing left and right to make sure no one's watching as I press the 'down' button. It's a smooth ride to the basement and when the doors open, I'm rewarded with a carpark.

'Let's hope there is something with keys in the ignition,' I murmur.

I scout around and it doesn't take long for me to find what I'm looking for. A sportscar. This sleek silver beast looks like it's built for a racetrack and when I test the handle, the door pops open with a hiss. I slide onto the leather seat and turn the key, then jump as the engine roars to life.

Easing the car towards the exit, I pray the carpark door will open automatically. It does, but the metallic shriek as the door retracts makes my fingernails curl.

Once on the road, I slot into the stream of traffic, keeping my eyes straight ahead. I don't want to risk catching the eye of any Kauri in the surrounding vehicles, nor do I want to be mesmerised by the dashboard display inside the car.

As I approach the palace, I'm almost sideswiped by a driverless garbage truck that cuts across three lanes to access the slip-lane entrance to the northern precinct. Instinctively, I yank on the steering wheel and follow him.

The truck disappears down a ramp but I swing my vehicle into a parking bay close to a pedestrian entrance. The tyres screech as I jam my foot on the brake and I narrowly avoid bashing my face on the steering wheel.

'Play it cool, Elvira,' I murmur to myself.

I've got a character who's perfect for this. Nat McGregor. She's not as calm or efficient as Beth, but she's got sass in spades, which is exactly what's needed here. Going undercover in enemy territory means being hyper-vigilant and highly adaptable to changing conditions. Nat is tough. She has a quick mind and a smart mouth. Frankly, she's a bitch.

I didn't use her before because Liberty didn't think we needed her.

I'm up for it, Nat says.

And now … *I* don't think we need her. 'Stand down, Nat,' I say. 'I've got this.'

I pop the door, climb out and kick the door shut again before running after the garbage truck. When I catch up to it, it's already backed up to the disposal chute.

Perfect.

I'm also relieved that it's a driverless vehicle. I don't need anyone to see this.

I race to the chute, kicking off my shoes while I wait for the truck to load its cargo. Then I slip off my dress and Shift. Clutching my stolen dress, I slip into the garbage chute just before the door shuts.

Phew!

The stench makes me dizzy but I have to focus. I need to get to Level 100 to find the gyrocopter.

The walls are smooth, but there is an alcove with a door at each floor level for the occupants to access the chute. Perfect for dragons to latch onto. Springing from floor to floor is going to give my legs a good workout and I hope that none of the building's residents are up for a garbage run just now.

It's slow going but I make it to Level 100 with my dress still in my grasp. I take a minute to steady my breathing so I can listen for signs of life outside the chute before I make my grand entrance.

I slide the door open and jump out onto the carpeted floor. A quick glance up and down the corridor reveals no Kauri, so I Shift and slip into my dress. Silently, I race to the landing pad which is also Kauri-free.

The gyrocopter is still there and, keeping my back to the wall, I approach it warily, scanning the walls and ceiling for CCTV cameras. Aerial vehicles stream past the building as I reach the gyrocopter. The door handle is in reach when I notice a piece of paper on the pilot's seat.

Heart hammering, I squint, but I can't read the note from here.

I crouch and crawl to the door, cracking it open just enough to slip my arm inside to retrieve the note, then scuttle back to my place against the wall.

E,

Go to Archie's Café.

I'll be waiting.

F.

It's Felix's writing, but how could he possibly know to leave a note here?

This smells like a trap.

But it *is* Felix's writing.

'Shit.'

I don't know where Archie's Café is but I could contact Gemini by pager and sort that out. But what about Liberty? I can't leave her for too long. Do I try to get her first and then meet Felix? Or see Felix first and then collect Liberty? Option B means Felix could do the heavy lifting. He'd think that was awesome.

Decision made, I slink into the pilot's seat and fumble under the chair for my pager. With trembling fingers, I send my message.

Can you reprogram next flight? Destination, Archie's Café.

The minutes drag by as I wait for Gemini's response. I sit as still as I can. My disguise is compromised so I definitely can't afford to draw attention from any passing vehicles. The blue dye and silver tattoos are fine, but the metal crescent I had on my head is gone; it didn't survive the Shift when we swan-dived from the window.

Ping.

I glance down at the pager. Gemini has responded.

Go.

I activate the remote access mode and flick the switches to start the engine, and as I buckle my harness, I whisper, 'Okay, Gemini. Let's fly.'

∞

As the gyrocopter touches down in a laneway between two skyscrapers, my stomach flutters. Archie's Café is in an abandoned part of the city. Good in one way – there most likely won't be any Kauri around but, on the other hand, a lone vehicle departing the main traffic stream for a location like this could draw attention.

Pager in hand, I exit the gyrocopter and, from the shadows, scan the street.

Felix is standing across the road – a few doors down – beckoning to me.

Shoeless, I jog across to him. By the time I reach him, he's holding open a door to a boarded-up shopfront.

'Quick,' he says, in a low voice. 'Inside.'

I duck into the gloom and Felix follows me.

He switches on a torch. 'I'm not sure about the new look, Elvira.'

'It's a disguise,' I say. 'A necessary disguise – to save your arse!'

'Right. Follow me.'

I pick my way through the broken furniture – challenging in the measly light – until we reach a staircase at the far end of the room.

'What is this place?' I ask.

'Nightclub,' Felix replies, turning to me. In the low light, his frown lines look like deep crevices. 'Before we go downstairs, I need to warn you about something.'

'Which is?' I say.

'There is a Kauri down here, but she's an ally, so don't freak out.'

I snort. 'Have you ever known me to freak out?'

'Yes,' he says, turning and clomping down the stairs.

I follow and when we reach the next level, I see the Kauri woman sitting at the bar – stroking a cat.

I catch Felix's arm. 'Grim? You found him?'

Felix grunts. '*He* found *me*.'

'He was still on the *Allegro* when they captured you?' I say.

'Yep.'

When we get to the bar, Felix indicates a stool for me to sit on while he strolls behind the bar. He reaches under the counter for a glass, which he fills with water and places in front of me.

'Elvira, this is Kauri-Rose,' he says, gesturing towards the blue woman beside me. 'Kauri-Rose, this is Elvira.'

'Kauri-Rose?' I say.

'Liberty's mother's consciousness in a Kauri body,' Felix explains.

'*What!*'

'It's true,' Kauri-Rose says. 'This body isn't really mine. I'm an unwilling tenant.'

'Uh-huh,' I say.

'You had a companion,' Kauri-Rose says to me. 'Where is she?'

My eyes narrow. 'How do you know I had a companion?'

Again, Kauri-Rose taps her index finger against her head. 'I am part of the Kauri matrix. I received the broadcast that a wehrdragon and a pale-skinned humanoid accomplice breached HQ.'

'Liberty,' I say. 'Liberty came with me to rescue Felix.'

'Liberty?' Felix and Kauri-Rose say in unison.

Felix adds, 'Where is she now?'

'In an apartment a few blocks south of the palace,' I say. 'She has concussion. The escape didn't go completely to plan.'

Kauri-Rose looks at Felix. 'I have to find her.'

Felix nods. 'We will, but we need to coordinate our plans first.'

I stare at Felix. He sounds calm, confident and in control. He can be that way with me, but generally not in front of people he doesn't know well – *or* people he has reason to impress.

'What?' he says, glaring at me.

'Nothing,' I say, raising my hands in surrender. 'Please continue.'

'Tell me what's happened since I saw you last,' he says. 'Did you find your grandparents?'

That feels like weeks ago now, but it's only been six days.

'I found them,' I say. 'We're currently recruiting all the wehrs we can find to take on the Kauri.' I turn to Kauri-Rose. 'No offence.'

'None taken,' Kauri-Rose says. 'I don't consider myself one of them.'

Returning my attention to Felix, I say, 'I've spoken to Karina, too. Gemini is—'

'Karina?' Kauri-Rose interrupts. 'Karina Warhurst? She's here?'

I nod. 'She's a wehrdragon – home at last.'

'Bitch,' Felix mutters.

'You know her?' Kauri-Rose says.

Felix glowers.

I say, 'She's his stepmother.'

'You're kidding! Really?'

'I *wish* she was kidding,' Felix says gruffly. 'Anyway, enough about Karina—'

'No, Felix,' I say, 'she's part of this. We have to talk about her.'

Felix sighs. 'Fine. What do we need to know?'

'Gemini is working with her at Gyoma Lake. He's working on a virus to infect the Star of Truth to destroy the Kauri.'

'Alvin's back there too?' Felix asks.

I bow my head. 'No,' I whisper. 'He died at my grandparents' home. The Kauri attacked us and …'

I can't get any more words past the lump in my throat. Felix puts his hand on mine and gives it a squeeze. 'Your grandparents … are they okay?'

I nod. 'Yep.'

'Good,' he says, withdrawing his hand.

'We're all to convene at Gyoma Lake in two days' time,' I say, 'so the final details of the assault can be thrashed out.'

Felix drums his fingers on the table before turning his attention to Kauri-Rose. 'What's the Star of Truth?'

'The Kauri Star of Truth is a … device,' Kauri-Rose whispers. 'Two interlocking tetrahedra – triangular based pyramids – that contain the collective knowledge of the Kauri. *Uno cognito sum* – one mind, many thinkers. Everything the Kauri have learned about the universe is stored in there. Everything.'

'The ultimate library,' I say.

'It's more than that,' Kauri-Rose says. 'It's not just storage – it is an evolving intelligence. Every individual Kauri can access this device – both to deposit knowledge and draw upon it.'

'Where is it?' Felix asks.

'At the palace,' Kauri-Rose replies.

Felix nods. 'Maybe we should steal that too.'

'Too?' I say. 'Were you planning to steal something else?'

Again, Felix nods. 'The Seed.'

'What's that?'

'A storage system for all the lifeforms they've encountered on their journey across the universe,' Felix says.

'Storage?' I say. 'What do they need storage for? Aren't they just wiping everything out?'

Kauri-Rose shakes her head. 'The Kauri mission,' she explains, 'is Optimisation of the Universe. Thousands of teams are sweeping the universe, cataloguing resources and capturing intelligent lifeforms. Once they've collected all their data they will apply the Prime Formula – the mathematical model of the universe that incorporates matter, energy, space and time. From that analysis, they will then redeploy the universe's assets in the most efficient way possible.'

'And the Seed?' I say.

'Seed*s*,' Kauri-Rose says. 'Each team has its own Seed. The Kauri who are here have their Seed which they have been adding to, from the galaxies they've visited – hundreds of thousands of planets. Once the

Prime Formula has been applied, those lifeforms deemed worthy will be reinstated in a place and time of Kauri choosing.'

'That's nuts!' I say.

'I agree,' Kauri-Rose says, 'and it needs to stop.'

'Thousands of teams?' I whisper. 'How are we supposed to stop that?'

'We don't,' Felix says. 'For now, we work with what's in front of us. We'll deal with the Kauri here on Rhybor first.'

'Okay,' I say. 'We'll all fit into the gyrocopter. We'll pick Liberty up and then head back to Gyoma in plenty of time for the meeting.'

Felix and Kauri-Rose share a look.

'What?' I say. 'What was that look for? What's going on?'

Felix turns to me. '*You* need to take Liberty back, Elvira. Kauri-Rose and I have some preparations to do here in the city.'

I frown. I can't go back empty-handed. I can't.

'What preparations?' I say.

'We're going to steal the Seed and the Star of Truth – and hopefully some weapons as well,' he says.

'But …'

Felix leans forward, resting his elbows on the bar. 'I'll be back in time for the meeting. Two days' time, you said?'

I nod.

'I'll be there.'

'Promise?' I whisper.

Felix winks at me. 'Promise.'

Chapter 30

Liberty

I peek around the black curtain to survey the crowd filing into the auditorium. 'It's almost full,' I say.

'Can you see Felix?' Elvira asks.

'No.'

The meeting is about to begin and Elvira and I have been relegated backstage. Since I'm not a wehr, I have no interest in sitting in the crowd patriotically punching my fist in the air. I'm in no condition to do so anyway. My head is still sore from our crash landing in the city two days ago.

Elvira's in no state to be out there either. The blue stain on her skin will eventually fade, and her hair will regrow to cover the silver tattoos on her head. But for now, her life is in danger if she walks among her fellow wehr. Her hooded jacket gives her limited protection from scrutiny.

'He promised he'd come,' Elvira says.

'I'm sure he'd be here if he could,' I say, surprising myself by actually believing it.

From what I've learned about Felix, his heart is in the right place – even if his execution of any task is cringy and clumsy. I hope his absence isn't an indication of something sinister. As more wehr fill the seats in this subterranean auditorium, I scan them more closely, willing myself to spot Felix amongst them.

'Hey, girls,' my father says, snaking his arm around my shoulder and planting a kiss on my head. 'Almost ready?'

'Ready for what?' I ask as Gemini, Aeon and Karina file in alongside him. 'It's not like we actually have to do anything – except stay out of sight.'

'It's an important job nonetheless,' Aeon says, smiling at Elvira.

I want to vomit at Aeon's forced attempt at paternal kindness, but at least he's trying to be nicer to his daughter.

'Is Felix here?' Gemini asks.

Elvira shakes her head. 'Not yet.'

Karina scoffs. 'That's certainly no loss.'

I know she's a wehr with superhuman strength and enhanced agility, but that doesn't stop me fantasising about dropping her with a well-placed jab to the sternum. She makes Aeon look like father of the year.

Aeon squeezes Elvira's shoulder. 'Don't worry, Elvira. When we reclaim the city, we'll find him.'

'If we're to reclaim the city,' Karina says, 'we've got a job to do first. Shall we get this show on the road?'

Aeon gestures to her to take the stage. 'After you.'

Karina strides onto the stage with Gemini and Aeon behind her. She checks the massive screen at the rear of the stage and appears to like what she sees. Herself. This auditorium can seat five hundred, and there won't be anyone – thanks to the AV system – who can't see or hear what's happening on the stage.

The crowd settles as Karina takes centre stage.

'I should have dragged Felix out,' Elvira mutters, wringing her blue hands.

'You respected your friend's decision,' I say. 'Had you dragged him out, that'd be like telling him you don't trust his judgement.'

Elvira sighs. 'I gotta tell ya, Liberty … in all the years Felix and I have been friends, he's given me plenty of reasons to *not* trust his judgement.'

Karina is about to launch into her speech so I let Elvira's comment slide.

'Rhyborians! Dragons! Welcome!' she cries.

'Welcome home!' someone from the audience calls.

Karina beams as cheering erupts inside the auditorium. 'Thank you,' she says when the noise subsides. 'It's great to be back, isn't it, Aeon?'

Aeon nods. 'Certainly is.'

As the cheering starts again, Aeon raises his hands. 'But of course, we are shocked and saddened by what has happened here in our absence. Our people have been persecuted … and the Kauri must be made to pay.'

This time there is no stopping the raucous shouting, clapping and whistling, which drags on for almost a minute.

It is Karina who signals for silence. 'Friends,' she says, 'we have a big job ahead of us to make the Kauri pay for their crimes. This is a formidable foe; one that won't be easily vanquished. This is not an enemy that can be conquered by hand-to-hand combat—'

'Which is just as well,' someone from the audience shouts, 'because there aren't enough of us left to fight anyhow!'

'Correct,' Aeon says. 'We must find a way to outwit them.'

'Not an easy task either,' Karina acknowledges. 'As you are the ones who have endured their tyranny over the last two decades, you will know that this enemy is highly intelligent, sophisticated and cunning.'

'*Aye!*' the audience cries as one.

'So, we must be *more* intelligent, sophisticated and cunning!' Aeon says.

The cheering is less enthusiastic this time.

'They don't sound confident about that, do they,' my father says quietly.

'No,' I say.

'Probably not surprising,' Elvira says. 'They've spent twenty years witnessing what the Kauri can do.'

Another voice from the audience calls out. 'How do we do that?'

'Good question,' Karina says, gesturing for Gemini to step forward. 'We would like to share with you a suggestion about how we might rid ourselves of this threat. Gemini Holmes is from Earth and was integral in stabilising the portal between that planet and ours. He has developed a weapon we can use against the Kauri. Gemini?'

I pinch my Liberty coin, rubbing it between my fingers as Gemini steps forward.

'As you're aware, the Kauri are cyborgs,' he says, 'and therefore susceptible to computer viruses. If we can set one loose in their Star of Truth, that will compromise the core of their system. From there, as each individual accesses the system, it will be digitally dismantled.'

'Surely they'll figure out that the Star of Truth is infected and stop connecting?' someone calls out.

Gemini nods. 'I have a backup solution – an algorithm that will replicate the virus and transfer itself wirelessly as Kauri make contact with each other.'

'We can infect the entire population and wipe out the scourge of the Kauri for good,' Karina says.

'And the universe will be a safer place – for all species,' Aeon adds.

The cheering is deafening, which is surprising given there are only a few hundred bodies in here.

'I think he's won them over,' my father says.

'Yes. Gemini is definitely charismatic,' I admit.

I feel Elvira's gaze on me but I don't acknowledge her. Whatever her issues with Gemini are, I don't want any part of them.

A chant starts up in the crowd. *'Death to the Kauri! Death to the Kauri! Death to the Kauri!'*

'The war has begun,' Elvira says.

I turn my head, expecting to see her fist clenched over her heart. It's not quite that bad. She *is* smiling though.

I feel like I'm on a Hollywood movie set – like this isn't real life – and my father and I are extras. We don't belong here. This isn't our fight. I remind myself that part of my decision to come here was because I didn't want to sit at school while my classmates were doing something exciting. In hindsight, that was a pretty lame reason to embark on such a crazy mission. But I'm here now and I can't back out.

And there's something else. A niggling truth that's becoming harder and harder for me to ignore. Felix and Elvira have each other's backs. I have lots of acquaintances at school, but no friends like them. None who would try to rescue me from a city overrun by a superior foreign enemy. None that I'd put my neck on the line for that way. Maybe it would be nice to have friends like that? Or maybe it's more downside than upside. Elvira is pretty cut up that Felix isn't here.

Elvira's gasp snaps me out of my musings.

'Felix!'

My stomach clenches as I watch him negotiate the central staircase. I hope he doesn't trip over. My eyes flick to the screen above the stage to check Karina's reaction. Her face betrays nothing.

Gemini is the only other person to move. He strides forward and embraces Felix once he makes it onto the stage.

Elvira clutches my forearm but her eyes are on Felix. 'What's he doing?' she says.

'I have no idea.'

Felix and Gemini exchange words but I can't catch anything of what they're saying from here. Gemini inclines his head in our direction and Felix's gaze follows. I duck behind the curtain as Elvira waves to him.

'Elvira, tell me what's happening,' I say.

She glances at me before returning her attention to the stage. 'Felix is still talking to Gemini. I wish I could lip read – but I can't, so I have no idea what they're talking about. They're both frowning a lot though.'

'Uh-huh.'

'Felix just nodded to Karina,' Elvira says, 'and she nodded back. No words exchanged. God, she's a bitch. Sorry, Dr Fox … didn't mean to swear in front of you.'

'It's fine, Elvira,' my father says. He winks, adding, 'I'm inclined to agree with you.'

Elvira's brow creases as she puts her hand over her heart. 'Now Felix is introducing himself to my father … they're shaking hands. Felix is leaning in closer, probably saying something he doesn't want Karina to hear.'

I nod.

'Oh my God,' Elvira whispers. 'He's going to talk.'

Nothing I have seen from Felix to date leads me to believe that public speaking is his forte. My instinct is to stay hidden behind the curtain because this promises to be a train wreck, but curiosity gets the better of me.

'I take it this wasn't part of your arrangement?' I say to Elvira as I peek around the curtain.

'No.'

'At least he kept his promise to come back.'

'Yeah.'

Felix walks to the far side of the stage, away from Karina, Aeon and Gemini – and those of us who are hiding offstage. Hundreds of eyes follow him and I wonder if he feels like one of those exotic fish in the elaborate tanks in fancy restaurants, where diners, in their quest for the most delectable victim, scrutinise every creature in the tank with murderous intent.

Felix plunges his hands into the pockets of his chinos and then pulls them out again before folding them awkwardly across his chest. He clears his throat and drops his hands to his sides. I can barely watch. If he does manage to force any words past his larynx, I hope they aren't an octave higher than they should be.

'Ladies and gentlemen,' he says, 'my name is Felix Dangerfield. Like Gemini, I'm from Earth, but I've spent the better part of the last week in Ilion. I have some information that might be useful if you're planning to retake the city.'

As far as starts go, it's not bad.

'The Kauri have taken everything from you,' Felix continues, 'your people, your city, your elenium. If you destroy the Kauri, you'll get you city and your elenium back, yes. But there is something you won't get back if you succeed in destroying the Kauri – your people.'

There is silence before a voice cries, 'They killed our people. There is no getting them back.'

'They killed *some* of your people,' Felix says, 'and you're right, those people aren't coming back. But there is something you don't know. Many wehr were taken by the Kauri and ... stored.'

'What the hell are you talking about?' a female wehr calls.

Felix clenches and opens his fist several times. 'The Kauri have the technology to store intelligent lifeforms. Their grand plan is to redesign the universe. They plan to bring the wehr they've stored back to life sometime in the future. Not here though – in a place they deem to be more suitable for the species.'

'That's ridiculous!' one voice cries.

'They've brainwashed him!' another calls.

My stomach churns as Felix folds his arms across his chest again. What he is saying sounds insane, but he appears calm and rational. And sincere.

'I have not been brainwashed!' Felix says. 'I'm telling you the truth. The Kauri can store living beings. I can prove it. I've got—'

Before Felix can finish his sentence, Karina pins him to the floor, facedown, with her knees in his back. I hadn't even seen her move! Murmuring in the crowd intensifies as Felix struggles. He wriggles like a lizard caught under a cat's paw, making no sound I can hear.

A rush of air at my side alerts me to movement, but Elvira is out of reach before I register she has bolted. She races across the stage, her hood falling back midway. For a moment there is silence, but it is quickly erased as the wehrs react to the sight of a Kauri in their midst.

'Kauri!'

'Get it!'

'Kill it!'

'Where did that come from?'

Everything happens so fast. Aeon catches Elvira by the wrist and twists her arm up behind her back as Gemini closes. Karina knocks Felix unconscious with a punch to the head and then drags him to the far side of the stage with Aeon, Elvira and Gemini right behind her.

'What the hell just happened?' my father says as pandemonium breaks out in the auditorium.

'I think what *just* happened is the least of our problems,' I say. 'I'm more worried about what happens next.'

My father turns to me, worry etched in the creases on his forehead. 'What are you going to do?'

'Find out where they're taking Felix and Elvira.'

'I'll help you.'

'No,' I say, shaking my head. 'I think you should prepare the portal – we might need to make a hasty exit.'

'Please be careful, Liberty,' he says. 'Karina and Aeon are ruthless.'

'I know,' I say. 'That's why I can't just let them take … my friends. I'm worried they might …'

I can't finish my sentence. My father pats my shoulder.

'Go. Be careful. I'll stand by the portal.'

'Copy that.'

Chapter 31

Felix

'It's sexist,' I say, jangling the chains attached to the metal bands around my wrists, 'that you get more bling than me.'

Elvira glares at me through the gloom of our accommodation. 'What are you talking about?'

'You have a lovely choker,' I point to my throat since the chains aren't long enough for me to physically reach it, 'but I don't.'

'You're an arse,' she says. 'You don't need the extra restraint. You're not going to turn into a dragon.'

Cruel. But I guess I asked for that.

My eyes roam the room but the candlelight doesn't make it to all its boundaries. The walls I can see look like they've been carved from rock, though the builder should have lost his registration for the poor workmanship.

Chains dangle from metal spikes at irregular intervals and I couldn't guess at the last time the rusted manacles on the ends of them had been secured to a living being.

'I'm surprised wehrs even have accommodation like this,' I say. 'Did they used to burn witches too?'

Elvira sighs and rolls her eyes.

'How long do you think they'll keep us here?' I ask, wriggling to get comfortable on the rocky floor.

'I anticipate two options,' Elvira says. 'They'll either leave us here to rot … or, if they can be bothered, they might send Gemini to finish us off.'

Elvira is always so dramatic.

'Your father's not going to leave you to die – or have you killed,' I say.

'Perhaps not,' she concedes, 'but Karina absolutely would.'

'Your father will come looking for you though?'

Elvira sighs again. 'I hope so,' she says, 'but this is Karina's doing. She wouldn't want him to find us.'

'Well,' I say, 'I reckon Gemini's loyalty is to your father. He won't come after us.'

'Felix, Gemini is an assassin. He claims to be loyal to my father, but he's not to be trusted. I'm sure his loyalty lies with the highest bidder.'

That's disappointing, but she could be right. We played right into Karina's hands. This is the perfect way for her to get rid of both of us.

'I'm glad you came back though,' Elvira says.

'What?'

'You promised you'd come … and you did. Thanks.'

'Yeah,' I say. 'Okay.'

'So … where is Kauri-Rose? Did you get all the stuff you stayed in Ilion for?'

I nod. 'Having a Kauri on your team certainly makes life a lot easier. We've got an OP-MA Starlifter parked a little way north of here – loaded with weapons. As well as the Star of Truth *and* the Seed.'

Elvira frowns. 'And you got it all … just like that?'

'Yep.'

'Don't you think that seems a little *too* easy, Felix? The Kauri are the smartest creatures in the universe and you pretty much just waltzed in and stole their two most precious treasures. As well as a plane load of weapons?'

'I had an insider helping me!'

'An insider who's been in that body for a few days!' Elvira says. 'Are you sure she's on our team?'

'Are you sure *who's* on our team?' Liberty says, appearing in the doorway and drawing a blaster from the holster at her hip.

She strides across to Elvira and takes aim.

'No!' I yell. 'Don't—'

A bolt of white streaks from the blaster, followed by another – and then two more in quick succession. Then there is silence.

Until Elvira says, 'Okay, you're a pretty good shot,' she inspects the manacles on her wrists which are no longer attached to the wall chains, 'but I'm not sure I want you shooting at my throat.'

Liberty offers her the blaster. 'DIY?'

Elvira's mouth twitches. 'Maybe not. Just … be careful. Okay?'

'You got it,' Liberty says, nodding.

I hold my breath as Liberty points the tip of the blaster at Elvira's throat. In the gloom I can't see if her hand is shaking or not. At least she's taking her time to line up this shot. I hope she has recovered from her concussion.

'Get on with it already,' Elvira says.

Her words are barely out when Liberty fires again.

Elvira gets to her feet. 'Thanks.' She gestures towards me. 'And Felix?'

'Not so fast,' Liberty says, returning the blaster to its holster. She looks at me. 'Who was Elvira talking about? Who is "on the team" that we're not sure about?'

I look at Elvira. 'You didn't tell her?'

Elvira shrugs. 'I didn't want to say anything until she was … here.'

Liberty crouches in front of me and my heart pounds inside my chest. *Who is … "she"?*

'A Kauri cyborg who has your mother's consciousness,' I say.

'What!' Liberty says. 'How is that possible?'

'The Kauri can extract a lifeform's consciousness,' I say, eyeing Liberty's blaster. 'They extracted your mother's consciousness from her remains – and implanted it in a Kauri body.'

Liberty holds my gaze. 'And where is she now?'

'Guarding an aircraft north of here.'

'Aircraft?'

I tell Liberty what I've just finished telling Elvira about the Star of Truth, the Seed and the weapons.

'And what's the plan?' Liberty says.

I take a deep breath. 'The plan,' I say, 'is to *not* wipe out the Kauri, but to store them.'

'Because?' Liberty says.

'Because this team here on Rhybor is one of thousands of teams roaming the universe,' I say. '*If* we can destroy this one, we're going to attract a whole lot of attention to ourselves that we don't want. We need to contain this – not pick a fight with the rest of the Kauri population.'

'That's a ludicrous story,' Liberty says as Elvira stands alongside her. 'You'd better not be making it up.'

Liberty stands, takes aim with the blaster again and with four shots, I'm free of the chains, if not the manacles.

I inspect the metal bands on my wrists and ankles. 'I look like a character from a sci-fi movie.'

'No,' Elvira says. 'You don't.'

'Well, I *feel* like I'm in a sci-fi movie,' I retort. 'Like Liberty said, the story I just told is ludicrous – but it's all true.'

'I want to see this cyborg you reckon has my mother's consciousness,' Liberty says to me. 'There's just something we need to collect on the way.'

'Which is?' Elvira prompts.

'Gemini Holmes.'

'Because?' I say.

'Two reasons,' Liberty says. 'Firstly, he's too dangerous to be left unsupervised for long and, secondly, it's better that we have him rather than Karina.'

∞

Liberty

'Well, isn't this cosy?' Gemini says. 'The whole team together at last.'

Seven of us are sitting in the belly of the biggest aircraft I've even seen. The Starlifter is a military transport aircraft that couldn't actually 'lift' a star, since it doesn't have any hands, but I suspect it could tow one. This ship is massive and there are thousands of weapons onboard. And then there are the two Kauri treasures sitting on top of the stack of crates before us.

My gaze flicks around the 'team'. Aeon is wedged between Elvira and Gemini, who've spent the last two hours following our escape from Karina's clan at Gyoma Lake competing for his attention. Felix is next to Elvira, cradling Grim in his arms. My father is beside me, separating me from the Kauri who claims to have my mother's consciousness.

My eyes lock with hers.

'Liberty,' the Kauri says. 'Please say something.'

'Okay … How did you steal an aircraft, an arsenal of weapons, the Kauri Star of Truth *and* the Seed?' I ask.

The Kauri's shoulders sag. 'I was hoping for a "Gee, Mum, I'm so glad you're alive",' she says.

'You're not my mother,' I say. 'Answer the question.'

My father clears his throat and, in my peripheral vision, I see Felix and Elvira exchange a glance but I ignore that, keeping my focus on the Kauri.

'It's not hard to steal from the Kauri,' Kauri-Rose says at last. 'They don't monitor anything because they don't think there is any threat. No one has ever escaped from them, no one has ever broken into their stronghold, no one has ever stolen from them … so it doesn't even occur to them that it *could* happen. It just hasn't been on their radar.'

'Until now,' I say.

'Because I escaped from them,' Felix says.

'And because Liberty and I broke in to their research facility,' Elvira adds.

'And,' Gemini says, pointing at Kauri-Rose, '*you've* now stolen from them.'

'Do you not think, after everything we've done in the last couple of days,' I say, 'that they won't retaliate?'

Kauri-Rose nods. 'We've managed to do all this stuff because they haven't been in the habit of monitoring things. But I think they're getting the idea. And they *will* notice – soon – that their prized possessions are gone, which is why we need to strike quickly.'

'We've already struck,' Gemini says.

All eyes turn to him.

'What are you talking about?' Elvira says.

'The virus,' Gemini says with a shrug. 'I've already deployed it. Kauris should be dropping like flies as we speak.'

'What!' Felix says. 'You only just got here! How could you possibly have downloaded the virus into that,' he points to the Star of Truth, 'already?'

Gemini scoffs. 'I did it hours ago,' he says. 'I didn't need that thing *here* to do it. I hacked the Kauri satellites and downloaded the virus remotely.'

I stare at the two interconnected pyramids of the Star of Truth as all the colours of the rainbow swirl lazily through the device, reminding me of a lava lamp. The collective knowledge of the Kauri contained in something I could hold in my palms. And right now, it's killing them all.

'This is bad,' I murmur.

'This is *war*, Liberty,' Aeon says.

'It's genocide,' Felix says.

I look up at him and he blushes, but he holds my eye.

'I am totally onboard with wehrs fighting to get back something of what they lost,' Felix says, still maintaining eye contact, 'but … I just don't know that genocide is the answer. The one thing I did learn in history classes is that future generations take a dim view of the mass slaughter of entire national or ethnic groups.'

'I'm sure future generations of wehrs will be thankful not to have to worry about the threat of the Kauri,' Aeon counters.

'Until the rest of the Kauri come for vengeance,' Elvira says, folding her arms across her chest.

'The rest?' Gemini says.

'The Kauri who invaded here,' Kauri-Rose says, 'are just one tribe. There are thousands of tribes replicating this work all over the universe. Wipe these ones out, and others will eventually come looking for the

Star … and,' she leans forward and picks up a thick chain with a dark crystal sphere attached to it, 'this Seed.'

The Seed dangling from the chain is like an oversized crystal ball, almost the size of a soccer ball, and its dark belly swirls with tiny, dazzling pearls of light. The finger-width strip of gleaming silver metal encircling the sphere is studded with a series of indentations, like miniature light-bulb sockets – function unknown.

'Are you saying there are more of these?' my father asks, pointing to the Star of Truth and then the Seed.

Kauri-Rose nods. 'Yes, Caspian. That's exactly what I'm saying.'

A look passes between them and my stomach clenches. 'Gemini,' I say, 'can you stop it?'

'The virus?' Gemini says.

'Yes,' I say, nodding. 'The virus.'

Gemini shakes his head. 'There is no stopping it. That's kind of the point of a virus.'

'Well, how about an easier question,' Felix says. 'Can you extract the wehrs who have been stored in the Seed?'

Gemini glances at the Seed before turning his gaze back on Felix. 'You're telling me that there are wehrs in there?'

Felix nods. 'There are probably millions of lifeforms in there – not just wehrs. We don't want *everyone* brought out *here* though. Just the wehrs.'

Gemini inhales deeply and exhales slowly. 'That'll be tricky.'

'Really?' Elvira says. 'The legendary genius Gemini Holmes has finally found something that's "tricky"?'

Kauri-Rose puts up her hand. 'You're going to need a quantum physicist. I'm good to go.' She winks at my father. 'An astrophysicist would come in handy too.'

'Sounds like fun,' my father says, rubbing his hands together.

Aeon clamps his hand around Gemini's forearm. 'I'm up for a new challenge.'

A sly grin splits Gemini's face. 'Then what are we waiting for?'

'How many wehrs are we talking about?' my father asks.

'The wehrs here assumed the Kauri were slaughtering them, not capturing them,' Aeon says, 'but if what Felix says about the Kauri's mission is true, there could be millions of wehrs in there.'

'Four billion,' Felix says.

All eyes turn to him.

Felix clears his throat. 'The Kauri who was … testing me told me that.'

'And by the time we get them back,' Elvira says, 'the Kauri will be destroyed.'

Gemini checks his watch. 'Once the virus has done its job – yes.'

'Well, since the grownups are going to tinker with the tech,' Felix says, eyeing the Seed, 'looks like the rest of us can have the afternoon off.'

'How do you figure that?' I ask. 'Won't the other Kauri tribes come?'

'I don't reckon they'll be here for a good while yet,' Felix says, scratching Grim under the chin.

Meow.

'Grim seems to agree,' Elvira says, looking at me. 'You, me and Felix can stand down.'

∞

Elvira

The sunset is spectacular from up here. Gliding south over the grasslands between Gyoma Lake and where Kauri-Rose parked the Starlifter, I am thoroughly enjoying some quality solo dragon time while my father and the others try to extract the trapped wehrs from the Seed. I've left Grim to chaperone Felix and Liberty, and hopefully the Ice Queen won't say or do anything too awful to Felix while I'm gone. She seems to have thawed since we first came to Rhybor, so things *should* be okay until I get back.

As I adjust my wings to catch an updraft, I marvel at the freedom of a world without the Kauri. Imagine being able to fly like this all the time! I continue my southward trajectory without any particular destination in mind, gazing at the pink and orange strips of cloud to the west that the sun has stained as it slips from the sky.

Turning my gaze south again, I am surprised to find that I recognise the landscape here. I've flown further than I'd intended – I'm approaching the hillside home of the Gyoma Lake dragons. Karina's clan. Time to turn around if I want to get back to the ship before dark.

I dip my right wing to wheel round when I spot lights south of the hill. The distant roar of engines floats up on the breeze and I turn a full circle till I'm heading south again. I lower my altitude. Peering between the tree branches, I can make out the source of the lights. Hundreds of motorbikes and land speeders are surging south. It looks like the wehrs have abandoned the Gyoma Lake stronghold and are heading for Ilion.

Shit. What's Karina up to now?

Avoiding detection is a priority, so I swing north and make my way back to the Starlifter. Flying into the breeze saps my strength quickly but I ignore the lactic acid building up in my muscles and flap my wings harder.

By the time I reach the Starlifter, night has fallen, and Felix and Liberty have returned. Felix is engrossed in a stash of weapons and Liberty is massaging Grim's ears.

Felix looks up from the range of blasters laid out on the floor before him. 'Have fun?' he says.

I shrug. 'Yes,' I reply. 'Even managed to do some "high-level spying".'

Felix groans as Liberty rolls her eyes.

'And what did you find out?' my father says, sitting up straight on his crate and tilting his head to his left to stretch his neck muscles.

'The wehrs have left Gyoma Lake,' I say. 'Looks like they're heading for the capital.'

My father looks at Gemini, who winces.

'What?' I say.

'That's a problem,' Gemini says.

'Why?'

'Karina probably thinks she's going to claim a city where the enemy lies dead, but ...' My father shakes his head.

'What *is* it?' I cry, exasperated. 'Can you just *tell* me what is going on?'

Gemini sighs. 'The virus failed.' He points to the Star of Truth. 'The Kauri AI has neutralised the virus. I don't know how many Kauri succumbed, but you can bet there are still plenty out there – and now they'll be really pissed.'

'So, Karina's walking into a trap?'

Felix grunts. 'Couldn't happen to a more deserving person,' he says.

My father's eyes narrow. 'Except that she's not the only one heading into danger. My parents are with her – along with many of our clan. We need to help them.'

Caspian eyes the Seed. 'We need to work faster then,' he says.

Kauri-Rose nods. 'We've miniaturised a portal to extract lifeforms,' she says, 'but we haven't finished the calculations to the exact extraction point for the wehr population in the Seed.'

'The model's locked,' Gemini says, tapping his tablet. 'We just have to wait for it to finish.'

'And we still have to address how to "expand" them again,' Caspian adds. 'Even if we can get their matter out, it'll remain compressed until we can figure out how to insert space back in the right places.'

'The Kauri must be able to reinstate lifeforms,' Liberty says, looking at Kauri-Rose. 'Can't you access the Star of Truth for that information.'

'I could,' Kauri-Rose says, 'but if I access the system, they'll be able to track me.'

'We can't risk the Kauri knowing where she is, Liberty,' Caspian says, 'because if they find her here – we're all cactus.'

I frown as I stride across the floor to where Felix is sitting. When I reach him, I swipe a squidger from his stash of weapons.

'Have you tried using this?' I ask.

My father's brow crinkles. 'No,' he says. 'Why—'

I interrupt before Gemini can. 'This is what the Kauri use to compress lifeforms,' I say.

My father nods.

'And *this* part,' I point to the cartridge on top of the device, 'is where the matter is stored before being transferred to the Seed.'

Again, father nods – along with Caspian and Kauri-Rose.

I screw off the cartridge and inspect both ends. 'Surely,' I say, 'if you attach these cartridges to that metal strip around the Seed and reprogram it to *reverse* the process the Kauri are using to *store* the lifeforms – you should be able to *re*store them.' I toss the cartridge to Gemini. 'Should be simple for a genius like you.'

Gemini snatches the cartridge from the air without taking his gaze from me. 'Yes,' he says. 'Should be a piece of cake.'

'Great,' I say, turning to Kauri-Rose. 'You flew this bird here?'

Kauri-Rose nods.

'Okay, let's get her in the air again. Destination – Ilion.'

'Hang on,' Felix says. 'We don't have a plan.'

I lock eyes with my father. 'By the time we reach the city, we will have. We need to get there before the others. Before the Kauri massacre them.'

Chapter 32

Felix

I nudge Elvira. 'I like Kauri-Rose's landings better than Gemini's,' I say.

'Agreed,' she says, unbuckling her harness and pushing up to her feet. Elvira extends her hand. 'Let's get this done, comrade.'

I take her hand, without asking which character she's channelling at the moment, and let her help me out of my seat. I don't need help; it's easier just to go with the flow sometimes.

'Several hundred wehrs assembling on the edge of the city,' Kauri-Rose announces as she strides from the cockpit. 'About a kilometre from here.'

'They couldn't have missed our landing,' Liberty says. 'This isn't a stealth craft.'

'No,' Caspian says, 'and the Kauri in the city won't have missed it either. We're on the clock now.'

'Can you release the wehrs inside the Seed?' I ask as Grim winds around my ankles.

Gemini shoulders his bulging rucksack and tucks his tablet under his arm. 'Only one way to find out,' he says. 'Let's take this outside.'

'Everyone, kit up,' Aeon says. 'Chest holsters, hip and thigh holsters – whatever you can. Fill 'em up. Blasters *and* squidgers. Catch what we can, kill what we can't.' He turns to Kauri-Rose. 'Stay inside here until I give you the signal.'

I'd fitted my holsters before take-off, so I just load up with blasters and squidgers. 'I'll start rolling out the extra crates,' I say once I've got what I need.

Aeon salutes. 'We'll release a few thousand wehrs here – enough to utilise the weapons you and Kauri-Rose managed to steal – and they can then breach the city.'

'Along with the wehrs Karina brought?' Liberty says.

Aeon nods. 'Yes. We'll arm whoever came with her.'

With half a moon as their only ally against the darkness, Karina's crew approaches the Starlifter on foot as we unload crate after crate of weapons. They reach us as I roll out the final crate. Like Elvira and Aeon, the wehrs are barefoot and dressed in robes.

'Aeon?' Karina says, blaster in hand. 'What are you playing at?'

Aeon strolls forward to stand toe-to-toe with her. 'I was just about to ask you the same thing, Karina.'

From among the crowd of wehrs shuffling closer, two break clear and rush to Aeon – the woman hugging him fiercely.

'Aeon,' she says. 'I'm so glad you're here.'

'I'm fine, Mother,' he says as he winks at her companion. 'I'm relieved you and Father are safe.'

'I told you no harm would come to them, Aeon,' Karina says smoothly.

Elvira pipes up. 'I'm surprised you didn't lock them up. Or is it just *me* that you like to keep chaining up?'

'Don't forget she chained *me* up too this time, Elvira,' I add.

Elvira slaps her forehead with her palm. 'Oh, that's right. Very thoughtful of her to give me a friend to talk to this time. I suppose I should be grateful.'

Karina snorts. 'Yes, you should both be grateful that you're alive,' she says. 'What I've done is *save your lives.*'

Beside me, Elvira snorts. 'Seriously?'

'Your ridiculous Kauri "disguise" could easily have gotten you killed, Elvira,' Karina says, 'I locked you up for your own safety. But no more! The world has moved on and there are bigger priorities than children who continue to get in the way of events that are greater than them.'

Children? Elvira and I are *not* children. I feel my blood turn to fire.

'You're planning to take the city?' Liberty says, coming to stand beside her father.

'Yes,' Karina says. 'Today, Ilion returns to the wehrs.'

'You won't get things all your own way,' I say, clenching my fists at my sides. 'The virus failed.'

'What!' Karina hisses as she spins round to face Gemini. 'You told me it *would* work, that it *was working!*'

'It *was* working,' Gemini says, 'but the Kauri were smart enough to counter it.'

'So, we've got to fight what's left?'

Aeon nods. 'If we want our city back … yes.'

'We have a plan,' I say, stepping forward to stand beside Aeon.

As my stepmother sneers and looks me up and down, Elvira elbows her father aside to stand beside me while Liberty appears at my other shoulder.

My heart thumps inside my chest.

'I don't think we need children—' Karina begins.

'Arm yourselves,' I say, raising my voice so that all the wehrs behind her can hear me, 'and circle the city. We'll raid in small groups, working from the outside to the palace at the centre.' I point to the crates. 'Plenty of weapons for everyone. Some are blasters, some will vaporise the enemy. Take as many as you can.'

Karina glares at me. 'You think this is going to win you some kind of credibility?' she says, her voice low and menacing. 'You don't belong here, Felix. You're *not* a wehr! You're a half-breed.'

I ignore my stepmother and address the wehrs again. 'Teams of six to eight,' I call. 'Aeon will give you your entry coordinates.'

Karina scoffs. 'You won't survive this night,' she says. 'Whoever manages to rid the world of the stain you make here – I'll give them a medal.'

'Too gutless to do it yourself?' I say calmly.

'I wouldn't waste my time,' Karina says, turning her back on me.

'Wow,' Liberty mutters, shaking her head. 'She really is a piece of work, isn't she?'

'Yep,' I say.

Liberty wraps her hand around my forearm and looks up at me, her blue eyes sparkling in the low light. 'I know when she called you a "half-breed", that was meant to be offensive, but you should be *really* thankful that you have *none* of her genetic material.'

'I totally am.'

'And also … congratulations.'

I cock my head. 'For what?'

Liberty releases my arm to wave her hand. 'For having so many weapons at hand … and not shooting her!'

'And let me congratulate you too,' Elvira says, 'for lying convincingly about the vaporiser.'

'Um, thanks, I think,' I say.

Knowing the 'catch over kill' strategy would have been too hard to sell to the wehrs, telling them that they were vaporising Kauri rather than capturing them seemed like the obvious solution.

As wehrs swarm to the crates, Elvira says, 'We should get our quads from the aircraft and take our positions.'

'Agreed,' I say.

∞

Elvira

Gemini's voice sails over the assembled wehrs. *'Shit!'*

Felix, Liberty and I trade glances. 'That doesn't sound good,' I say.

I spin round to find Gemini lying on the ground next to his quad bike, clutching his ankle.

'Stupid cat!' he cries.

Grim springs up onto the seat of the quad before turning to hiss at Gemini.

My father rushes to Gemini's side and crouches beside him. 'Are you okay?'

Gemini winces. 'No. I tripped over the cat. My ankle is busted.'

I join them. 'Could we strap it?' I say.

'Even if we strap it,' Gemini says, 'I'm still not going to able to ride – or deploy the Seed.'

I clench my fists to stop my hands trembling. This is bad. Gemini was going to get the Seed back to the palace so that when the wehrs were released, they'd be close to the city's main weapons cache.

'I can take it,' I say.

My father turns to me and my pulse quickens as his chocolate-coloured eyes bore into mine. 'This is an extremely delicate and dangerous mission, Elvira.'

'I can do it.'

My father sighs and turns to Gemini. 'Give her your rucksack.'

Gemini props himself against the quad before handing over his rucksack containing the Seed. 'Be careful, Elvira,' he says. 'Message me when it's in place and I'll activate the release program,' he taps his tablet, 'from here.'

'Roger that,' I say, shouldering the bag.

'And I'll be wanting that bag back, Elvira,' Gemini says.

'Relax,' I say to him as my father wraps his arms around me.

'*I* won't be able to relax until you're back, Elvira,' he whispers in my ear.

A burning wave of emotion washes over me and I inhale deeply through my nose as I fight to maintain my composure. The scent of his ylang-ylang shampoo triggers memories from my childhood. Memories of being snuggled in my father's arms as he carried me to bed when I fell asleep on the sofa watching TV.

'I *can* do this,' I whisper back.

'I know you can.' He pauses. 'I love you dearly, Daughter. I hope you know that.'

'I do now,' I say.

A cloaked figure appears beside me, ruining our moment. 'I see I have a new companion for this mission,' Kauri-Rose says, keeping her voice low so as not to draw the attention of the wehrs.

'*Three* new companions,' Liberty says. She points to Felix, me and then to herself. 'We're a team.'

I hope my surprise doesn't show. It seems we've made some real progress in thawing our Ice Queen.

'Yeah,' I say to Kauri-Rose, 'we're a team.'

'Then on your bikes,' she says, 'we need to get ahead of the others.'

With Gemini's bag on my back and his pager in the inside breast pocket of the knee-length wrap dress I stole from Karina's clan's hideout, I jump aboard my quad and gun the engine.

Wind whips my face as I roar along the runway towards the city. Kauri-Rose appears to my left while Felix and Liberty come up on my right. As we enter the city from the north, I am instantly on edge. The city buildings are lit up but there is no traffic. Not on the roads or in the sky. I roll off the throttle.

'They're waiting for us,' I say.

'Yep,' Felix says, drawing a squidger from one of his holsters. 'Maybe we should have waited for the others. We're sitting ducks out here.'

'Should we split up?' Liberty asks.

Gemini would make this work.

I push that thought aside. 'No, we're a team,' I say. 'We stick together.'

I draw a squidger and open the throttle on my quad again, hurtling forward. The roar of our engines shatters the city's silence. With each block we pass without any sign of Kauri, my chest tightens a little more.

Just bring it already.

Then, I sense it before I see it – a Kauri on a balcony to my left. I wave my squidger at the building and pull the trigger. The squidger hums, the Kauri disappears.

'*Yes!*' I hiss.

'Got one!' Liberty cries.

'I've got two!' Felix yells.

Kauri-Rose pulls ahead of us and turns, squidger pointed in our direction. 'Zip it!' she says. 'Taunting them is not a—'

Blaster fire rains down from buildings on both side of the roadway and I wrench the handlebar, swerving dangerously close to Felix's quad.

'Look out!' Liberty yells.

I push the handlebar forward again – tricky to do one-handed – and try to correct my course. My quad skids, tyres squealing. I point my squidger at a building and squeeze the trigger. I don't bother to aim because I can barely see through the smoke from my tyres. What *is* clearly visible, though, is the blaster fire.

I've no idea if I'm capturing any Kauri so I shove the squidger in my thigh holster and focus on the palace, which is still at least two dozen blocks from here.

'Cover me!' I yell.

We make it two blocks without blaster fire. But when it comes again, it's ferocious. A luminous bolt blasts Kauri-Rose's rear right tyre, sending the quad somersaulting down the roadway. Kauri-Rose sails into the air … and rotates through three cartwheels before landing on her feet.

I zoom past, then check her in my mirror. Legs pumping, she draws another squidger from her hip holster and takes aim with two weapons as she sprints down the roadway. I swivel to find Felix closest to me.

'Double back!' I yell. 'Get Kauri-Rose!'

'On it!' he yells back, peeling off to the right.

Liberty pulls alongside me. 'Lean forward!' she says. 'I'm going to jump onboard with you!'

I nod. Better idea to have her on my quad. She can fire with two hands.

I lean forward, but not enough. The front wheels flick up when she lands behind me.

'*Lean!*' she cries as she throws her weight against my back.

'I'm leaning,' I shout, 'but it's really hard to steer like this.'

'You watch the road,' Liberty yells. 'I'll watch the buildings.'

'Got it!'

We make another few blocks before Felix catches up. We're down to two bikes but, with two dedicated shooters, we've a better chance of making the palace.

The sporadic blaster fire continues for several more blocks and I try to do my part by swerving occasionally – varying my trajectory so the Kauri can't line up a shot.

'*Crap!*' Liberty cries. 'I'm hit!'

'*Liberty!*' Kauri-Rose screams. 'Are you okay?'

'My neck! That bloody hurts! Am I bleeding?'

'The wound's cauterised,' Kauri-Rose calls. 'You're good for now!'

Liberty leans in close to my ear. 'Gun it, Elvira!' she hisses. 'And just go straight!'

'Are you sure?' I call back. 'We're easier to hit on a straight line!'

'Do it!'

I grip the handles tighter and tuck my head down as I commit to the straight line. My blood runs hot. My dragon wants out.

Not now!

I contain my dragon and we make it three more blocks before we're hit again.

My tyre this time.

As I'm catapulted through the air, I shrug off Gemini's rucksack and toss it to Kauri-Rose, who has to dangle herself over the back of Felix's quad to snatch it before it hits the ground.

Then I release the buckle on my dress, letting the garment flutter to the ground as I Shift.

I see Liberty pitching head first towards the roadway. 'Not again!' she cries.

No, I think, *definitely not again.*

My rear claw catches her ankle and I beat my wings downwards as hard as I can. Her hands scrape the road, but that's better than her head. She doesn't need another concussion.

I wing my way to a first-floor balcony and deposit Liberty on it before landing beside her.

'Thanks,' she says with a nod.

I return the nod before casting my gaze over the railing to the roadway below. Felix and Kauri-Rose leap from the quad and race through the building's entranceway. I turn my attention south, towards the palace. We're four blocks away.

Damn.

Gemini would have made it, my brain taunts.

As I wait for Felix and Kauri-Rose to join us, I scan the streetscape, assessing different options. My eyes land on my discarded dress on the road. The dress with Gemini's pager in the pocket.

Damn.

Felix and Kauri-Rose burst through the doorway and out onto the balcony.

'Liberty,' Kauri-Rose says, 'are you okay?'

'I'm fine,' Liberty replies before turning to Felix. 'New plan?'

Kauri-Rose frowns as Felix nods.

'Elvira,' Felix says, 'could you fly the Seed to the palace from here?'

I shake my head. *They'll shoot me down for sure.*

Felix rubs his chin. 'Yeah, I think they've revised their mission. They want revenge. It's not capture anymore. It's shoot to kill.'

Kauri-Rose extracts the Seed from Gemini's rucksack and cradles it in her hands, the starlike lights in its belly twinkling mysteriously.

'We were so close,' she whispers, staring into the Seed. 'There are more than enough wehrs in here to conquer the Kauri, but we're four blocks from the weapons we need for them to get the job done.'

Four blocks. It's going to have to do.

I face Felix and tap one of my talons against his chest. *Wait here.*

'What are you doing?' he asks.

I don't answer. Instead, I leap over the balcony and sail down to the roadway, landing beside my dress. As I complete my Shift, I drape the dress around my shoulders and buckle it quickly. By the time I'm dressed, a cordon of Kauri is closing in on me. In groups of five and six, they silently exit the buildings close by and march towards me, blasters raised.

When several Kauri disappear, a group turns to face Felix, Liberty and Kauri-Rose on the balcony.

'Drop the weapons and come down here,' a Kauri bellows.

'Or what?' Felix yells back.

The answer is a barrage of blaster fire.

I hold my breath as I wait for the shooting to stop. It goes on and on – until the balcony is a smoking wreck. When the blasters finally fall silent, I peer through the dust, praying to see movement. But there is none.

My heart feels like it's being squeezed in a vice. *'Felix!'* I scream.

The ground level doors slide open and Felix, Liberty and Kauri-Rose walk through the entranceway with their hands in the air. The Seed is nowhere to be seen.

The cordon opens to let them through. Felix stands on my right, taking my hand and squeezing it gently.

'Still a team,' he whispers.

I clutch his hand. 'Thanks.'

'You have killed and stolen from us!' a Kauri says. 'This is unacceptable. You must die.'

'If you kill us,' I say, 'you won't ever get your stuff back.'

The Kauri scoffs. 'Once you are all dead, we will have no trouble finding our possessions.'

'One of our possessions is right in front of us,' another Kauri says. 'The prototype with the human consciousness.'

The first Kauri nods. 'Yes. We'll take that one now.'

Two other Kauri stride forward, each taking one of Kauri-Rose's arms and forcing her to her knees.

The lead Kauri smiles. 'Kill the others.'

Chapter 33

Liberty

My hands are sweating as I stare into the eyes of the Kauri closest to me.

'How many Kauri did you lose?' I ask.

The Kauri takes three steps forward and presses the butt of the blaster against my forehead. 'This one wants to die first,' he says.

'I don't really—'

A shriek splits the air.

'Elvira!' Felix yells.

Elvira crumples to the ground, clutching her stomach. *'Arrrgggghhhhhhh!'* she groans as she writhes on the roadway.

Pointing at Elvira, the Kauri closest to me says, 'Shoot the impostor! Put her out of her misery.'

'NO!' I say, trying to distract him. 'Me first – you promised.'

Elvira vomits over the feet of the Kauri lining up her shot.

'Disgusting,' the Kauri hisses as she fires her blaster.

Elvira is thrashing around now, moaning constantly – and somehow avoiding the luminous bolts the Kauri is firing at her.

Felix kicks the Kauri in the sternum then drops to the ground, shielding Elvira as another Kauri steps up to finish the job. I unleash a kick too – a roundhouse that collects my Kauri in the temple. As he staggers back, I duck, anticipating the barrage of bolts that will come in retaliation.

'What's that?' I hear a Kauri ask.

I chance a peek at our captors, who are staring at the balcony they've destroyed. Actually, they're not studying the balcony. They're captivated by the pulsating glow that is coming from somewhere further inside.

Before they recover their wits, a sonic pulse knocks us all to the ground.

I roll onto my back, fighting for breath. The acoustic shockwave has winded me as well as knocking me off my feet. As I stare at the sky, my vision blurs. I blink several times, trying to get a clear view.

And then it happens.

Thousands of lights – *hundreds of thousands* of lights – erupt all around us. On the ground, in the buildings, and even in the air over our heads. They wink out as quickly as they appeared but then wehrdragons appear in their place. Most are in human form, but many are dragons. I watch several human wehrs overhead Shift to dragon form as they plummet towards the ground.

'It's like the Big Bang, Liberty,' Kauri-Rose says, crawling towards me. 'Do you remember what I told you about the beginning of our universe? How it wasn't a single explosion? That it happened everywhere … all at once?'

On my hands and knees, I stare at her, nodding. When I was younger, my mother tried to explain the universe's origin many times. And now I get it. But right now, that's not the biggest revelation.

'Mum,' I whisper. 'It really is you!'

Kauri-Rose smiles. 'Yes, Liberty. It really is me.'

'Gemini did it!' Felix says, snatching weapons from the stunned Kauri. 'He brought them back.'

'The wehrdragons are everywhere!' Elvira says. 'How are we supposed to coordinate them?'

'It didn't exactly go to plan,' my mother admits. 'The return field was supposed to be much smaller. There must have been an error in the anchor point calculations – maybe our coefficients for the state vectors were a bit off.'

Felix fills his holsters with blasters as wehrdragons continue to rain down. 'Yeah,' he says. 'That's just what I was thinking.'

I watch as the wehrs quickly dispatch our Kauri captors, then I look at Felix who is standing in front of me with his hand out.

I accept his hand and pull myself to my feet. 'Thanks.'

'You're welcome,' he says, offering me two blasters.

Is this really the same guy who interviewed me for the *Indigo Times? That* guy stumbled through all his questions, didn't take his eyes off my chest the whole time, and even forgot my name at one point. *This* guy has got his shit together.

His green eyes lock with mine. 'Do you reckon you and Kauri-Rose can get the Seed back to the Starlifter?'

I glance at my mother, who nods. 'Mission accepted,' I say, smiling. 'What are you going to do?'

'Elvira and I will go to the palace – try to sort this mess out.'

I unclasp my pendant and step towards him. 'Lean forward,' I say.

'Why?'

'Just do it … please,' I say.

When he's within reach, I secure the silver chain around his neck with trembling fingers.

'Liberty,' my mother says, 'what are you doing?'

Felix stares at me, cradling the coin in his hand.

'It's always brought me good luck,' I say, 'and I think you're going to need it.'

Felix nods. 'Thanks. I'll bring it back when we're done.'

I smile at him. 'I'm counting on it.'

∞

Elvira

I stuff Gemini's pager back into the pocket of my dress. That job's done. The wehrs are here. I'm relieved Gemini's remote release actually worked. But with so many wehrs around – and I really hope all four billion of them aren't coming – it's not safe for me to be blue. So I Shift.

I survey the scene. Kauri stream from the buildings and, although they are outnumbered, the wehrs are unarmed. Razor-sharp teeth and claws, and the ability to breathe fire, are great – but only if you can avoid the blaster fire long enough to use them. The wehrs need weapons. We have to get to the palace.

Felix is talking to Liberty and Kauri-Rose, but it's a male wehr behind them that catches my attention. Three Kauri are running towards him, blasters raised. He spots them, dodges their fire as he Shifts, shredding his chinos and t-shirt as he transforms into a dragon the colour of blood oranges.

The dragon roars, spewing a wall of flame at his assailants. It slows them down but doesn't stop them. I launch myself into the air and head straight for them. Claws out, I grab the first one. My momentum carries both of us, knocking down the next two like bowling pins.

His voice is in my head as I land beside him. *Thanks.*

You're welcome.

What's your name?

Elvira.

He nods, smoke curling from his nostrils. *What the hell is going on here, Elvira?*

Long story. Can we fight first and have story time later?

The dragon nods.

We need to get to the palace, I say.

For weapons? he sends back.

Yes.

Follow me then.

Without waiting for a response, he leaps into the air. Who does he think he is?

I leap after him, slower, because I need to grab Felix on the way.

'Hey!' Felix cries as my claws grip his biceps. 'What are you doing?'

Taking you to the palace, I reply. *That's the plan, isn't it?*

'I'd have preferred a quad,' he says.

I can't ride a quad like this. And we need to stick together. We're a team, remember?

'Sure,' he mumbles.

The blood orange dragon – I should have asked him what his name was – is pulling ahead of me in the chaos. Wehrs are still appearing all around. It's like New Year's Eve fireworks. And the noise is deafening. The Kauri are now airborne, zipping between the buildings on their speeders and firing at anything that isn't blue. Higher in the atmosphere, bigger ships are on the move, but they're not engaged in the fight.

They're leaving.

'Some of the Kauri are escaping,' Felix yells.

I grunt. *We can't do anything about that.*

'Three speeders closing in!' Felix says.

I'll dodge what I can, but you've got blasters, right?

'Bullseye!' Felix yells as the first speeder explodes.

The shockwave sends us somersaulting towards a building.

'Elvira!' Felix yells.

I stretch my wings, fighting for control; however, it's Felix who comes to the rescue. As we're about to slam into the building, Felix twists and plants his feet.

'Arrrrgggh!' he grunts as he pushes off the outer wall.

Two more blocks.

'If you could avoid plastering us against any buildings on the way, that'd be great!'

As long as you stop blowing up speeders at close range, we have a deal!

Dodging obstacles becomes more difficult the closer we get to the palace. In the air, on the ground, the city is swarming. Even without marshalling, the wehrs are gravitating towards the palace.

I follow my companion to the top level of the palace. He soars onto a landing bay and slides to a graceful halt. My landing is compromised by having to dump Felix first, though it's still not my worst.

The dragon Shifts. 'Who's that?' he says, pointing to Felix.

'I'm Felix,' Felix says, leaping to his feet. 'I'm from Earth.'

The naked man nods. 'That explains why you didn't Shift and fly yourself up here.' He extends his hand. 'My name's Helion.'

I shuffle closer but I'm not going to Shift. He might be comfortable with nudity, but I'm not.

'Elvira,' Helion says. 'Are you going to Shift?'

Not bloody likely, I send to him. *Not until I have some clothes.*

He smiles. 'That can be arranged. We'll pick up something on the way to the armoury. Follow me.'

Helion punches in a code to the keypad at the door to the penthouse.

'How do you know the code?' Felix asks.

Helion turns his head but doesn't stop. 'Because this is my house, Earthling,' he says. 'I'm the king of Rhybor.'

King Helion? This guy does *not* look like a king. Maybe it's his frohawk. Maybe it's because he doesn't look like he's seen many more summers than I have. Or maybe it's because he's strutting around naked.

Helion turns to me, frowning. 'You're a wehr,' he says. 'You should know your king.'

I was born on Earth, Your Majesty, and only arrived here about a week ago. They told me you were dead.

'Dead?' Helion says, crossing the floor to a set of doors. He opens a cupboard to find it empty. Slowly, he surveys the room. 'It's different. I feel like I've missed something here.'

'Twenty years,' Felix says.

Helion's eyebrows arch. 'Pardon me?'

'You've missed twenty years,' Felix says. 'The Kauri invaded twenty years ago and have had you … in storage.'

Helion's gaze falls on me. 'That "long story" you mentioned,' he says. 'I think I need to hear it … as soon as I find us some clothes.'

The noise and lightshow outside continues as we hunt for clothes in the king's penthouse. Eventually, we find a stash of garments in an anteroom. When he hands me a linen robe, my heart races.

I should warn you, I say, *that I will look like a Kauri when I Shift.*

'This *is* going to be a "long story", isn't it?' Helion says.

I Shift, and with Felix's help, we fill the king in on what we know of the Kauri invasion of Rhybor.

'Capture what we can, kill what we can't,' he murmurs when we're done.

Helion looks up, his gaze flicking between Felix and me. 'I approve of your strategy. We will continue it. I will make it happen.'

I sigh with relief.

He points at me. 'You can't go out there though, Elvira. Not looking like that. Stay here. I want to make sure you're safe.'

'I feel like I should be helping somehow …' I say.

Helion walks over to me and takes my hands in his. 'You have already helped immeasurably,' he says. 'And I hope you're planning to stay on Rhybor now, Elvira – since it is your true home – so you'll have more opportunities to help in the future. Once the blue fades.'

'Stay?'

'I'll need good people like you – and Felix,' Helion says. 'Once I've dealt with the Kauri, I'll have to sort out the Crusaders. What do you say?'

'Um … sure,' I say.

'Felix?' Helion says. 'You in?'

'Ah, I don't think my stepmother will like that,' Felix says.

'Your stepmother?' Helion says, frowning. 'Is she important?'

Felix shakes his head. 'She is best described as "insanely dangerous" – and, as a Crusader, probably your biggest enemy.'

Helion scoffs. 'A Crusader, huh? Well, I have ways to deal with Crusaders, so leave her to me.'

'Cool,' Felix says.

'So, you'll stay?' Helion says.

'Sure,' Felix says. 'Sounds like fun.'

∞

Felix

I roll off the throttle of my quad as I approach the Starlifter. Dawn has arrived. Sunlight crawls over the gargantuan aircraft as it creeps towards the broken city behind me.

I park the bike outside before I find Grim at the bottom of the ramp. 'Hey, Grim,' I say, scooping him off the ground. His rumbling purr is almost louder than a quad bike.

'Miss me?' I say.

Meow.

'I missed you too.'

Liberty strolls down the ramp towards me.

'I brought your pendant back,' I say. 'It worked.'

'Glad to hear it.' Liberty frowns. 'Where's Elvira?'

I snort. 'Don't you worry about her. She's settling herself into her new royal penthouse accommodation in the city.'

'Royal penthouse? What do you mean?'

I fill her in on our meeting with King Helion and details of the wehrdragon victory over the Kauri.

'Sounds like the king knows what he's doing,' Liberty says.

'He was all over it,' I say. 'The king was keen for Elvira to stay with him – considering she saved his life.'

'And Aeon?'

'With Elvira.'

Liberty nods. 'I hope he's being nice to her.'

'They were hugging when I left.'

'Do you know what happened to your stepmother?'

I smile. 'The king is hosting Karina too, though not in his penthouse – if you get my drift.'

'She's in jail?' Liberty says, eyebrows arched.

'Yep.'

'Sweet.'

I nod towards the aircraft's ramp. 'Is it safe to come onboard?'

Liberty sighs. 'Only if you're up for a nerdfest,' she says. When I frown, she adds, 'Now the Kauri are gone, it is safe for Mum to access the Star of Truth, so she's pulling everything she can on their portal intel.'

'Gemini?'

'I reckon we're lucky he's injured. Otherwise he'd have nicked off with the Star by now. Dad is watching him like a hawk – just in case.'

'What would he do with it?' I say.

Liberty shrugs. 'I think after it neutralised his virus, he is keen for revenge. He's found – in his eyes anyway – a worthy adversary.'

'Sure.' When I bend down to put Grim on the floor, he claws at my shirt. 'Geez, Grim,' I say. 'Being a bit needy, aren't you?'

'He really did miss you,' Liberty says.

'Well, I was going to give you your pendant back, but that's difficult to do with an armful of cat.'

She crooks her finger, gesturing for me to come closer. 'Come here. Let me help you.'

I lean forward and she clasps her hands behind my neck. As she fumbles with the clasp, her lips press gently against mine. My blood rages through my veins and despite my compromised genetics, I feel like I could Shift.

Liberty pulls back, securing her pendant around her neck. She smiles at me. 'Thank you for bringing it back … safely.'

I bow. 'My pleasure.'

Liberty glances over her shoulder. 'Bit stuffy in there,' she whispers, gesturing over her shoulder towards the interior of the Starlifter. 'Would you like to join me to watch the sunrise?'

'As long as you don't mind Grim coming too?'

'I think I can deal with that.'

Epilogue

Kitchen of Dr Caspian Fox, Astrophysicist – Thursday 9 December, 2021 – 04:15 pm

Harry Jones twists the cap off his beer and drops it in the pouch hanging from the armrest of his wheelchair, then raises the bottle to his host. 'To your portal, Dr Fox!'

Caspian Fox raises an eyebrow but says nothing as he puts his own bottle to his lips. He's been back on Earth less than forty-eight hours and has had little sleep, so imbibing beer – a drink not to his taste – is unwise. But he needs Harry Jones.

'Your portal is stable, isn't it, Dr Fox?' the veteran journalist says.

'Yes, Mr Jones,' Caspian says. 'The portal is stable.'

Harry grins. 'I'd love to see it.'

Caspian places his bottle on the kitchen table. 'You may see it on one condition.'

'Which is?'

'You don't just look at it,' Caspian says. 'You go *through* it.'

Harry leans forward. 'And where am I going?'

'Rhybor.'

'You're running tours?'

'Selective tours,' Caspian says. 'We think you'll be useful.'

Harry's eyes narrow. 'We?'

Caspian smiles. 'Me and my wife, my daughter and her friends.'

'Friends? Liberty, Felix and Elvira … are all on Rhybor?'

Caspian nods.

Harry slams his fist on the arm of his wheelchair. 'I *knew* it.' He slurps on his beer, celebrating the confirmation of his hunch. 'Hang on … *useful*? Useful for what?'

'You like big stories, right?' Caspian says.

Harry grunts. 'I'm the anchor of the *Indigo Times*. I don't waste my time on small stuff.'

'Well, Rhybor has finally succeeded in repelling the race of cyborgs that took their planet hostage twenty years ago.'

Cyborgs? Harry's eyes twinkle at the prospect of solving the twenty-year-old mystery of the portal collapse. 'I'm listening.'

'The Rhyborians repelled the invading cyborgs—'

'Hang on,' Harry says, plucking his phone from his pocket. 'Mind if I record this?'

Caspian waves his hand. 'Go ahead.'

Harry sets his phone on the table. 'You were saying, Dr Fox?'

'The Rhyborians repelled the invading cyborgs but didn't defeat them. The Kauri will regroup and return for vengeance with a greater force. Rhybor won't stand a chance.'

'And the cyborgs? What's their endgame?'

'Universal domination.'

'Uh-huh.'

'This is real,' Caspian says. 'The cyborgs – the Kauri – are the apex predator in our universe and are sweeping every planet, systematically harvesting and storing the intelligent lifeforms they encounter. When they are done, they plan to create their version of utopia. Rhybor is now a thorn in their side and the Kauri won't fail a second time.'

'And what do you want me to do?'

'Interview, document, report – everything you can,' Caspian says. 'The story needs to come back here. The Rhyborians will need Earth's help in order to have any chance of defeating this foe.'

'A fight like that sounds expensive,' Harry says. 'Who here do you reckon would be up for a fight like that?'

Caspian shrugs. 'I don't know, but we'd better find someone because once the Kauri are done with Rhybor ... Next stop?' He takes a long swig of his beer. 'Earth!'

Did you love *Wehrdragon: Liberation*?
Leave a review on Goodreads or your preferred platform!

For the latest on new releases, connect with Sarah:
www.sarahfisherauthor.com

Or on Facebook or Instagram
@SarahFisherAuthor

Titles by Sarah Fisher

The Dragonscale series

The 13th Key
Firestone
Redemption

The Wehrdragon series

Liberation

About the Author

Sarah Fisher lives west of Brisbane, Australia. When she's not corralling her collection of unruly fictional characters, she teaches real characters at local schools. She is living proof that while growing older is compulsory, growing up is not.

9 780648 182467